SCOUT'S DUTY

HENRY VOGEL

Published in the United States of America by Rampant Loon Press, an imprint of Rampant Loon Media LLC, P.O. Box 111, Lake Elmo, Minnesota 55042. "Rampant Loon Press" and the Rampant Loon colophon are trademarks of Rampant Loon Media LLC.

www.rampantloonmedia.com

Cover art by Jeff Doten.

ISBN: 978-1-938834-45-5 (ebook)

ISBN: 978-1-938834-46-2 (print)

First publication: October 2015

*Dedicated to the memory of Edgar Rice Burroughs
and Leigh Brackett*

LIGHTS IN THE SKY

The nights in Morda had just started turning cool and fall was fast becoming my favorite season. Though the purple and gold leaves were glorious to behold, fall's status rose because Callan and I had taken to reclining out on the balcony and gazing at the stars.

And by recline, I mean we lay in each other's arms. Absolutely nothing drives away the night's chill like a beautiful woman sharing her warmth with you. Trust me on this.

"Have you figured out which star you came from, David?" Callan's soft, warm breath tickled my neck.

"It's slow going without the instruments I usually rely on. The astronomers at the Royal College get amazing results with their telescopes and, with their help, I'm narrowing it down." I pointed to a cluster of stars right above us, far away from the bright planetary ring. "I'm pretty sure it's one of those stars. The first thing a scout should do after exiting a wormhole is to take astronomical readings and determine exactly where he is. Of course, I was too busy dodging asteroids after popping out in the middle of the planetary ring to have time for that."

"You were just in a hurry to get down to the ground and rescue me from the trogs." Callan snuggled in even closer, though I would

1

have sworn that was impossible. "And stop me from marrying Prince Rupor."

Remembering my frantic efforts to stay alive within the planetary ring, I said, "Plus saving you from having Raoul as a brother-in-law. So sure, let's go with that."

"Our children, when we have them, will hear my version of the story. It's much more romantic." Callan gave a contented sigh. "When I was a little girl, I'd have been beside myself with excitement if someone told me a story like ours. I can't wait to see the excitement shining in little eyes as they hear about their heroic father."

"Well *I* can't wait until they hear how their brave and brilliant mother concocted the plan to save the city of Faroon and defeat the trog army." I pulled back and looked into Callan's eyes. "You were going to include that part, weren't you?"

"When it comes time to tell the story, perhaps we should tell it together. That way we can make sure the whole story gets told."

"As always, your wish is my command, Your Highness."

We were silent for a few seconds, gazing into the heavens and lost in our own thoughts. Then Callan pointed toward the planetary ring. "Look at that, David!"

I looked where she pointed. Strange lights flared and vanished within the ring. Then bright trails blazed through the upper atmosphere as tiny asteroids fell from the heavens and burned up in the atmosphere.

"I thought I'd seen every sight the ring has to offer, but I've never seen anything like those flashing lights before," Callan said. "It's beautiful. Do you have any idea what it is?"

A knot of excitement and apprehension formed in my gut. I knew exactly what we were seeing.

"It's a spaceship blasting its way out of the ring!"

I whooped and pulled Callan into a kiss. "My emergency drone must have reached the wormhole and gotten through to the Federation Navy."

Callan propped her chin on one hand. "What is an emergency drone?"

"I never told you about launching the drone?" When Callan shook her head, I continued, "A drone is an unmanned spaceship that carries a message. In my case, the drone carried the coordinates of the wormhole to this system as well as the initial sensor readings when I exited the wormhole. The drone launched from my scout ship, but my sensors couldn't track it through all the asteroids. I hoped it flew into the wormhole safely, but had just about given up that hope."

"Then the drone flew out the other side of the wormhole and waited for someone to find it?" Callan puzzled through the idea. "So it's a lot like a message in a bottle?"

"That's sort of right, if the bottle could set sail for the nearest port. When the drone got through the wormhole, it would have flown back to the nearest Scout base."

"How does the drone know the way to the base if there's no one flying it?"

"It's complicated." How could I explain astrogation and autopilots to Callan? "Let me think a bit about the best way to explain it to you."

"Martin already understands, though." Callan waved her hand toward the flashes in the ring. "Whoever is on that ship already understands. And just about everyone in your part of the galaxy understands." Her next words were so soft I almost didn't hear them. "But *I* don't understand."

"That's not your fault, Callan. You just don't have the background for it and I'm not sure I can do a good job explaining it."

Callan laid her head on my chest and I felt a splash of warm liquid. Was that a tear?

Cupping her chin, I lifted Callan's head so I could look into her eyes. A second tear spilled from her eye and rolled down her cheek.

"Hey, why are you crying?" What had I said to make her suddenly sad?

"When that spaceship lands, the whole galaxy will be open to you again. Why would you stay on my backward planet when you could go back to exploring the stars?"

"Callan, why would I leave you just to explore a bunch of stars? I'll stay here *because* this is your planet. I'll stay here because *you* are here." I pulled her close and kissed her. "It's going to take a lot more than a sleek spaceship to lure me away from the life we've made together. And even if I am lured away, I'll miss you terribly and come home as soon as humanly possible."

Callan gazed into my eyes for a second. I willed the truth of my words to reflect in them. With a sigh, she snuggled even closer to me. "You do realize you're in serious hot water with me?"

I felt a jolt of alarm "You don't believe what I just told you?"

"I believe it." This time I could hear the smirk in her voice. "But if you think you're leaving me behind when you fly off to the stars, you've got another think coming."

"My deepest apologies, dearest. Of course I'll take you with me. If nothing else, I'd love to introduce you to my parents."

"And your little sister, Sandra?" Callan prompted. "From your stories about her, I'm certain she and I will become good friends."

"Yeah, sure, I'll introduce you to my little sister, too." I kept my tone light, but I hadn't seen my family in over two years. They must be worried about me and I missed them terribly.

"Now, shouldn't you be rushing off to tell Martin about the spaceship?" Callan asked.

"Not yet. We can't do anything until it breaks atmosphere, anyway." I stood up, pulled Callan up beside me, and looked toward our bedroom. "So, a while back you said something about children?"

Callan laughed, soft and sultry. "Well, if you insist..."

Bright light flared above us as an explosion lit the ring and the flashes stopped. An asteroid must have hit the spaceship!

WHERE'S MARTIN?

As the explosion faded away, a new red trail blazed to life in the upper atmosphere. I assumed it was wreckage or asteroid fragments and expected the trail to streak towards the ground. Instead, the angle of descent lessened and the red trail diminished as the object slowed. It was under intelligent control.

I jumped to my feet. "Some of the ship's crew must have survived that explosion. They're bound to have wounded among them—and there will probably be more when they hit the ground. We've got to gather a search and rescue team to find and help them."

Callan and I watched the red trail moving across the sky. "It looks like it's going to come down in the lands between Mordan and Tarteg. David, go alert Martin and Tristan and whoever else you want to have with us on this rescue mission. I'll speak to Mom and Daddy and make arrangements for a naval escort."

With a nod and a quick kiss for Callan, I ran off to find Milo. Milo didn't have any skills we'd need on the team—though he'd more than earned the right to join us if he wanted to do so—but Milo has a knack for knowing where everyone is at any given moment. When I found him, I was not surprised to find several young ladies-in-waiting vying for his attention. Not bad for an orphan who'd grown up on the streets of Faroon.

I bowed politely to the girls. "Please pardon my interruption, ladies, but I must speak with Milo for a moment."

The girls' eyes widened. They knew Milo had saved my life more than once, but apparently they never expected me to come to him. I guess it *is* more common for royalty to summon people, but I was in a hurry and still wasn't comfortable with the whole 'royal' thing.

Adopting a serious expression, Milo stood. "Of course, Prince Consort. Ladies, would you please excuse me?"

A chorus of yeses followed as Milo and I stepped just out of earshot. Once the girls could no longer see his face, Milo grinned broadly. "Thank you, David. You've given my reputation a bump upwards."

"What are friends for?" I asked. "And mentioning friends, do you know where I can find Martin?"

"Sure. At this hour on a Thursday you'll find him at the Drum and Fife on Waterford Street."

"For a former raider, Martin is awfully predictable." I shook my head in mock disapproval. "Is palace life making him soft?"

"Soft in the head, maybe. Or, more accurately, the heart," Milo replied.

"Martin has a girlfriend?"

"He usually has three." Milo grinned. "The pages are all in awe of his prowess with the fairer sex."

"Usually? That's not the case anymore?"

"Not since he met Megan, it isn't. She's very pretty."

"Does she work at the Drum and Fife?" I asked.

"Sort of. Megan's a very talented musician, too. She sings there every Thursday," Milo said. "She's at the Broken Barrel on Tuesdays, so that's where Martin goes every Tuesday."

"Well, I hope Martin will forgive me for pulling him away from his lady love."

"What's up, David?"

In a few short sentences, I brought Milo up-to-date on the crashing spaceship. "I hate to pull you away from your young ladies, too, but I need you to round up Tristan and Nist. Tristan should gather any medical supplies he thinks he'll need and Nist should start preparing the *Pauline* for flight."

Milo offered apologies to his female admirers as I struck out for the Drum and Fife. Two guards fell in behind me as I left the palace, something I was still getting used to. Waterford Street was but a few blocks away. The guards and I covered the distance in under ten minutes.

I opened the tavern door to find a sea of angry patrons blocking my way. Over their heads I saw the object of their rage. A defiant red-headed woman—Megan, I assumed—clasped a guitar to her chest and glared at the crowd. Sword drawn, Martin stood between the mob and the musician.

MEGAN

I wanted to call on some of that royal authority I didn't like using to calm things down, but I couldn't be heard over the crowd noise. I had to find a way to get to the stage and hope some of the crowd recognized me. I had no other hope for getting their attention. My guards were still nervously assessing the situation when I did the one thing I knew they didn't want me to do. I plunged into the crowd and began worming my way toward the stage.

I had gone but a few yards when someone in the crowd threw a bottle at the stage. Martin swept the bottle aside with his sword, otherwise it would have smashed into the woman's head. A crowd shouting and waving fists in the air could be calmed. A mob shoving and throwing bottles was a different matter.

Boost!

About to shove through the crowd, I suddenly remembered how, years ago, Martin had leapt over a line of Tartegian guards in the trading post cellar. I leapt into the air, hoping to fly over the crowd. It didn't work so well. With people packed around me, I couldn't jump as high as I needed, nor as far forward. Finding myself about to come down in the crowd, I tucked and pushed off from a couple of sturdy shoulders. I completed a flip and landed next to Martin.

Raising my arms, I yelled for quiet. The mob fell silent and I dropped Boost.

"What is the meaning of this?" I demanded. "How dare you attack this woman? You're acting like a lawless gang of Beloran tunnel rats."

A big man back in the crowd hollered, "Come down here and say that to my face, pretty boy! Ain't no way you'd say that to us if you knew anything 'bout tunnel rats."

I guess they didn't recognize me. "I know exactly what I'm saying, since I've been into the tunnels of Beloran and faced the tunnel rats."

The big man barked, "Ha! Only one Mordanian man has been into those tunnels and lived to tell about it."

I looked at the man, my eyebrows raised in inquiry. "And?"

The crowd looked at me, blank expressions on their faces.

"Take your time," Martin added helpfully. "It'll come to you."

My guards pushed their way to the front of the crowd, pained expressions directed my way. At sight of their green and gold uniforms, one man's face cleared.

"That man is David Rice, the Prince Consort."

Heads bobbed in agreement, even the big man who'd challenged me.

"Now that we've cleared that up, I'll return to my question." I glared out at the crowd. "What is the meaning of this demonstration?"

A voice from the crowd called, "She provoked us!" A chorus of voices added "Yeah!" and "Right!"

"One woman armed with nothing but a guitar provoked such a violent demonstration? How?" When no one answered, I looked to Martin. "Would you care to fill me in?"

"The crowd asked to hear new songs, ones they'd never heard before. She toured Tarteg before coming here, so Megan chose to

9

sing some songs currently popular there," he said. "She led off with *Rupor's Lament*."

"Never heard of it."

"I'm not surprised, David. It's about Callan and Rupor and is strongly slanted to the Tartegian point of view. The song questions the prince consort's motives, his honor, and his off-world origins." Megan snorted at this, causing Martin to give me a half smile. "But the real trouble started when the song called Princess Callan a rather rude name. It...ah...rhymes with rich."

Even this cautious approach to the word brought mutters from the crowd. Megan chose to make it worse by saying, "From everything I've been told, the song doesn't go far enough."

I stepped between Megan and the crowd just in case another bottle was thrown. "Martin, can you please shut her up? We've got vastly more important matters to deal with than Megan's thoughtless song choices."

"No one shuts me-"

Martin clamped his left hand over Megan's mouth, wrapped his right arm around her waist, then picked her up. "What's going on?"

"Less than an hour ago, another spaceship came through the wormhole."

NO BARDS REQUIRED

Upon hearing my words, Megan snorted again. Even with her mouth muffled by Martin's hand, Megan had no trouble making her opinion quite clear. Her eyes spoke volumes as well and made me happy it was Martin's hand within range of her teeth rather than mine.

I glanced at Martin. "Does she know who you are and where you came from?"

Megan's flashing eyes turned to Martin and her eyebrows drew down. Was she giving him the evil eye for silencing her or trying to puzzle out where he was born?

"Our relationship hasn't really advanced to such personal revelations." Martin turned his winning smile on Megan and was rewarded with a steel-melting glare.

"That explains a lot. Meanwhile, we've got things to do." I turned to face the crowd. "Clear a path, please. We're leaving."

Most of the crowd moved aside, but one man planted himself in front of me. "Didn't you hear what that woman called our princess? We can't forgive an insult like that."

"Yes, my good man, I heard. And if I can forgive the singer, so can you," I said. "After all, I *am* married to the princess."

The man smacked his forehead and stepped aside. "Of course, sir. Please forgive me, sir!"

"There's nothing to forgive." I clapped him on the shoulder.

My guards took up position on either side of me as we exited the tavern. Outside, I filled Martin in on the spaceship's arrival. With Martin's hand no longer covering her mouth, Megan kept trying to interrupt with questions. I plowed ahead with my explanation, overriding her comments and ignoring her questions. I will say this for Megan, she didn't give up easily.

"So," Megan said when I stopped speaking, "you and Martin are heading off after one of these 'spaceships' you claim to have arrived in?"

"Martin, I'm tired of listening to this woman rant and rave about my origins and crashed spaceships." I shook my head in disgust. "Then again, there are none so certain as the truly ignorant."

Megan's head whipped up, her eyes widened, and her mouth opened and shut several times without a sound emerging. I found it a welcome change.

"Yes, Megan, we're heading off after a spaceship," Martin said. "I know you're well educated, so I truly don't understand why you're so determined to cast David as a liar or conman."

"He's part of the royal family and royals always lie." The fire in Megan's eyes and voice faded as she spoke, as if she spoke out of a long-ingrained habit.

Martin shook his head in mock sorrow. "I must say that you're quite cynical for one so young."

"Travel as much as I have and you'd be cynical, too," Megan replied.

"I've been on seven other inhabited worlds," I said, "and traveled extensively on this world, yet I'm not cynical in the least."

"No doubt due to the rapture of true love." Megan's voice was drier than the desert where I'd crashed.

"People say travel broadens the mind, Megan, but that only

works if the mind is open." I stopped at the palace gate. "You're safe now, Megan. Run along home."

"And miss out on the great spaceship hunt and the chance to broaden my mind? Not on your life." Megan linked arms with Martin. "I'm coming with you."

"Whoa there, Megan," I said. "You most definitely are *not* coming with us."

"Why not? I'll stay out of the way." Megan widened her eyes and pouted, an effect designed to melt the heart of any man who faced it. From the look Martin turned on me, Megan's pout certainly worked on him. It might have worked on me, too, if I hadn't married the most beautiful woman on eight planets.

"That pout won't work on me." I made shooing motions. "Scat. We don't need in-flight entertainment for a rescue mission."

Megan dropped her wide-eyed pout and went back to glaring at me. "Are you afraid I'll find out the princess isn't nearly as sweet and beautiful in real life as *Rice's Rescue* claims she is?"

I turned to Martin. "What is *Rice's Rescue?*"

"It's the Mordanian counterpoint to *Rupor's Lament.* As you might guess, the crown prince of Tarteg isn't portrayed in the best light in the Mordanian version." Martin looked back and forth between Megan and me. "But I think you should reconsider your position concerning Megan. There are definite advantages to bringing her along."

I snorted. "Name just one and I'll let her join us."

"Songs will be written about this event. Everyone will benefit if those songs are more accurate than either *Rupor's Lament* or *Rice's Rescue.*" Martin patted Megan's arm. "Who better to write some of those songs than an actual eye witness?"

He had a point—a minor point, but a point nonetheless. I sighed. "Fine, Megan can come along. But I'll warn you right now, if she insults Callan I'm throwing her overboard."

Megan smiled in triumph. "Well, if your princess is as sweet as you Mordanians say, that won't be a problem."

"Well, even if you can't stop yourself from throwing insults,"

Martin added, grinning, "rest assured David will land the airship before giving you the old heave ho."

"Wait—you're saying he's serious about that?"

I headed into the palace and didn't hear Martin's reply. Whatever he said didn't deter Megan. The two of them caught up with me just before I found Callan.

The palace swarmed in a controlled frenzy as pages, guards, and naval officers dashed about. The activity centered on Callan, who made quick decisions followed by crisp orders. The king and queen sat to one side, watching their daughter with proud smiles. They waved as I entered and approached Callan. She signed some order or requisition then turned to me. Rising up on her toes, Callan gave me a peck on the lips and one to Martin on his cheek.

Callan turned a welcoming smile on Megan. Eying Martin's and Megan's linked arms, Callan said, "Martin, is this lovely lady the reason you've declined my last two dinner invitations?"

"She most definitely is," Martin smiled. "Megan, this is Her Highness, Princess Callan."

Megan surprised me by dropping into a curtsey. "Your Highness."

Callan took Megan's hand and drew her up. "We don't stand on ceremony unless we're in formal court. At least, not among friends." Callan turned to Martin. "You know you could have brought her to dinner with you."

"Megan is a musician and was performing both nights," Martin replied.

I added, "Martin thinks she should accompany us and chronicle this mission in song."

"What a splendid idea," Callan smile grew wider. "It will be refreshing to have another woman on board the ship. Most of my trips with David are overwhelmingly masculine."

"Why thank you, Your Highness."

"Now Megan, I told you we don't stand on ceremony among friends. Call me Callan." Callan turned to me. "I've ordered four escort ships for the *Pauline*. The naval ships are already airborne. We can leave as soon as you're ready."

"I'm ready now." I waved my arm around us. "But what about all of this activity?"

"Oh, they're just working out logistics for the follow-on forces. I'm sure the admiralty will be quite happy to handle that without any guidance from me." Callan slipped her arm through mine. "Let's go."

Milo and Tristan were already aboard the airship. Seconds after we boarded, Nist piloted the *Pauline* into the air and the rescue mission was underway.

CRASH SITE SURPRISES

"Why must all of our escort ships be so...stately?" Nist groused. 'Stately' was Nist's current euphemism for 'slow.'

"Seven hours and twenty-three minutes," called Martin. Several guards groaned and one cheered.

"What's that all about?" Megan asked him.

"Nist always chafes at the top speed of Callan's escort airships," Martin said. "The guards like to bet how long it will take before he voices his frustration aloud."

I tuned out their conversation as Callan came out of the airship's cabin and into the dawn light. She had retreated there with Megan shortly after lift-off. The two women passed the intervening hours chatting. I busied myself discussing rescue contingencies with Martin. Distracted as I was, I only realized I hadn't once heard shouting from the cabin when a quiet and thoughtful Megan returned to the deck. Considering how abrasive Megan was when I'd first met her, I'd expected Callan to adopt her icy, court-proper princess persona at least once during the trip. Yet Callan emerged all smiles from the cabin.

Seeing the direction I was looking, Callan said, "Megan is quite a talented and passionate woman."

"Lucky Martin," I murmured.

"Passionate about her *beliefs.*" Callan rolled her eyes before musing, "Though if their relationship ever becomes seriously romantic then yes, lucky Martin."

"You *like* her? I admit you've spent more time with Megan, but I found her rather irritating."

"You met her during her confrontation with an angry mob. One where people truly were ready to hurt her—and in my name, no less." Callan grimaced. "Fear rarely brings out the best in people, David."

"She was afraid?" I shook my head. "Megan hid it very well. I thought she was angry."

"She won't admit it, but Megan simply wasn't thinking when she started playing *Rupor's Lament*. She should have simply stopped playing when the tavern fell silent. An apology followed by a spritely tune probably would have settled the crowd. But she's a stubborn woman whose pride forced her to keep playing the song."

"Megan told you all of that?" I asked.

"Not directly, no, but any woman could have heard it in Megan's voice and seen it in her face." Callan looked up at my face. "So, did you and Martin figure out what you're going to do when we find this spaceship?"

Before I could answer, a shout rose from a lookout on one of the escort ships.

"Unknown object twenty-three degrees to starboard."

I looked in that direction and immediately spotted the line of broken trees and churned dirt. It extended over a mile. At its end, the crashed starship lay with its nose buried in the ground. It was a big ship, with at least a hundred and sixty yards of fuselage angling up above the tops of the trees.

A shout rang out from the lookout on board the lead escort. "Tartegian warships dead ahead."

I turned my gaze toward Tarteg and easily spotted the approaching warships.

"This is not good, David. They outnumber us seven to four."

Martin, far more experienced with airships, assessed the situation before I'd finished counting Tartegian warships.

"Don't you mean seven to five?" Megan asked. "Did you forget to count the airship you're riding in?"

"I didn't forget the *Pauline*," Martin replied, "I left her out of the count on purpose."

"Why?" Megan asked. "This seems like a perfectly fine airship."

Nist beamed at the compliment to his pride and joy.

"She's a splendid airship—but she's not a warship. She has neither weapons nor a contingent of marines," Martin replied. "If it comes to a fight, Nist will drop David and me on the command ship then take Her Highness and you away from here at top speed."

Megan bristled. "Is that because we're women? Are you saying women can't-"

Callan interrupted the argument, "Nist, I wish to speak with the Tartegian commander. Please raise a white flag and then slowly fly forward."

Megan glanced at Martin and me, obviously expecting us to voice an objection. When we didn't say anything, she threw up her hands. "I don't get it. If you have to fight the Tartegians, you're going send us away. And it's all because we're women and this isn't a warship. But neither of you have any problems with this same non-warship—protected by nothing but a piece of white cloth— sailing in alone to parlay with those same Tartegians."

"While our two countries have their differences, Tarteg is a civilized country. Its navy will honor the flag of truce. I doubt their commander is any more anxious for battle than we are." As I finished speaking, a Tartegian airship raised a white flag and flew to meet us.

"Well, I must say that's quite a relief," Megan's incredulous expression said otherwise. "If it comes to a fight, I'm sure all of those who die will die a happier death knowing their killers followed the rules of war like proper gentlemen."

"Megan, the rules of war exist to protect the living by avoiding needless conflict and unnecessary loss of life." Suddenly, Callan turned her icy princess persona on the musician. *"Those rules succeed because they insure we can talk to each other safely and without fear."*

"I realize this situation is outside of your experience," I said, "but you asked to come with us as an observer. Watch in silence or I'll have one of the guards take you below deck."

Megan's eyes blazed at me but she kept quiet.

"Ahoy, Mordanian vessel!" a familiar voice called from the Tartegian airship.

The Tartegian commander was Prince Rupor.

A VIABLE SOLUTION

"Awkward," Megan sang softly.

Ignoring Megan, Callan called, "Hello, Rupor. How have you been doing?"

"Callan?" Rupor couldn't keep the surprise from his voice. "What are you doing out here?"

"The same as you, Rupor. I'm investigating the crashed spaceship."

"I'm surprised your *consort* let you come to the unsettled lands," Rupor said. "Isn't he afraid you'll be kidnapped?"

"Point to Rupor," Megan said under her breath.

"With your step-mother and half-brother in exile," Callan shot back, "my *husband* doesn't believe he has to worry about Tartegian kidnapping plots."

"Ouch! Two points to Callan," Megan added.

Callan turned an irritated glare on Megan.

I took the hint, even if Megan appeared oblivious to it. "Guard, take Megan below deck and keep her there until further notice."

Megan's protests interrupted Callan's exchange with Rupor. By the time Megan was out of earshot, the airships were within a few yards of each other.

"You've come with an interesting pair of companions, Callan," Rupor said. "While I can understand traveling with your consort–"

"*Husband.*"

"–I must admit I'll be damned if I understand traveling with Bane." Rupor finished. "Don't you find it rather ironic that I was deemed unfit to wed you because my relatives contracted for your kidnapping but your *actual* kidnapper is deemed a fit companion for the very princess he kidnapped?"

"Isn't it odd how my kidnapper has atoned for his crimes—in rather spectacular fashion, I might add—while your relative, Raoul, remains an extremely irritating thorn in my side?"

The bickering was getting out of hand. I interrupted with a change of subject before the truce failed and fighting broke out. "May I humbly suggest the two of you save the verbal sparring for court, Your Highnesses? People may be injured within the spaceship."

Callan reddened. "Thank you for reminding me of my duty, darling. David is right, Rupor. We must put aside our differences and decide how our two nations can best respond to the situation at hand."

"Yes, I suppose he is correct." Rupor's gaze swept the entire scene. "May I suggest an approach by a combined party of Mordanians and Tartegians? I believe it is the only viable solution. Your... husband...should be among those selected. He speaks our language and, I assume, the language of those within the spaceship. I prefer not to rely on second-hand reports, so will represent Tarteg myself."

"I agree with your suggestions, Rupor, but wish to suggest one more member of the party." Callan placed a hand on Martin's shoulder. "If he's willing, I'd like Martin to go along, as well. He speaks both languages and, like David, can Boost should an emergency arise."

Rupor thought for a moment. "Our differences aside, Callan, I know you are a sensible woman. I agree to your suggestion. Bane may accompany us."

Callan turned to Martin. "I realize I've put you on the spot, Martin, but will you go with David and Rupor?"

"Try and keep me away," Martin grinned.

After another round of discussions, Rupor joined us on board the *Pauline* for the descent. Ten minutes later, the three of us hopped down to the ground.

"Take the ship back up, Nist," I said. "I don't know what to expect, but if anything happens, get out of here as quickly as possible."

"Is there anything I should watch for in particular?" Nist asked.

"Airships falling out of the sky would be a good indicator of trouble," Martin remarked dryly.

We set off at a slow jog toward the spaceship. Within minutes we were forced to reduce our pace as we scrambled over broken trees and mounds of dirt. It took ten more minutes to reach the crash site. When we came close enough to see details on the ship, Martin stiffened.

I barely avoided crashing into Martin's back when he stopped. "What's the problem, Martin?"

"We could be in for some serious trouble, David." Martin pointed to designs painted on the side of the spaceship. "Those look like pirate markings."

PIRATES AND LASERS

"Are you sure?" I asked. I'd been out in the wider galaxy far more recently than Martin had and the designs meant nothing to me.

"My Master Scout and I had a run-in with pirates prior to crashing onto Aashla," Martin said. "Those markings are similar to the ones used by those pirates."

"Well, I believe you, Bane," drawled Rupor. "Vermin always recognize their own kind."

"You're not helping, Rupor," I said. "If Martin is right, we truly are all in serious trouble."

"It's only one ship," Rupor scoffed.

"You wouldn't say that if you had any idea what a single space-ship like that is capable of doing," Martin growled.

"If it's a simple matter of education, then by all means do enlighten me," Rupor replied.

"Put simply, if that ship is fully crewed and functional, then whoever commands it rules this world," Martin said.

"You must be joking," Rupor looked back and forth between Martin and me. "He *can't* be serious?"

"Do I look as if I'm joking, Rupor?" Martin's gaze bored into the prince. "If this is a pirate ship, our only hope for stopping them is for at least one person to insinuate himself into their good graces, bide his time, and wait for the opportunity to strike."

"Oh ho! Now the plot comes clear," Rupor cried. "You wish this super ship for yourself. Well, I-"

I clapped a hand over Rupor's mouth and an arm around his throat. "I'm sorry for the rough treatment, Your Highness, but we don't have time for this bickering. For what it's worth, I believe Martin's suggestion has merit. Martin, what should our first move be?"

"Assuming there are survivors—and from your description of the partially controlled descent, I'm sure some of the crew is still alive—I'm going to try to make contact with them." Martin shrugged. "If they're not pirates, great. We help with their wounded and take it from there. If they *are* pirates, I'll try to trade on my old reputation as a raider to join them."

"Um, Martin, those on the ship are not going to know anything about your past activities on Aashla."

"I know that, David, but I *do* have that experience to draw on. I'm confident I can convince them of my bona fides."

"What about Rupor and me?" I asked.

"If these are pirates, they must *not* learn you're an off-worlder, too, David. A military hero who can also fly their ship will be too much of a threat. They'd kill you without a second thought."

"So I pretend to be a local?" I asked.

Martin nodded. "That includes pretending like you don't speak their language." At my nod, Martin turned to Rupor. "Prince, you *must* follow our plan or these men may kill us all."

Rupor stared at Martin for a moment, then nodded. Relieved, I released Rupor.

"You two stay hidden," Martin said, then picked his way to the ship's airlock. He fiddled with the airlock controls. A minute later, the airlock door slid open and Martin stepped inside.

Immediately after entering the airlock, Martin dove back out and rolled to the left. A bright beam of red light lanced behind him, tracking too slowly to hit him before he was out of the line of fire. The beam cut deep, smoking lines into the broken trees piled up beside the spaceship. It sliced completely through smaller tree trunks, those only a few inches thick.

"By all that is holy, what was *that?*" Rupor stared, wide-eyed, at the damage left by the beam.

"It's called a laser." Since no language on Aashla had a word for 'laser,' I used the galactic basic word. "For simplicity, let's just say it's a highly focused beam of light."

"Light? Is that all?" Rupor asked. "Why didn't Bane just wear metal armor? Surely that would stop the light. Or he could have carried a mirror to reflect it."

"The laser would burn through metal armor in a heartbeat. It would do the same to a mirror. I realize this is all new and strange to you, but you have to believe me." I met the stare Rupor turned on me. "It gets worse, Your Highness. That is just a small laser, one a man could carry. The spaceship is armed with half a dozen much larger ones." I searched for a way to help him understand. "Think of the laser we just saw as a single-handed target crossbow. In comparison, the ship's lasers are ballistas."

"And Bane thinks these people may be pirates?" Rupor turned back toward the ship and stared with apprehension. "God protect us! No nation could stand against such power."

I placed a hand on Rupor's shoulder. "That is why you *must* follow our instructions in this matter. If these are pirates, our best —perhaps our only—hope is to infiltrate the pirate gang and bring them down from within. That means you're going to have to put aside your opinion of Martin and trust him to find a way to do just that."

Rupor wrinkled his nose as if smelling something foul. "And what of you, Rice? Are you certain they are pirates?"

"Certain? No. But I trust Martin and will follow his lead until we can learn more about our visitors," I said. "That means you *must* keep quiet about my background. If the pirates discover I am a crash-landed scout, they'll kill me out of hand."

"Why would pirates worry about a single scout? I've heard

you're a formidable fighter, but it's obvious you can't defeat these pirates single-handedly."

"You're right, I can't. But the very nature of scouting brings us in contact with pirates far more often than any of the other military branches. We're trained to deal with them and, at the risk of bragging, succeed more often than we fail." I smiled grimly. "As you might guess, Your Highness, pirates tend to dislike us scouts."

Rupor nodded. "I'll do my best, Rice. And you might as well call me Rupor out here. It's quicker and quick communication may save lives."

Back at the airlock, Martin got to his feet and dusted himself off. The hiss of an opening airlock door came from the ship. Footsteps clanged in the airlock and a huge figure appeared at the outer door. Our situation had just gotten far worse. The figure wore military-grade powered armor.

TAKE ME TO YOUR LEADER

Ignoring Martin standing next to him, the armored figure scanned the area. I pulled Rupor down behind a mound of dirt and broken trees. If we were lucky, the heat from the crash would mask us from infrared scanning. The armor whined faintly—the armored head swiveling to complete an infrared sweep, I assumed. I put a finger to my lips and motioned for Rupor to stay down. Eyes wide and his face deathly pale, Rupor nodded.

"Hey, you in the powered armor," Martin spoke galactic basic. "Take me to your leader."

The man in the armor took two clumping footsteps.

"Put me down," Martin shouted. "I can walk on my own, you know. All you have to do is give me a chance."

Footsteps clanged from the air lock.

"This is no way to treat a guest, you know," Martin continued complaining until the airlock hissed closed and cut off his voice.

I risked a peek over our hiding place. As I'd expected, there was no sign of the armored figure or of Martin.

Ducking down again, I whispered, "Martin has been taken inside. I guess that counts as a successful start to Martin's plan."

"What was that thing?" The color still had not returned to Rupor's face.

"It was a man wearing...you don't really have a word for it." I tried to think of something within Rupor's experience. "The closest I can get is armor with an engine."

"An engine?" Color slowly seeped back into Rupor's face. "I know quite a bit about engineering and that armor gave off no smoke and had no place for a boiler."

"The engine is based on science and engineering you don't have on Aashla." I started crawling away from the spaceship. "I'll try to explain in more detail, but not until we're far away from this spaceship."

Staying low and keeping dirt mounds between us and the ship, Rupor and I scrambled through the debris from the crash. Ten minutes later, we broke free of the trees and picked up our pace, waving at the ships floating above us. Within seconds, the *Pauline* dropped down to meet us.

Milo was the first person to realize Martin wasn't with us. By the time we reached the *Pauline*, he had alerted everyone else on board. Megan was among those waiting on the deck. Callan must have ordered her released.

Impatient Megan spoke first. "Where's Martin? What have you done with him?"

"*We* haven't done anything with him," I said.

"He was captured," Rupor added.

I gave a quick account of the events. Megan's hand flew to her mouth when I described the powered armor and everyone else looked grim.

"I could say things have gone exactly according to Martin's plan," I said, "but not even someone as optimistic as I am can convince myself that's true."

"What are we going to do now?" Callan asked. "We can't just abandon Martin inside that spaceship."

"No, of course not, Callan. Fortunately, I know exactly what we're going do to."

Megan stared intently at me, then asked, "And what is that?"

"First, all of you are going to fly several miles away and wait for my signal," I said. "That includes you, Rupor."

"I can't say as I approve of this plan, Rice. A Prince of Tarteg doesn't run away from a fight."

"This is a tactical withdrawal, nothing more. Until we know more about that ship, there's no point putting you at risk." Rupor opened his mouth—to protest, I assume—so I added, "You don't send generals to scout enemy positions, do you Rupor?"

"Of course not."

"Then we're sure as hell not sending a crown prince to do the same job."

Rupor sighed and nodded.

"And what are you planning on doing, David?" Callan asked.

I gave her my most confident smile. "I'm going back for Martin, of course."

KNOCK KNOCK

Callan looked into my eyes for a few seconds. At last she said, "Don't get yourself killed, David."

"Have I ever?"

"Well don't start now." Then she wrapped her arms around me and kissed me long and hard. When she released me, she wore her princess mask once again. "That signal you promised—I suppose we'll know it when we see it?"

"You know me well, dear," I unbuckled my sword and handed it to Callan. "I doubt whoever is on that ship, whether they're pirates or not, will allow me to go armed on board. Keep this safe for me. Rob will come back to haunt me if I lose his sword."

As Callan took the sword, Megan began humming a haunting melody. Eyes closed and head tilted back, she swayed slightly and her hands moved as if plucking guitar strings. Perhaps realizing silence had fallen around her, Megan opened her eyes.

"Sorry." Megan's face reddened.

"I've never heard that music before. What is it?" Callan asked.

"A theme for the ballad I'm composing about all of this. It's the lovers parting." Growing more self-conscious as we watched, Megan crossed her arms and her eyes flashed defiance. "Well, that is why you brought me."

"It's beautiful," Callan said, disarming Megan's defensiveness with two words. "I don't know how you did it, but you captured my exact feelings in that theme. I can't wait to hear the theme you compose for the lovers' reunion." Callan turned her gaze back to me. "Now you have two women awaiting your return, darling. That *is* something men dream about, isn't it?"

"Only in their nightmares," Rupor muttered.

"I shall strive mightily to avoid disappointing either my lover or the lyricist," I proclaimed. I gave one last look at Callan then turned to leave.

"How will you get into that metal monstrosity?" Rupor asked, sucking all the romance out of the moment.

I shrugged. "I'll knock on the door."

Fifteen minutes later, I did just that. I knew the knock couldn't be heard inside the ship, but the local I pretended to be would not. After a few seconds, I knocked again and called, "Hello? Is anyone there?"

I was on my third round of knocking and calling when the airlock slid open, revealing the same armored figure. I let my mouth go slack as a massive metal hand dragged me into the spaceship.

"Hey, let me go!" I cried in Mordanian. "I don't want to be dragged like an animal."

The armored man kept his grip, pulling me into the spaceship. I flailed about, acting frightened and out of my element. Under the cover of my flailing, I examined the ship and the members of the crew we passed.

The ship's interior was impeccably maintained. The captain and crew took very good care of their ship. In the history vids we'd watched in high school, pirates were always depicted as slovenly and their ships in such a state of disrepair it was a wonder they didn't simply fall apart in space. Even taking into account the Federation bias behind the vids, if Martin's suspicions were correct and this was a pirate ship, it certainly was an atypical one.

None of the crewman I saw, including the man in the powered

armor, did anything to dispel that notion. An unskilled or careless crewman wearing powered armor would crush my arm to pulp in his untrained grip. The armored man held my arm firmly, but did so without hurting me. That care didn't strike me as very piratical and I dared to hope that Martin's assessment was wrong.

The crewman dragged me to the bridge where I found Martin deep in conversation with another man. He was the captain. There was no doubt about that. The man stood almost as tall as Martin and me and had the look of a commander of men—confident, laser focused, missing little going on around him, and quite intimidating to those unused to dealing with such men. If it came to a fight, this captain would be a formidable enemy.

The captain turned my way and didn't see Martin scratch his head right over his implant. Then he extended his arms as if stretching. The hand he'd scratched with ended up pointing at the ship's computer. I nodded to Martin, as if in greeting, showing I understood. The captain obviously made Martin download his translation of local languages into the ship's computer. Somewhere, a crewman listened to a translation of our conversation. We had no secrets while on board the ship.

"Welcome aboard, young man," the captain said in galactic basic.

I shrugged, looked at Martin, and spoke Mordanian. "Captain Bane, what did he say?"

"This is Amaral Caudill, captain of this spaceship. He welcomes you aboard," Martin translated.

At the sound of the man's name, my blood ran cold. Mere feet from me stood one of the most vicious pirates ever to plague the Terran Federation.

CAPTAIN CAUDILL

Martin crashed on Aashla seventeen years ago. I couldn't remember when Caudill first appeared in news reports, but it was about the same time. Even if Martin had heard the name, he couldn't know of the death and destruction the pirate left in his wake. Caudill measured his legacy in thousands of butchered crew and passengers, vast fortunes in plundered riches, and a name that struck fear into the hearts of spacemen throughout Federation space and the frontier.

Struggling to block the horror Caudill's name conjured, I turned what I hoped was a pleasant smile on Caudill. "Captain Bane, would you tell Captain Caudill that I'm pleased to meet him and am most impressed by his ship of space."

As Martin relayed my greeting, I looked around the bridge. I kept my eyes wide and darting all around, as if I couldn't decide which instrument panel was the most wonderful. As my eyes flicked around the bridge, I had my implant record everything. The picture formed from the images indicated a bridge crew who all looked the worse for wear after their crash. Even Caudill favored his right arm and propped his right leg on a stool.

At a break in the conversation, I said, "The crew and the

captain look banged up, Captain Bane. Should we summon our doctor?"

The ship would certainly have a nano-tech med bay, but if I were in Caudill's position I'd save it for true emergencies. With no way of knowing how long he'd be stuck here, I had no doubt Caudill would ration high tech medicine with extreme care—probably saving most of it for himself.

"In my experience, medical care on primitive lost colonies such as this one is dicey at best. Is your doctor as likely to kill my men as heal them?" Caudill asked after Martin completed translating my question.

Martin held out one of his hands, pointing to the scars left from a tammar slash to the hand. "Our doctor saved my hand after a tammar—that's a damned big native predator—cut it to the bone in three places. The hand is a bit stiff, now, but otherwise as good as new. Tristan is good by most any standard—including what you'll find on rim and frontier worlds—and is superb for a primitive planet like this one."

Caudill peered at Martin's hand with interest then turned to one of the crew. "Have you got a final casualty count?"

"Yes, Captain. We have one hundred and twenty-six dead and thirty-six injured."

"Good God, you lost one hundred and twenty-six men in this crash?" Shock showed on Martin's face. I was shocked, too, but didn't dare show it since I wasn't supposed to understand gal base.

"One of the inertial dampeners failed during our exit from the wormhole. Everyone in the aft half of the ship disintegrated. At least it was a quick death." Caudill shook his head slowly. "The dampener shouldn't have failed like that. We keep them in good repair. And, yeah, send your man to get your doctor."

Martin, wincing at the thought of malfunctioning inertial dampeners, turned to me and switched languages. "That's an excellent suggestion, David. Please do go and fetch the doctor."

I nodded in acknowledgement, my mind already spinning

through plans. Could Tristan find a way to drug or otherwise incapacitate most of Caudill's remaining crew? If we couldn't find some way to eliminate the pirate threat, everyone on the planet was in serious trouble.

A SURPRISE ADDITION

"Considering the number of wounded, your doctor may need to bring a lot of supplies." Caudill spoke to the armored figure. "Orrons, go with the lad. Help carry the supplies if necessary and make sure nothing...unfortunate...happens to Captain Bane's assistant."

"That's very...generous...of you, Captain Caudill," Martin said.

"It's nothing more than the courtesy due a fellow professional," Caudill replied.

Of course, both of them spoke in galactic basic, so I just kept walking. I did stop at the first clumping footfall from Orrons, though. Casting an inquiring glance back at Martin, I asked, "Am I to have company on the trip to get the doctor?"

Martin switched to Mordanian. "You are, David. This man will provide protection and, should you require help carrying Tristan's supplies, will assist with that as well."

I looked Orrons up and down. "The man looks to be very heavy, sir. He'll likely break through the deck of any airship he boards."

"Your lad is either a tad slow or is planning something," Caudill said.

"Ah, so you *do* have the translation files I provided up and running," Martin said, his tone neutral. In Mordanian, Martin added, "You're not to board the airship, David. Just have Tristan and his supplies brought to you. That should solve the problem of Orrons' weight."

I nodded, waved to Orrons, and left the ship. The walk back to the clearing went much faster than my trip to the ship. That's because Orrons simply picked me up and smashed through the debris and trees. I hoped both the Tartegian and Mordanian commanders had spyglasses trained on me. This display of power would do more to convince them of the threat posed by the pirates than anything Martin or I could say or do.

Orrons put me down once we reached the clearing. Happy to be back on my own feet, I looked up at Orrons and waved. "Hey in there. Can you hear me?"

Orrons nodded.

"And you can understand me—even better. I need to signal that airship." I pointed to the command vessel for the Mordanian squadron. "Can you help me with that?"

With a nod, Orrons picked up a flaming tree trunk and waved it like I would wave a stick.

A moment later, the command airship descended. Of far greater importance, the *Pauline* stayed aloft. The last thing I needed was Callan or Megan drawing Orron's attention.

The squadron commander was at the bow when the airship came within easy hailing distance. He snapped off a parade ground salute.

"What can we do for you, Captain Rice?"

The commander, unaware of the mild deception Martin and I had played on Caudill, had just revealed my actual rank to the pirates.

Orrons' armored head tilted down to look at me. Was he reporting this revelation to Caudill? Of course he was. The question was, what kind of reception awaited me when we got back to the spaceship?

I hid my consternation from the squadron commander. He

could not know what Martin and I had done nor had he done anything wrong. The fault lay entirely with me. Had I explained the plan to Callan, she would have told her officers and told them how to address me. I could but hope lives were not lost because of my mistake.

"We have injured crewmen aboard the spaceship, Captain Subing," I said. "Please ask Tristan—Dr. Agrilla—if he would come with me to the ship so he may tend to them."

Captain Subing saluted again and his ship returned to the squadron. As the airship pulled alongside the *Pauline*, a mechanical voice issued from the suit. "Explain your deception. Why did you pretend to be subordinate to Captain Bane?"

The voice spoke in Mordanian, meaning the suit's translation system now included Martin's translation files. No doubt, Caudill was asking Martin the very same question. If only I knew how Martin would answer.

"Captain Bane is fully capable of commanding this mission and accompanied us by royal request. He speaks your language and knows your culture and your habits. A wise man defers to those with superior knowledge. That's why we had Martin make first contact with you," I responded. "When he did not return, I knew we must send someone to investigate. I came because I had to see your ship first-hand. Martin has told us of the ship's power, but seeing is believing. I treated him as a superior so your captain wouldn't see me as a threat—which I'm not. Now that I've seen your ship and that armor you wear, I realize no one on Aashla could possibly threaten you."

Orrons nodded but said nothing more. The two of us stood quietly, waiting for the doctor. Fifteen minutes later, Captain Subing's ship descended again. The crew lowered Tristan's medical kit, extra supplies, and then Tristan, himself, to the ground. As I worked to free Tristan from the harness, a commotion broke out on the deck above me. Amidst shouted commands from unseen officers, a lithe figure swung over the railing and slid to join us.

Wearing a wicked grin, Megan dropped the last few feet to the ground. Without a word, she helped me free Tristan from the harness.

"Captain Subing? Would you care to explain this woman's presence?" I called.

"It's nice to see you again, too, Captain Rice." Megan's voice simply dripped with honey.

"I do apologize, sir," called Subing. "We had no idea she slipped onboard. She must have crossed to my ship while the men were occupied with Dr. Agrilla."

"That's quite all right, Captain. I've been caught unawares by Megan, as well." I caught Megan by the arm. "Send some men down to fetch her."

"Don't you dare think you can have me manhandled back aboard that ship."

"Oh, I dare. I most certainly dare."

"No," The suit's mechanical voice startled everyone but me. "The woman will come with us."

HOSTAGE

Why did Megan have to do this? Caudill had enough leverage over us without having Martin's girlfriend as a hostage. There *had* to be a way to keep Megan out of the pirate spaceship. My mind raced, trying to find it. Leave it to Tristan to find the right approach.

"Do you have any medical experience, young lady? Training as a nurse or anything like that?" Tristan asked.

"I'm a musician, not a doctor." With no concept of the situation and the stakes, Megan got defensive. "How much experience have you got with the guitar?"

"I haven't played since my wife died." Tristan met Megan's challenging glare calmly. "So, definitely no more than forty years."

Megan's eyes widened and her mouth hung slack. I resisted the temptation to reach over and close her mouth.

"As you've no doubt heard, the woman won't be any help with your wounded crew mates," I said to Orrons. Looking up to the airship, I called, "Captain Subing, please send down a properly trained airman."

Orrons turned his attention on Megan and went still—conferring with Caudill, no doubt—then spoke in a booming voice. "Keep your airman aboard the airship. *I* want to bring this woman back to the ship and Captain Caudill has given me permission. He wishes to meet her, as well. Uninjured members of our crew will provide assistance for the doctor."

Megan flashed a triumphant smile and struck off toward the spaceship. I refrained from calling her an idiot, though God only knows how I managed to do it. Orrons lifted most of Tristan's supplies and the four of us trudged in silence toward the spaceship.

After we fought free of the debris and approached the airlock, I gave Tristan and Megan significant looks. "Please remember that none of the crew speak our language. Since Captain Bane comes from their civilization, we must ask Captain Bane to translate for us."

Megan gave me a puzzled glance. "But I thought you-"

Tristan pretended his foot caught on a root. Off balance, he stumbled into Megan and they both tumbled to the ground.

"Ouch!" Megan yelped, pushing at Tristan.

He flailed a bit, as you might expect from an old man, and used that as cover to whisper hastily in Megan's ear. Only then did he manage to push himself up and off of her.

"I am *most* sorry, my dear," he said, offering his hand to Megan to pull her back to her feet. "David, it will be rather awkward if I have to send for Captain Bane whenever I need a translator. Lives may be lost if I must wait for a translator to make my needs clear."

"That's an excellent point, Tristan. It is the first thing I will discuss with both captains when we get inside."

Orrons led us to the bridge. Once we stepped through the hatch, I noticed that Caudill's crew moved to block the hatch. Orrons stepped aside and I realized something had gone seriously wrong.

Caudill stood behind Martin holding a fully charged blaster to Martin's head.

Tristan glared at Caudill. "If this is some twisted form of coercion intended to force me to work on your wounded, I assure you it is unnecessary."

Caudill listened as the computer translated. "I do not threaten

Captain Bane in the vain hope it will make you perform miracles. I trust pride will make you to do your best."

Tristan gave a start as the computer translated Caudill's words into Mordanian. "Then why do you hold a...I assume that's a weapon?"

"Yes, doctor, it is a weapon. It crossed my mind that you and your deceitful friend here," Caudill pointed at me with his free hand, "might take this opportunity to drug my crew and me. Unconscious men are *so* much easier to capture than conscious ones." Caudill turned a smile on Megan. "Wouldn't you agree, young lady?"

When the translation singled her out, Megan paled and squeaked, "Me? How should I know about these things?"

"Because it's one of the oldest tricks in the book. The bumbling but beautiful young assistant—that's you, my dear—provides a welcome distraction for a crew too long in space. While the crew concentrates on the obvious charms of his lovely assistant, the doctor administers incapacitating drugs to said crew. Didn't these fine gentlemen tell you the plan before asking you to accompany them?"

Megan looked back and forth between Tristan and me.

"Megan," I said, "not only did I *not* request your company on this mission, I quite specifically told you to stay on the airship."

Caudill shook his head as if in admiration. "Masterful manipulators always make you believe it was *your* idea, Megan."

"Remember who overruled me and insisted you accompany us?" I pointed at the armored figure. "Orrons did, with the added comment that Captain Caudill gave him permission to bring you."

"Captain Caudill, what is more important to you—arguing with Captain Rice or seeing your men receive medical care?" Tristan's stern doctor's voice cut off whatever Caudill was about to say.

Anger flashed in Caudill's eyes. "My crew matters most, of course."

Tristan stared down the angry pirate without expression. "Then perhaps you would be so good as to direct me toward your wounded men?"

"Morrison," Caudill pointed to a crewman, "will take you to them. Captain Rice will accompany you as an assistant. The lovely Megan will stay on the bridge. Captain Bane and I will be glad of such delightful company."

The look on Martin's face said no such thing, but there was nothing I could do. Megan fidgeted as Morrison helped Tristan and me gather the medical equipment. Her eyes darted around the bridge, perhaps searching for a place to hide. As irritating as her impetuosity was, I pitied her.

"Orrons told me that you're a musician, Megan." Caudill smiled, once again the charming and congenial host. "Perhaps you would grace us with a song?"

Megan nodded, the jerky movement of someone unsure of what to do. Then, her voice quavering but still beautiful, Megan began to sing. With horror, I realized the song she'd chosen was *Rupor's Lament*.

EMERGENCY DRONE

As she sang, Megan's posture straightened and her voice gained strength. Singing obviously calmed the woman. If only it would calm me, as well.

There once was a prince,
Handsome and gay,
Who loved a princess,
Lovely but fey.

I could not allow Megan to continue singing this song. The minute she sang the verse ridiculing the story of my arrival on Aashla would be my last. But I could think of no way to stop her without arousing Caudill's suspicions to the point he would kill me anyway.

"By all that's holy," Martin cried, "I beg you to kill me now so I don't have to listen to that insipid song one more time."

Startled, her face coloring red, Megan stopped singing.

Caudill looked at Martin, an eyebrow cocked. "From what little I heard, it was but a love song. Do you have a problem with love songs, Bane?"

"Oh no, not at all. Who wouldn't love such a song?" Martin

sneered. "It's all about a handsome prince who falls in love with a beautiful princess. But the princess jilts the prince and marries a member of her royal guard. If you've got any lovestruck teenage girls in your crew, summon them forthwith! I have no doubt they will love every single sentimental verse."

"Fine," Megan snapped. "If you dislike it so much, I'll sing something else."

Megan's next song was a traditional ballad with no mention of crash-landed scouts anywhere.

With the brief dramatic outburst over, Morrison motioned for Tristan and me to follow him. He led us through the ship to a cargo bay that had been adapted to hold the wounded. Close to forty men lay within, some as still as death, others fidgeting and impatient to leave.

Tristan pointed to three men. "David, please have these men moved to those tables across the room. They're in the most danger."

The computer translated Tristan's words for Morrison, who frowned. "Four of the men are in worse shape than those three. Start with them."

When the computer finished with speaking the translation, Tristan turned a frosty look on Morrison. "Are you a doctor young man?"

"No, but it's obvious to anyone who isn't blind who's worse off, old man."

"Those four men are beyond my help. I will not waste time with them while there are those I can help." Tristan turned back to me. "Begin triage once you've moved those three men."

For the next hour, I worked my way through the room, rearranging the wounded as instructed, while Tristan did what he could for those who might be saved. When I finished, I stood and stretched my sore back—and spotted lights flickering against the back wall. Curious, I took a closer look.

A Space Forces decryption machine—stolen, no doubt— churned through a decryption routine. A metal tube—one I recognized immediately—was connected to it. The tube was the emergency drone I'd launched when my scout ship exited the wormhole.

Morrison, Caudill's representative in the cargo bay-cum-sickbay, saw me staring at the decryption machine and emergency drone. "Hey, you. We don't have any wounded crew over there. What do you think you're doing?"

I turned at Morrison's call but dutifully waited for the computer to finish translating his words before answering. "I just saw these things glowing and blinking and got curious. I've never seen anything like it before. What does it do?"

"That's none of your business. It's too advanced for a yokel like you and doesn't have anything to do with medicine." Morrison pointed toward Tristan's makeshift surgery. "Now get back to helping the old man with the surgery. I don't want any of my friends dying because you were too busy gawking at pretty lights to help."

"It looks like the doctor has everything under control, but if that's where you want me..." I shrugged and went over to Tristan.

"Our gracious host sounded irritated. What was that all about?" he asked.

"I have no idea, Tristan." I hooked a thumb over my shoulder toward the decryption machine. "They've got a machine over there that has some kind of lights that glow and blink. Morrison says it's beyond the understanding of a yokel like me. I'm sure he's right."

Tristan raised his eyebrows. "Is that so? Well, if they're so smart why do they need a yokel doctor to tend to their wounded?"

That was a very good question—one I hadn't given much thought to. Any ship this size should have at least one docbot— maybe even a human doctor—plus a plentiful supply of medical nanites. Caudill might want to conserve his supplies, but he'd already lost half of his crew to the inertial dampener failure. The pirate captain couldn't afford to lose any more crewmen if he ever hoped to fly this ship again. Most of their medical supplies must have been lost along with the men. The transition out of the wormhole would have pulverized those supplies along with the men. That thought got me wondering what other equipment and supplies might have been lost, as well. Maybe Caudill's position wasn't as strong as I had feared.

Later, when Tristan and I were tending to the last few wounded crewmen, Caudill came to inspect our work. Caudill worked his way through the room, speaking to every crewman who was conscious. When Tristan reported that five of the men probably wouldn't survive, Caudill bowed his head in sorrow. If he was acting, he did a masterful job of it. Caudill knew how to inspire loyalty in his crew.

"My men will need food and better accommodations than this cargo bay," Caudill said to me. "I want to send a message to Prince Rupor and Princess Callan informing them that I wish to negotiate for the care of my men."

NOT STUPID

It took all the control I had to keep my expression neutral until the computerized translation ended. How had Caudill found out about Callan and Rupor? I trusted Martin to keep silent and, impetuous and thoughtless as she could be, I doubted Megan would talk, either. Not voluntarily, at least. Had Caudill forced one of them to talk by threatening the other? I'd find out soon enough.

I had to keep Callan and Rupor as far from Caudill as humanly possible. I played the only card I had. "Tell me what you need, Captain Caudill. I am authorized to negotiate on the behalf of their Highnesses."

I longed to speak in gal base. Waiting for translations I didn't need wore on my nerves.

Caudill turned an appraising look on me. "I suspect you really could negotiate for one of the countries. What's the one with the princess?"

"Mordan."

"Yes, Mordan. And the country with the prince?"

"Tarteg."

"Right. Them, not so much, I think."

"I'm sure the two kingdoms will work together to take care of you and your men," I said.

"I doubt that. You remember Orrons, of course. The man in the big suit of armor?"

"He's rather hard to forget. What of him?"

"You saw how easily Orrons waved that tree trunk? It's the armor that makes that possible."

"I assumed as much."

"You did?" Caudill looked closely at me. "For a man from a backward planet, you have a surprising grasp of modern technology, Captain Rice."

"No, I have a surprising grasp of common sense." I put a little irritation into my voice. "I may be ignorant of your worlds and your machines, but I'm not stupid."

"Stupid, no. Dangerous, yes."

"Was there a point to your comment about the armor, Captain?"

"There was. As you probably guessed, using the armor for brute strength is so easy even you could do it."

Of course I could. I'd received plenty of training in powered armor at the academy.

Caudill continued, "The real skill is handling fragile things without breaking them. Very few people can do that. Orrons is a master. No, it goes beyond that. He's a true artist." Caudill held his palms a foot apart. "Imagine a pretty musician's head between armored hands. Slowly—so slowly the human eye can't discern the movement—the hands press together. Inexorable pressure builds in the skull, causing exquisite pain. How much pressure can a human skull take before it cracks? For a former pirate, Captain Bane proved surprisingly uncurious about the answer. And he succumbs to persuasion rather easily." Caudill shook his head in mock disgust. "All it took was one scream.

"As a native of this planet, you know Tarteg and Mordan have warred for centuries. Now I know as well. And that's information a man like me can put to good use. You see, Rice, I'm not really negotiating with the prince or the princess. I'm selling my ship and services to the highest bidder."

Caudill's smile was as cold as his eyes. "With me backing one of those kingdoms, the next war between Tarteg and Mordan will also be the last war between them."

SUBTERFUGE

"Decades have passed since the last war between Mordan and Tarteg," I said. "You're counting on an enmity that doesn't run very deep anymore."

Caudill laughed when the computer completed translating my words. "How very optimistic of you, Rice. Old enmities can lay dormant for ages and then, when you least expect it, spring back with full vigor. And a peace that is desirable when neither country holds a military advantage becomes a burden when you can crush your enemy."

"Are you so certain your experiences on other planets apply here? I doubt you've ever been on a world like Aashla."

"Men are men wherever they live. And some men will always seek power over their fellows. It's our nature."

Caudill was right, something I knew from bitter experience. But I hoped he was wrong about Tarteg and Mordan. "I'll defer to your extensive experience in that matter. Meanwhile, are you sure you want to send someone as dangerous as me to deliver your message?"

Caudill turned an appraising eye on me. "Now that is an interesting question, Rice. You've piqued my curiosity—who would you send?"

"I'd send Megan. Her skills are of no use to you nor to the prince and princess. Your position is not weakened and theirs is not strengthened." It was a long shot, but worth trying.

"That's an interesting and accurate analysis." Caudill rubbed his chin. "Except you left out one vital point. Megan has great value as a hostage against Bane's good behavior. And, if I read you and the old doctor right, she'll insure your good behavior as well. While sending her doesn't strengthen the prince and princess, it does weaken me. No, you'll deliver my message."

"Fine. Give me the message then Orrons and I can leave."

"As long as I have your friends, I see no reason to waste Orrons' time. I'm sure a fine young officer such as yourself can deliver a message without supervision."

Five minutes later, I picked my way through the debris outside the spaceship, trying to figure out why Caudill hadn't sent Orrons with me. There were many possible reasons, but only one that fits our current situation so neatly. Caudill wanted to conserve the suit's power. Had his armor recharging unit been destroyed in the crash? It seemed likely.

Perhaps Caudill's position wasn't nearly as strong as he wanted us to believe.

As before, it took fifteen minutes to work my way clear of the debris from the pirate ship's crash landing. Once I reached clear terrain, I waved to the airships floating in the distance. Almost immediately, one of the Mordanian ships broke formation and descended.

When the airship was close enough, I called, "Captain Subing, drop a line so I can come aboard. I must speak with Their Highnesses."

The ascent seemed to take forever but lasted no more than ten minutes. Captain Subing smartly maneuvered his ship alongside the *Pauline*. Callan and Rupor leaned against the little airship's railing, all signs of the earlier tension gone. The two future monarchs chatted amicably and tried to hide their apprehension over the news I brought. Callan gave me a dazzling smile that did not wipe away the concern in her eyes. Rupor wore a neutral expression, but I saw tension lines in his brow.

"Callan, greet me as you would any other naval officer." I saluted as the sailors tied the airships together. "Holding Megan gives Caudill leverage over Martin and led to unfortunate, though understandable, revelations. Caudill is certain to watch this meeting. As I must return to him after our conference, I don't want him getting the idea he can use me to gain equal leverage over you."

I vaulted over to the *Pauline* and bowed respectfully to Callan and Rupor, just as any officer would do. Callan wore what I called her court face, which she adopted whenever she sat in royal court. It gave her that serene, knowledgable look subjects want to see in their monarch. The court face must be something royal family members learn in the nursery, as Rupor wore the male version of the expression.

I outlined what I saw inside the spaceship as well as the situation with Megan, Martin, and Tristan. I spent a lot of time explaining the destructive power of Caudill's weapons. But I spent the most time trying to explain what it meant if Caudill couldn't recharge the powered armor. Callan and Rupor concentrated hard on my explanation, asking several questions.

"If I follow what you're saying," Callan mused, "it's like tossing the last of your fuel into a boiler while your airship is flying in the middle of a desert. You can run the steam engine for a while, but once you're out of fuel the engine becomes nothing more than a useless hunk of metal."

"That's a fair description of the situation, Callan." I said. And Rupor nodded, his furrowed brow clearing after listening to Callan's analogy.

"In that case, our course is obvious." Rupor smiled, definitely happy to be back on more familiar ground. "As part of these negotiations, Callan and I must convince this pirate to burn what fuel he has left for his armor."

SIGNALS FLAGS AND RADIOS

"That's a great idea, Rupor, but have you got any idea how to get Caudill to do it?" I asked.

"No prince—or princess—worthy of the title would ever purchase someone's services without personally observing their capabilities," Rupor answered. "Waving a tree trunk around, while quite impressive, is hardly a sufficient demonstration to warrant the kind of money Caudill no doubt wants."

"That's an excellent point, Rupor," Callan responded. "David, tell Caudill we will only consider bidding after we've seen what his armored man can do."

"*I* know what that man can do and I don't want either of you getting anywhere close to him," I said. "For your own safety and the safety of your kingdoms, you two must watch Caudill's show from afar. You must also watch from different ships which hold positions far from each other."

"If you think that's best, David, Rupor and I will do as you suggest."

Rupor nodded his agreement. "But that still leaves us with a problem. Callan and I must have some way to communicate with this pirate. How else can we tell him what we wish to see?"

"Devices exist that allow people to talk across long distances.

Captain Rice isn't supposed to know about them, so I'll have to make sure Caudill thinks to suggest them." I saluted and then hopped across to Captain Subing's ship. "Take me down, Captain."

Twenty minutes later, I presented Their Highness's demand for a demonstration to Caudill. It did not surprise me in the least that the idea had no appeal to him.

"How dare those spoiled, inbred barbarians make demands of me. They have *seen* the powered armor at work." Caudill stood inches from me, his shout filling the small bridge. "Can anyone on this backward planet wave a tree trunk around like it's a twig? No, they cannot!" Caudill pressed his thumb on the arm of is chair. "I could squash them and their pathetic kingdoms, if I so desired!"

I kept my face impassive and waited for the translation to complete. "If you are so powerful, Captain Caudill, why even bother offering your services to the highest bidder?"

Martin chuckled, "The lad has you there, Caudill. These people may be technologically primitive, but they are not stupid. The two kingdoms may *want* your services, but they do not *need* them. You, alas, are in the exact opposite situation."

"I hold the four of you hostage," Caudill shot back. "Those arrogant royals should pause and consider that."

"Sorry, old chap, but we're all Mordanian. I'm sure Her Highness will be quite put out if something happens to us, but I doubt Prince Rupor could care less. You're the one counting on old enmities returning in full force yet you expect a Tartegian to temper his demands to save the lives of Mordanian subjects?"

Caudill turned back to me. "Earlier, you said you could negotiate for both countries. I accept your offer. Let's negotiate."

I shook my head. "I could have negotiated before Their Highnesses got involved. I no longer have that authority. You negotiate with them or you don't negotiate at all."

"And if you don't negotiate," Martin added, "you don't get the food and medicine you need. That's quite a quandary you've landed yourself in, Caudill."

Caudill ranted and raged for another ten minutes, but my

refusal to negotiate blocked his every suggestion. In the end, he agreed to the demonstration.

"Have the prince and princess land so we can get on with this circus." Caudill turned away, thinking our conversation was at an end.

I dutifully waited for the translation before speaking. "Their Highnesses will be viewing the demonstration from their airships."

Caudill whirled back to me, his face red. "After all of this, they aren't even going to come down and watch? No. Absolutely not."

"The royal heirs of the two most powerful kingdoms on Aashla do not endanger themselves needlessly." I put every bit of offense I could muster into my voice. After listening to this murderous pirate denigrate my wife, I found I had quite a lot of offense to draw upon.

"Then how will they communicate with me?"

"We'll use signal flags. The ships have skilled flagmen. Demands and comments will fly between their ships and us in a matter of minutes."

"Minutes? Tell me you're joking."

"Not at all Captain Caudill."

"Oh for God's sake, Caudill," Martin snapped, "give them a couple of handheld radios if you're too impatient for the flags."

Eyes blazing, Caudill called for radios. I could only hope the rest of the plan went as smoothly.

REMOVE HIS HELMET

The logistics of the power suit demonstration took a while to setup. I took the radios to Callan and Rupor and explained how they worked. Then I offered a suggestion.

"After Caudill shows you a few basic things, Rupor should ask for a demonstration of weapons systems."

"I agree we should see this man's weapons at work, but what if Caudill asks how we know about... Drat, what was the red light called?"

"Stick with calling it a red light. Martin is the only one who knows the name and he never had a chance to tell you," I said. "Since you've seen that in person, it's easy to explain your curiosity. Seeing one weapon in action will pique your curiosity over other weapons."

Callan nodded. "I'll let Rupor ask about weapons first, but we'll both demand to see more."

"Good. One final thing—have your ships keep moving. They don't have to move too fast, just fast enough to make targeting difficult."

Rupor scratched his head. "Don't they have some machine that makes aiming easier? It seems like they have a machine for everything else."

"They do, but they're designed to target other spaceships. I can't go into the details now, but those machines aren't designed to target steam-powered airships. In simple terms, the machine can't see the airship. That means aiming manually, which is a lot harder." I looked back and forth between Rupor and Callan. "Just promise me you'll turn and fly away if the pirates fire at you."

They both gave me their assurances, as did the captains of the ships they'd be aboard while observing. Then I was returned to the ground, where I contacted Caudill by radio.

"Everything is set for the demonstration, Captain Caudill," I radioed.

"Very well, Orrons and I are coming out."

That was unexpected. I hadn't expected Caudill to step foot outside the spaceship any time soon. Perhaps I could find some way to turn this to our advantage.

"Remember my crew holds your three friends," Caudill growled, as if reading my mind. "And, of course, Orrons can break you into little pieces. So don't get any ideas and don't try anything."

Moments later, Orrons tromped out to join me, Caudill riding on his shoulder. Orrons gently lowered Caudill to the ground and then awaited orders.

Caudill proved to be quite the showman, putting Orrons through a range of impressive maneuvers. And Orrons proved to be the powered-armor artist Caudill said he was. The longer I watched Orrons, the more I found myself praying the armor's charge would run out soon—*very* soon.

After ten minutes, Caudill spoke into his radio, "That's more than sufficient. Do either of you have any questions before the bidding begins?"

I expected Rupor to ask for the laser demonstration, but Callan got in first and with an unexpected request.

"Yes, have him remove his helmet. I'd like to see Orrons' face."

"Why would you care what he looks like, princess?" Irritation crept into Caudill's voice. "What's important is what he can *do*, not what he looks like."

"Martin has told us of mechanical men. How do we know this isn't some machine that will always do your bidding?"

"I find myself concurring with Callan," Rupor said. "I also wish assurances Orrons is not some form of construct."

Caudill pondered then sighed. "Fine... Take off the helmet, Orrons."

Callan's request created a crack in the powered armor. I only had to find a way to exploit it.

HE'S A SCOUT

Orrons lifted his hands toward the neck of the powered armor and the metal fingers danced and tapped around the seam. Slide locks opened and button locks depressed. After a few seconds, the helmet popped up a fraction of an inch. Orrons grasped the helmet and lifted it off of his head.

I don't know what I expected to see—the scarred and hardened face of a pirate, I suppose. I did *not* expect to find a boy, no more than sixteen or seventeen, looking down at me. I wasn't the only one surprised by the sight.

"Why he's no more than a child!" Callan's voice exclaimed over the radio.

Teenage annoyance filled Orrons' face after hearing the translation.

"Boy he may be," Caudill said, "but Orrons is highly skilled with the powered armor and will follow my orders to the letter. Be it crushing your foes or crushing that musician's head, Orrons is man enough to handle the job."

Orrons smiled with pride and nodded to his captain. "Aye aye, Cap'n."

Rupor's voice crackled from the radio. "Unlike Her Highness, I'm not concerned over the lad's age. I *am* concerned that you speak of the lad obeying your orders. If I employ him, I expect him to follow my orders, as well."

"That's an entirely reasonable expectation, Prince Rupor." Caudill smiled broadly at this more traditional question. "All I need to do is order Orrons to obey your orders and he will do it. You do understand that he won't turn against me or any of my men."

"Of course." Rupor's tone said this was perfectly right and natural. "I wouldn't trust a turncoat, anyway."

"All right, I believe we've had more than enough talking," Caudill said. "It's time to get down to the bidding."

"I did have one more request-"

The radio crackled to life, interrupting Rupor. "Captain? You requested a call if a certain task was completed while you were outside. It's done."

"Excellent! There were times I feared it never would end." Caudill said. "What have you got for me?"

With Caudill distracted by the call and Orrons watching his captain, I studied Orrons, looking for a weakness. It didn't take long to determine the boy's head was his only weakness. If I kept him from donning the helmet again, I could knock him out.

"I've got something very interesting, indeed," came the reply. "I think you should return to the ship and hear my report in private."

"There is no need for me to go to all that trouble," Caudill said, impatience in his tone. "Just turn off the translator and spit it out. Whatever you have to say will be private enough."

"That's just it, Captain," the voice responded. "The report won't be private at all."

With a sinking feeling, I suddenly realized they'd broken the encryption on the emergency drone launched by my ship.

Caudill's bantering tone vanished. "What do you mean by that?"

The radio crackled. "That man with you isn't a native of this planet. He's Terran Scout First Class David Rice."

YOU'VE GOT HIM NOW

Caudill spun around and stared at me, his eyes as warm and filled with humanity as the eyes of a snake. His gaze flicked to Orrons. In a voice as devoid of emotion as his eyes, Caudill said, "Kill him."

Upon hearing the order, Orrons' face transformed. Pride in Caudill's compliment fell away as Orron's lips spread in a feral grin. His eyes went cold as the flash of humanity faded. Looking into that face, it was no longer possible to think of Orrons as a normal teenager. Before me stood a sick and twisted human being—one who could crush me without even trying.

"And Orrons," Caudill added in a conversational tone, "we're trying to make an impression on an audience. So please do your best to make his death messy."

Now emotion flowed into Orrons' eyes, but it was not comforting in the least. No one could take solace from the anticipation shining in Orrons' eyes.

I only had one possible response to the threat Orrons represented.

Boost!

Time slowed as my implant poured adrenaline into my body. Orrons, already slowed by the cumbersome powered armor, moved in extreme slow motion as he lifted his arms to replace the helmet. If I was going to have any chance in this fight, I had to keep that helmet off of Orrons' head.

I charged Orrons, grabbing the helmet and swinging my feet up to plant on Orrons' chest plate. The armored boy shifted his grip, anticipating that I would pull the helmet from his hands. The suit's mechanical muscles made that impossible. Even Boosted, my strength couldn't match his. But I had a lot more experience than the young Orrons and went with something he never expected. I shoved the helmet at Orrons' head. With Orrons already pulling the helmet toward himself, the helmet slammed into Orrons' face. Blood spurted from his smashed nose and he instinctively released the helmet to hold his nose.

Helmet in hand, I shoved off the chest plate, flipping to land ten feet from the boy. Spinning, I flung the helmet as far from the three of us as possible.

Flowing blood and burning rage turned Orrons' face a mottled crimson. With a bellow, Orrons rushed toward me, his teeth bared, a guttural snarl on his lips. I held my ground, diving to the right just before the armored boy trampled me under his metal feet. Orrons thundered past but dug in his feet and, leaving twin furrows in the ground, slid to a stop far more quickly than I liked.

I had hoped to draw Orrons far out of position, giving me an opening to charge Caudill. If I got my hands on him, the fight was all but over. Orrons obviously worshipped Caudill and wouldn't do anything to risk his piratical father figure. But my hope was in vain. Caudill moved constantly, always keeping Orrons between us.

Orrons charged again. I dodged again. And, damn him, Caudill moved again. This fight reminded me of my fight with the trog leader in Faroon, back before Callan and I were married. I couldn't afford to let the trog get his hands on me then and I definitely couldn't let Orrons get hold of me now. The difference was Orrons had but one vulnerable spot—his head. And, because the pirates frowned on armed guests aboard their spaceship, I didn't even have a sword.

"Calm down, Orrons. You're just running around like a child. Slow down and take your time," Caudill called. "The scout can't use his Boost for much more than a minute. Be patient and wait him out."

And there was my one minor advantage. Caudill knew nothing of my extensive history with Boost. Could I draw Orrons in close by pretending to lose Boost? If I sold the act well enough, I'd have one chance to sucker punch Orrons. To have any hope of knocking him out with one blow, I had to hit him with something harder than my fist. I found that something the next time I dived and rolled away from Orrons. Pain lanced through my back as I landed on a rock twice the size of my fist. Ignoring the pain, I grabbed that rock and a smaller one close by.

Coming out of the roll, I flung the smaller rock at Orrons' head. He brought his arm up and the rock clanged off the armor. Then I staggered, held a hand to my head, and bent over.

"What did I tell you, lad?" Caudill crowed. "You've got him now. Remember to make his death messy."

Orrons grinned, stomping up to me. After chasing me all around the clearing, the teenager simply could not resist the temptation to gloat. A nasty smile on his face, Orrons leaned in close.

Grinning myself, I rose from my crouch and smashed the rock into Orrons' head.

SATISFACTION

Driven by my Boosted strength, I expected to hear the satisfying thunk of stone on bone. That would be followed by Orrons toppling to the ground, unconscious. None of that happened. Instead, I heard the clunk of rock on metal.

Orrons yelled in pain and flailed his arms at me, knocking me away from him. An arm caught a glancing blow against my chest, knocking the wind out of me and sending me flying from him. I crashed to the ground a good thirty feet from the armored figure. Then I tumbled heels over head for another ten feet.

When I stopped rolling, everything hurt. I could do nothing but gasp to draw breath into my empty lungs. Dazed, I couldn't concentrate well enough to override my implant's safety protocols. Those protocols, incapable of judging anything but my physical condition, decided Boost was more harm than good and shut it off. Unable to move, I could do nothing but stare into the bright sky. Absently, I noticed several of the airships break from their holding patterns and descend under full power. To my dismay, I recognized the *Pauline* leading the way. No doubt Nist acted under orders from Callan. Why couldn't she understand how much I needed to keep her safe?

"That was quite a show you and Orrons put on, Rice. You should have seen the look on your face when you hit Orrons metal skull plate. It was priceless." Caudill laughed as the heavy tread of armored feet started toward me. "Do you want to know why Orrons is so skilled with the armor? I had his brain wired with a direct neural interface when he was five years old. That kind of interface gives a man astounding control over the armor. As an added bonus, Orrons got a metal skull. He's had a dozen years to practice since the operation, too. Add all that together and you get a true artist with powered armor."

I knew of many people with neural interfaces, but they got theirs as adults. No reputable doctor would even consider installing one in such a young, still-developing brain. The child was almost certain to die a hideously painful death.

"Are you insane? How many children died before you succeeded with Orrons?" I wheezed, finally starting to regain my breath.

"Let me think. Four boys, two girls. So, only six."

"Only? *Only*? How can you live with yourself?"

"Quite easily. After all, I did succeed with Orrons."

Then Orrons loomed over me, blocking the sun. He raised his foot, planning to stomp the life out of me, I assumed. Instead, Orrons rested his foot on my chest. The weight of the foot, alone and without any pressure from Orrons, sent pain shooting through my bruised ribs. Meanwhile, I scrambled to discover some way to escape from this with my life.

"I'm going to take my time killing you." Orrons' smile twisted in a sick imitation of joy. "This will be like squeezing that woman's head between my hands. I'll build the pressure so slowly you won't feel it at first. Second by second, the pain will build until your bones begin to crack. Then it will continue building until your organs pop. And all the time, I'll be right here, looking you in the eye as you die."

"You are one truly sick and twisted boy, Orrons." I looked at Caudill. "You must be so proud of him."

"Indeed I am, Rice." Caudill regarded the armored boy with

something akin to paternal pride. "Orrons is absolutely loyal and he never questions my orders. In many ways, Orrons is the son I never had."

"Like any sane woman would ever have a child with you," I spat through teeth gritted against the pain. "How much do you have to pay them to be with you, Caudill? Or are you the type who prefers a woman in a drugged stupor?"

All emotion fled Caudill's face. Dead eyes met mine and, in a flat tone, he said, "You'd be surprised just how many women want a man exactly like me, Rice. They may deny it, but I can see the desire in their eyes. But enough of this chit chat. This game grows tiresome. My time is valuable and yours, alas, is short. I believe it's past time to finish you. Orrons-"

The radio crackled to life and Callan's voice burst forth. "Spare David's life and I'll give you everything you're asking for!"

Caudill's eyebrows rose and he gave me an appraising look. "David? Not Captain Rice? Well, Your Highness, that *is* an interesting development—one I find very intriguing. Princess Callan, would you care to elaborate on the true nature of your relationship with the nearly deceased captain?"

Silence stretched for several seconds.

"No? Then perhaps you would allow me to make a guess. Forced to marry against her wishes and now trapped in a political marriage—to the prince of a troublesome neighboring kingdom, perhaps—the young princess found true love in the arms of the dashing and mysterious Captain Rice." Caudill's smirk returned in full force. "How am I doing, princess? Please do let me know if I've gotten the wrong idea."

Once again, Callan held her silence.

"I'm sure your story would have quite a romantic ending if you didn't already have a husband." Caudill shook his head in mock dismay. "That's quite an unfortunate detail—unless you and Captain Rice have plans to do away with the unfortunate fellow. Am I on the right trail?"

Callan's continued silence kept Caudill heading down the wrong path.

"And what of poor, betrayed Prince Rupor. I wonder if he will reward me better for killing Rice than you will for sparing him?"

"I most certainly will not reward you for killing that man!" Rupor's voice burst from the radio. "But if you grant me the satisfaction of killing him myself, I'll give you everything you're asking for and more."

Caudill's smirk broadened into a smile of true pleasure. "That, Prince Rupor, is an offer I simply cannot refuse. Captain Rice is yours to kill."

A FAIR FIGHT

Orrons sulked at Caudill's order to remove his foot from my chest, but he did as he was told. Obeying a second order from Caudill, Orrons stood straddling me, insuring I stayed put.

"Prince Rupor," Caudill said, "I suggest you have Her Highness attend this event along with you."

"I see no reason for that," Rupor replied.

"You don't? Then perhaps you have earned the disrespect she shows to you." Caudill's voice took on an edge, "If you coddle Princess Callan and shield her from witnessing the end result of her infidelity, you will simply encourage her to stray again."

"There is no need to order me to attend. I *insist* on witnessing this duel, Rupor!" Callan replied. "I will take great pleasure in watching David slice you to pieces."

"Foolish woman, where did you get the idea that Rice would be armed?" Caudill snarled. "I promised Prince Rupor he could kill Rice. I did not promise Rupor could duel with him."

"That is unacceptable, Captain Caudill." Rupor struck a perfect tone of effrontery. "Rice *must* be armed and I must slay him in a fair fight. It is the only way I can restore my tattered honor."

Caudill stared at the radio in disbelief, but he desperately needed Rupor's aid and good will. "If you say the fight must be fair, then fair it shall be. Her Highness may bring a sword for Rice."

With an annoyed shake of the head, Caudill turned off his radio and turned to me. "Don't think you've earned a reprieve, Rice. Should you manage to win this duel, I will have Orrons kill Princess Callan. After you've seen your lady love ripped apart by Orrons, I'll have him do the same to you. So, if you truly love Princess Callan, I very strongly suggest you let Rupor slay you. Orrons will do the same thing if you make any attempt to warn her. Are we clear on this matter?"

I nodded.

"Oh, and I hope I don't need to remind you to make this look convincing."

I shook my head.

"Good. Enjoy the next few minutes. They're all you have left."

With that cheery comment, Caudill fell silent as we waited for Their Highnesses to arrive. The *Pauline*, bearing Callan, began descending when Caudill discovered my real identity. The fast little ship was minutes ahead of the others and was the first to arrive.

Nist brought the *Pauline* to within three feet of the ground and flew toward us. The airship moved slowly compared to an aircar—so slowly that I doubt Caudill ever realized just how fast the airship was flying. As the ship came adjacent to Orrons and me, Nist twisted the controls and spun the *Pauline* sideways. The stern swung around and smacked into Orrons back.

Small for an airship, the *Pauline* still greatly out-massed the armored boy. Orrons flew ten feet away, landing in a sprawl. Like an angel from heaven, Callan dropped my sword into my hand.

NO OTHER CHOICE

I drew my sword and sprang to my feet as Nist threw the *Pauline's* throttle wide open and twisted the ailerons up. The airship nosed up but it would be long seconds before it was too high for Orrons to jump to it.

Servos whined as Orrons shoved off the ground with mechanically enhanced strength. Popping up and onto his feet, the boy's eyes smoldered and his face went white with rage.

"I'm going to pull off your arms and legs and then laugh while you die, Rice!" Orrons' voice cracked as he screamed my name.

"Hey, at long last you've hit puberty." I could only hope goading worked as well on the boy as it had on Raoul.

Orrons roared wordlessly and lumbered toward me. Good, better me than the airship.

"Rice has already Boosted, Orrons. He's just a normal man, now. I can handle him," Caudill yelled over the roar of the *Pauline's* steam engine. "You go teach the crew of that airship what it means to mess with a man wearing powered armor. I want the princess alive but you can do what you wish with the rest."

Orrons turned toward the rising *Pauline*, flexed his knees, and jumped. He caught hold of a piece of the airship's ornate trimming. I hoped the trim would break off in Orrons hand, but the airship was too well made. It held and Orrons climbed toward the deck. I didn't even pause to consider my next action.

Boost!

Orrons and Caudill were in for quite a surprise. I leapt after Orrons, catching hold of a foot. Then I used Orrons like a ladder and climbed over him to the deck. As Orrons pulled himself over the railing, I bounded to his shoulders and jumped to the deck ahead of him.

Sword drawn, one of Callan's guards rushed at the armored figure. With a bellow, Orrons backhanded the guard, sending him crashing against the cabin. Knowing there was no reasoning with the boy, I charged. As expected, Orrons' swung his fist at me. I ducked under the punch, grabbed Orrons' elbow, and swung around the arm and onto his back.

My sword flashed in the sunlight as I swung at the only unprotected part of Orrons' body—his neck. The blade sliced through flesh and bone with ease. In terrible slow motion, Orrons' head spun through the air before dropping over the railing.

The powered armor stumbled forward a few steps, following the residual impulses left after Orrons' death. The headless figure hit the far railing and tottered off balance. Before the internal stabilizers could restore the balance, two of Callan's guards slammed into it from behind. The armor tumbled over the side of the airship and fell from sight.

I dropped Boost as I collapsed to my knees and buried my head in my hands. Tears stung my eyes as the full impact of my actions hit me. Orrons was barely older than Milo—a child with his whole life ahead of him. My mind replayed the scene, searching for anything I could have done to save Orrons. In a grotesque mockery of reality, in my mind the severed head spinning away belonged to Milo rather than Orrons.

Then a pair of arms wrapped around me and rocked me in a tight embrace. I felt warm breath on my cheek and soft lips kiss away my tears. Callan.

In ragged gasps, I said, "He was just a boy, Callan. But I didn't hesitate to kill him."

"You had no other choice, David," Callan whispered fiercely.

"How can you be so sure?" I asked.

"I looked into his eyes and recognized what I saw in them," Callan said. "I saw the same thing in the eyes of King Rat when he tried to kill you. And I saw it in Raoul's eyes when he thought Sarn had killed you. I'm sure I'd have seen it had I ever looked Windslow in the eyes, too. You cannot reason with madness, David."

My reply died in my throat as a red beam of light blazed overhead. The laser punctured the *Pauline's* gas envelope and then the beam tracked along the taut fabric. The beam easily burned a long cut in the envelope. The envelope collapsed and the *Pauline* dropped out of the sky.

MY UNDIVIDED ATTENTION

I wrapped a protective arm around Callan and grabbed a line with my free hand. Next to me, Nist worked the ailerons furiously. Surely he realized the airship was falling from the sky. What did he hope to accomplish? We weren't more than thirty feet above the ground. The fall probably wouldn't be fatal but it was far enough to cause serious injuries.

"Everybody, slide when we hit the ground!" Nist shouted.

I had just enough time to wonder what he meant by that when the *Pauline* tilted sharply to starboard. I suddenly understood Nist's plan and my respect for the man's skill as a pilot—already considerable—rose several more notches. The tilt would allow the airship to land on its hull rather than the much stronger keel. Then the collapsing hull could absorb much of the force from the impact. The angled deck allowed us to slide to the ground, dissipating even more of the force in the slide.

The *Pauline* struck the ground and my ears were filled with the sounds of breaking timber and shouting men. I released the line and wrapped my other arm around Callan. Then I lifted her off the deck, protecting her from splinters, scrapes, and cuts as best I could. My feet slammed into the starboard railing and my knees flexed to absorb the impact. Pain shot up my legs and agony burst anew from my bruised and battered chest. Then all was quiet except for the groans of the *Pauline* and her crew. With a soft rustle of fabric, the gas envelope settled over us and blocked everything from view.

"Callan, are you all right?"

"I'm a little shaken up, but fine. What about you?" she said.

"Never better." I eased my grip on Callan. "Nist?"

"Over here."

"That was brilliant flying."

"But I broke the *Pauline*."

"Callan and I will see that she is rebuilt as good as new. You have my word," I assured him.

Fighting our way clear of the collapsed envelope, Callan and I emerged into the sunlight. Before us stood Caudill, his laser pistol trained on me. Knowing the pirate could burn a hole through my head before I could do anything to stop him, I went very still. Then Callan wriggled out next to me.

"I found your sword, darling. You-" She broke off as she noticed Caudill.

"Have her slide the sword to me," Caudill said.

"You're trusting me to translate accurately?" I said. "Why don't you turn on your radio and let the ship's translator handle that for you?"

"You've already Boosted twice today, something I'd thought impossible until now. If I split my attention between you and the radio for even a second, you might Boost a third time and take my laser."

Yeah, my plan was exactly that.

Caudill continued, "Instead, I'll just give you my undivided attention and let you translate. Oh, and tell your guards to stay where they are or I'll burn both of you down."

"What about the pilot?" I asked.

"That was quite a clever job he did landing this tub. I'd say he's much too clever to leave where I can't see him. He will come out as well. Hands empty and where I can see them, of course."

"Callan, slide my sword to Caudill." I raised my voice. "Everyone besides Nist, stay under the envelope. Nist, show empty hands first, then you can crawl out into the open."

Caudill's eyes flicked to Callan as she slid the sword to him but were back on me in an instant. Leering, he said, "She's quite the lovely paramour, Rice. I can certainly see why you risked your neck to be with her. Once my ship is repaired, I do believe I'll take her with me. Her sale price will almost cover the cost of replacing Orrons."

Nist's empty hands poked out a few feet away. He pulled himself halfway out and sat up. Pulling his knees up, Nist pivoted on his backside. As his feet swung free, I realized something was clamped between his feet. Nist's legs kicked out and sent Orrons' head crashing into Caudill's chest.

The hardened pirate recoiled from the severed head of his young crewmen. Caudill uttered a cry of mingled horror and disgust as he stumbled back a step. The head splattered blood over Caudill's chest and the pirate wiped at it out of reflex. In that split second, the laser pistol swung down to point at the ground. Finally, his attention wasn't on any of us.

Boost!

And nothing happened. Time did not slow and adrenaline did not flood my body. There was no time to wonder why Boost failed. I still had to act while Caudill was distracted.

I launched myself into a somersault toward Caudill, grabbing my sword as I came out of the roll. Surprise and horror made Caudill continue backing away, but I saw his laser pistol already tracking back toward me. Lunging as far as I could, I struck the pistol with the flat of my sword. The force of the blow sent the gun flying from Caudill's hand.

Grinning in triumph, I pulled my sword back for another thrust and stepped toward Caudill. "Surrender or die."

Caudill's shoulders slumped and his hands raised. Then he leapt forward, a vibroblade humming to life in his left hand. I jumped back. The vibroblade missed, but I heard the buzz of the blade as it passed.

I thrust wildly with my sword, but my backpedal gave Caudill the same opening I'd needed from him. Dropping the vibroblade, he dove for his fallen laser pistol. Rolling up onto his knees, Caudill raised the gun and trained it on me.

I tensed for a dive of my own—and then a crossbow bolt ripped through Caudill's throat while another buried itself in his back. Two of Callan's guards lay just under the collapsed envelope, spent crossbows in hand.

Caudill dropped the laser pistol as both hands flew to his throat in a useless attempt to staunch the spurting blood. As Caudill thrashed and gurgled, I picked up the laser pistol and turned toward my wife and men.

With no one to see his death throes, the most feared pirate in the galaxy breathed his last.

A ROYAL SECOND-IN-COMMAND

Callan, Nist, and the guards rose to their feet as I approached. I had nothing more in my mind than sweeping Callan into my arms. As I reached toward her, she turned to her guards and Nist.

"Thank you for your quick thinking and quicker actions, gentlemen." She kissed each of them ceremonially on the cheek. "Without the three of you, I'd be a widow now."

The younger of the two guards actually blushed. "We were just doing our job, Your Highness."

Callan crossed her arms in mock disapproval. "David, can you believe what Voss just said?"

"Never, ever say you're 'just' doing your job—especially when your job may mean sacrificing your life to save ours." I took Voss's hand and shook it. "Callan and I are honored to have men such as you guard us."

While smiling and making similar comments to Nist and the other guard, I queried my implant to discover why Boost failed me for the first time. I found the answer and my concentration returned to the real world—where I found Callan watching me.

"Well, what does your implant have to say for itself?" Callan asked when I looked up. I must have looked surprised, because she added, "You get an introspective look when you're talking to that machine in your head, darling. I assume you asked it why Boost didn't work?"

"You knew I tried to Boost?" I asked.

"Of course I did, David."

"Is that another look of mine?" Callan nodded and I continued, "It turns out the implant has a safety override I didn't know about. Apparently, Boosting several times close together—even if the Boost only lasts for a few seconds—is as dangerous as one long Boost. I'd already Boosted twice within just a few minutes, so the implant blocked my third attempt. But don't worry, I'm pretty sure I can find a way to turn the override off."

"Don't you *dare* think about doing that, David Rice!" Callan's green eyes flashed with anger and...fear? "Boosting is dangerous. Those overrides exist for a very good reason and you are not to fiddle with them. Consider that a royal decree, if you must"

"But, Callan, Boosting has saved our lives many times."

"No, David, *you* have saved our lives. Boosting is a tool, just like your sword is a tool. What matters is the man who uses the tool, not the tool itself." Callan wrapped her arms tightly around herself. "David, Tristan can heal many wounds, but we both know Boost burnout is beyond anything he can heal." Loosening her arms, Callan flashed her sweetest, most dangerous, husband-pay-atten-tion-to-me smile. "So leave those safety overrides alone or you'll spend the next month sleeping in the guardhouse."

"You had but to ask, my dear. You know I can refuse you noth-ing." I lifted her hand to my lips. "But now we've got to figure out how to rescue our friends from the surviving pirates."

"Do you think a rescue is possible?" Callan asked. "Won't the pirates on the spaceship know their captain is dead and be preparing for an attack or a siege?"

"I don't think they know anything that just happened. Caudill turned his radio off so he could threaten me without you and

Rupor hearing. He didn't turn it on again after you and Rupor played on his suspicions. And the wreck of the *Pauline* blocked their line of sight from the spaceship. Caudill's men don't know he's dead yet, but they will get suspicious if they don't hear from him soon."

"Could you wear the powered armor? With the helmet on, couldn't you just march right onto the spaceship and smash anyone who refused to surrender?" Callan asked.

"I'm afraid not," I replied. "Only Orrons could control the armor. It's another machine-in-your-head thing, but it's a different one than I have."

At that moment, Rupor's airship glided into position above us and began venting gas. Rupor, I realized, was onboard a Tartegian warship rather than a personal craft like the *Pauline*.

Looking at the descending ship, I asked, "Callan, do you think your ex-betrothed would lend me a few of his marines to lead against the pirate ship?"

Callan sighed. "You're the only one of us who's been inside the spaceship. And you're the only one of us who knows how to open the doors. I don't like the idea of you going back in there, but you're the only person who can lead. Rupor won't like it, either, but he'll agree."

Callan was right about Rupor on both counts.

After reluctantly agreeing, Rupor added, "Of course, I'll be there as your second-in-command."

I opened my mouth to talk him out of it, then looked at his determined face. "I will be honored to have you at my side, Your Highness."

Callan gave me a smile and a nod. Apparently, I'd given the correct response. Shortly, the marines from Rupor's ship gathered around me.

"We have too many unknowns to consider anything but a simple plan." I gave a feral grin to the marines. "And this one is as simple as it can get. Once inside the ship, you capture or kill everyone who doesn't speak your language."

"Direct and to the point, Rice." Rupor nodded his approval. "I like it."

"Am I safe in assuming there are no questions?" At the marines' laughter, I gave them a tight smile. "Now, let's go capture a pirate ship."

A PRINCESS-STEALING NE'ER-DO-WELL

Of course the plan had more detail than I'd said, but not a lot more. Nist rounded up a canvas sack from the wreckage of the *Pauline* and I put Orrons' head in it. Next, I pulled on Caudill's bloody shirt and donned his hat, which was blessedly free of blood stains. Mixed in among Rupor's men, I hoped to pass myself off as Caudill. The deception only had to last long enough for us to get inside the spaceship.

"How do I look?" I asked Callan, spreading my arms wide and striking a pose.

Callan studied me with a critical eye. "Quite a lot like a dead man walking."

"With Rupor's marines packed around me, none of the pirates will see the blood stains. How does the hat look?"

"Is that hat fashionable out in the wider galaxy?"

"I've been away from galactic civilization for a few years," I answered, "but it was all the rage before I left."

"Then let us desperately hope that galactic fashion has come to its senses."

"You don't think it gives me a rakish look?"

"I love you, David, but no." Callan smiled, shaking her head. "If you pull the brim low and keep your head down, it will hide your face. That is your primary reason for wearing that monstrosity, isn't it, darling?"

"Of course."

Perhaps my face displayed disappointment, because Callan rose on her toes and kissed me lightly. "You don't need a hat to look rakish to me, David."

I heard laughter behind me. Turning, I found Rupor and his marines watching Callan and me with amusement.

Callan crossed her arms and glared at Rupor. "Shall I tell your men what *you* wore when we met for the first time, Rupor?"

Rupor's men laughed all the more as their prince's face reddened.

"All right, men, you've had a good laugh," I called. "Now it's time to get serious. Let's form up."

Rupor's men gathered around me. Rupor assumed a prideful look and, the bloody sack held before him, struck out toward the spaceship. I prayed the flash of laser fire would not be the last thing we saw.

The men marched with quiet purpose appropriate to the true situation. My plan hinged on the marines' ability to convince those aboard the spaceship that they were celebrating, not attacking.

"You're supposed to be happy, men. Laugh and joke," I said quietly. "Keep your hands away from your weapons and act as if your prince has won a great victory over that princess-stealing ne'er-do-well, David Rice."

As I'd hoped, that brought a laugh from the men and even Rupor chuckled.

"That's the spirit, lads," I said. "Rupor, try swinging that sack in a jaunty manner, as if it held a treasured trophy. These pirates think you're all a bunch of savage barbarians, anyway. Have some fun and live down to their expectations."

That did the trick. The marines strutted and capered, laughing all the while. One man moved ahead of the group with an exaggerated march more appropriate for the stage than the battlefield. He bowed low to Rupor and requested the honor of carrying the sack.

Rupor presented the sack to him as if awarding him a medal for valor. Each man stepped forward for his turn; some hoisting the sack like a trophy, others swinging it in time to a few dance steps, and one peeked inside and cackled. Through it all, we drew closer to the spaceship.

Grinning, one of the marines spun past me and asked, "Won't these pirates just cut us down with weapons like the one their captain used on your airship?"

"You'd think so, but no. Every bulkhead in a spaceship is crammed with vital machinery or conduits for vital machinery. No spaceman uses a laser inside the ship if it can be avoided."

"What weapons will the pirates use?" he asked.

"They'll use swords. That's one of the few things adventures stories get right about combat aboard a spaceship." We climbed over the last pile of debris and the pirate ship loomed above us. "When we get to the hatch, keep up your chatter and pack tightly in front of me. The noise will help cover the difference between my voice and Caudill's. Packing tightly will also give me an excuse to ask for someone to open the hatch."

Seconds later, we entered the airlock. The ruse had gotten us this far. Would it get us inside the spaceship?

SURPRISE ATTACK

Rupor led the way into the pirate ship's airlock, his men crowding in behind him. It was tight in the airlock and I couldn't step forward to give the crew a clear look at my face. The men continued their boisterous celebration, with the close confines of the airlock amplifying their noise. Rupor ignored the comm next to the door and, with a flourish, knocked on the airlock. Several long seconds crawled by before the knock drew a response.

"Yeah, what is it?" The voice spoke galactic basic and was barely audible over the din caused by the marines. After a short delay, the computerized translation repeated the question in the language of Tarteg and Mordan.

"Your captain has brought us to your ship to celebrate my victory and cement our alliance with you," Rupor yelled over the ruckus, holding up the sack. "Open this door and let us begin the celebration in earnest."

We endured a pause as the computer translated back to galactic basic before we received a reply. "If the captain wants you in the ship, he can open the door when he gets there."

It was time to see if the noise would help mask the differences between my voice and Caudill's. Without waiting for the translation,

I deepened my voice and rasped, "Did you even bother to look at your view screen? If I could reach the blasted airlock, I would open it."

The next few seconds felt like hours. At last the voice replied, "My apologies, Captain. I didn't see you back there. I've sent someone to open the airlock." There was another brief pause, then the voice added, "Uh, Captain, the bottom of that bag is red and looks wet. What's in it?"

"The bag holds that scout's head. Turn off the translation for a minute, would you?" I said, sticking to the deep, rasping voice.

"It's off."

"Taking the head is some kind of local ritual. We need these barbarians right now. Order the crew to just smile and nod when the savages show it off."

"Will do, sir."

Machinery hummed to life and the airlock door slowly slid open. I thought our ruse had worked, right up until I saw a squad of armed pirates waiting for us.

I feared the entire squad would be armed with laser pistols. We were in serious trouble if they had modern weapons. Fortunately, old shipboard habits die hard. Either the pirates never considered arming everyone with lasers or too many of the laser pistols were destroyed when the inertial dampeners failed. Whatever the reason, only the leader held a laser. The rest of the pirates held drawn swords. The leader could still burn us all down with the laser. We needed a distraction and needed one quickly.

Gambling that the translator was still turned off, I said, "Rupor, give the pirates a stern and disapproving look, then shrug and pull the head out of the bag. Men, when their leader is distracted, all of you must duck. Stay down until I give the word."

Rupor straightened, his stance radiating royal disapproval of this breach of protocol. The squad leader, irritated that he couldn't understand what I was saying, called out to the intercom, "Turn the translator back on."

Then Rupor pulled Orrons' head from the bag and thrust it

toward the leader. Every one of the pirates recoiled at the sight of Orrons' head dangling before them. Then Rupor added to their horror by tossing the head to their leader. All pirate eyes followed as the head arced toward their leader.

He instinctively fended off the head with his hands. "Yaaaah!"

The man's laser pistol swung away from the airlock and I called, "Duck!"

The marines before me dropped into a squat and I raised Caudill's laser pistol and fired. The bright beam flashed over the marines' heads and burned the leader's gun hand off at the wrist. Gun and hand fell to the floor as the leader screamed in pain. Clutching his wrist, the man stumbled backward into his squad.

"Now!" I cried.

Scooping up the fallen laser pistol, Rupor shouted, "Up and at them, men."

With a roar, the Tartegian marines charged from the airlock and into the squad of pirates.

Stuck toward the back of the pack of marines, I could only watch as Rupor and his men slammed into the squad of space pirates. Disorganized by the flailing of their one-handed leader, the pirates tried to regroup in the face of the onslaught. But Rupor picked his boarding party well. The men in front blocked the pirates' desperate attacks and slammed them into bulkheads or down onto the deck. The marines behind them stabbed, hacked, and trampled the pirates as they passed. Lastly, those bringing up the rear finished off the wounded before rushing to rejoin the boarding party.

The attack was brutal and deadly. The pirates, used to fighting poorly trained merchant spacers and terrorizing space liner passengers, had no response for the efficient, organized violence dealt by Rupor's boarding party.

Bloody sword held high, Rupor voiced a savage cry of triumph. His men joined in and the metal bulkheads reverberated with the din. Rupor charged down the nearest passageway, he and his men deaf to my shouted instructions to take the next corridor, the one leading to the bridge.

The Tartegian's tactics, skill, and enthusiasm would only carry them so far. The pirates still outnumbered us four or five to one and knew the ship's layout intimately. Eventually, superior numbers and superior knowledge would carry the day. Our sole hope lay in controlling the bridge, the heart of the spaceship and from where the crew would direct the defense of the ship.

With a sigh I could just barely hear over the fading cries and footfalls of the boarding party, I jogged in the opposite direction. After all, someone had to take control of the bridge.

I had no allies. I had no Boost. I had no plan. But I had a laser pistol and, more importantly, I had the sword Rob had given me as he lay dying. It was enough to win the day. It *had* to be.

SHHH!

The clash of weapons echoed up the corridor as Rupor's boarding party found more pirates to fight. As a distraction, the Tartegians had the full attention of the pirates aft of the airlock. But would the fighting behind me distract the pirates in front of me?

I reached the ship's main corridor, running from stem to stern right through the middle of the spaceship. Aft held crew quarters, ship's stores, and the cargo bays. Forward lay officer's territory and the bridge. At least, that's the layout found on a military or merchant spaceship. Since pirates tended to steal their ships rather than have them built under contract, chances were this ship didn't break from that mold. I was gambling my life—and the lives of Martin and Megan—that Caudill was a traditionalist.

The Scout Academy requires courses on space piracy for all cadets. Scouts travel far from the space lanes, it's pretty much our job description. Even though the Scout Corps is much smaller than any of the other military branches, scouts are far more likely to encounter pirates. A scout's survival could depend on knowing pirate tactics and recognizing the signs of a pirate lair. In other words, I knew more about pirates than most people. Martin did, too, but added personal experience to the mix.

Shipboard discipline among pirates is vastly different than among law-abiding crews. There is usually one punishment for breaking the pirate compact—spacing. That means a smart pirate captain finds ways to keep his crew entertained during the long, boring hunt for prey. Pirate ships are known to have well stocked bars, full emersion gaming consoles, and top of the line video rigs. Some even have live entertainment, usually provided by captives taken from space liners or from rim settlements.

All of this came back to me as I started up the main corridor toward the bridge. I moved in short dashes, slipping from one side passage to another, staying out of sight as much as possible. I had just ducked into an aft slanting passage when I heard the hiss of the bridge hatch sliding open. A second after that came the sound of footsteps pounding down the corridor toward me.

I pressed up against a recessed hatch but it provided little concealment. With the aft slant of the passage, I stood well within the peripheral vision of the approaching pirates. One of them was bound to see me.

The pounding of pirate footsteps grew louder and louder. I raised the laser pistol I'd taken from Caudill's body and readied my sword. If luck was with me, I could cut them down before they reached me. But I'd also warn the pirates on the bridge they had an enemy close by. So much for having the element of surprise when I reached the bridge.

With a soft sigh, the hatch behind me slid open and hands dragged me into the compartment. I spun, sword raised to strike, as the hatch sighed shut again. A single finger pressed against my lips.

"Shhh!"

A pretty, petite blonde stood before me. To her right stood a lovely brunette with startling blue eyes. To her left was a stunning redhead. Beyond those three, close to two dozen more women eyed me warily. All of them held makeshift knives and appeared prepared to use them.

One woman, her eyes locked on a vid screen, called, "All clear."

"Are you the scout who's got Caudill's men so scared?" the blonde asked.

"They're scared of me? That's good. Scared men make mistakes." I looked around the chamber the blonde had pulled me into. The women were quite pretty and every single one of them was dressed like a lingerie model, though ones with worse fashion sense than even I possess. Milo would almost certainly like their look, being a teenage boy, but Callan had long since taught me the difference between mere revealing clothing and alluring attire.

"We didn't choose the clothes," the blonde said, reading my expression.

"Of course not." I turned my attention to the blonde, making sure my eyes met hers. "I assume you're all Caudill's captives, no doubt brought on board to entertain his crew?"

She nodded, her eyes suddenly shining with unshed tears. My already considerable loathing for Caudill increased five-fold. "I'd kill Caudill over this outrage if he wasn't already dead."

Every woman in the room pinned me with a laser-like gaze as the blonde asked, "You killed Caudill?"

"No, my men killed Caudill before he could kill me. I found myself forced to kill Orrons."

The redhead threw her arms around me and kissed my cheek. "Oh, thank you so much!"

"We know *why* Orrons was a basket case, but he still had some sick interests—and a...thing...for redheads," the blonde explained. Then she blinked away her tears and was all business. "I assume you're trying to rescue your friends on the bridge?"

I nodded. "And take control of the bridge, so I can help the boarding party heading aft."

"We can help you with that, but in return you've got to agree to help us rescue our husbands."

"Of course I'll help you. It's what scouts do, you know. Are they being held forward or aft?"

The blonde shook her head. "I'm afraid they aren't on board

the ship. They're three wormhole jumps away, in Caudill's pirate base."

I shook my head. "I'm sorry, I can't help you. You're sitting in the only intact spaceship on the planet and I'm told it can't fly any more. I wish there was something I could do to help your husbands, but I can't." I looked around the room, locking eyes with several of the women. "Are you still willing to help me rescue my friends?"

"You know, all you had to do was tell us you'd do it," the blonde said. "We wouldn't have known the difference until it was too late."

My face must have given away my opinion of that course of action.

"Please excuse us. We've spent far too much time around pirates lately." The blonde met my gaze, a smile tugging at her lips. "Are there any more men like you at home?"

"That depends on which home you mean," I responded. "I don't know about my birth planet, but on this planet there are whole armies of honorable men who I struggle to emulate."

"I doubt you struggle over anything concerned with honor," the blonde said. "But your answer is just what we wanted to hear. We're going to need men like that to rescue our husbands."

"But I just told you I don't have a working spaceship."

The blonde reached up and patted my cheek. "Don't worry your handsome head over that. If you can take this spaceship, we'll make her fly again."

I could tell there was more to their story, but I could get the rest later—after we were finished dealing with the pirates. "You've got a deal. What I need most right now is to get to the bridge unseen. Can you help with that?"

"I've already got that covered," called the woman at the vid station. "I've got an override on the cameras in that passageway. Ever since you came aboard, all they've seen outside the bridge is an empty passageway."

"That's perfect." I thought furiously for a second. "Can you open the hatch to the bridge from here?"

Fingers danced over the makeshift control panel. "I can now."

"Good. Open it just before I reach it."

The blonde opened the hatch out of their chamber and I slipped into the passage. Sword and laser at the ready, I charged full speed toward the bridge.

FREE MARTIN

The bridge hatch loomed large as I sprinted down the passageway. Ten feet from the hatch, my brain yelled for me to stop before I slammed into the hatch. Then the hatch slid open and I charged onto the bridge.

From various bridge stations, half a dozen pirates directed the ship's defense against Rupor and his boarding party. On the far side of the compartment, a seventh pirate stood guard over Martin and Megan. Martin's arms twisted behind his back, no doubt with his hands bound. But Megan's hands were free and clasped together in her lap. Obviously, the pirates did not consider a musician from a primitive world any kind of threat. If all went according to plan, they'd regret that decision.

The closest pirate looked up at the sound of the hatch sliding open. I swung my sword, slashing his throat as I charged past. He collapsed to the deck, gurgling, as blood sprayed across his console. The remaining pirates stared at me, shocked disbelief written on their faces. Their hesitation only lasted for a second, but that was all I needed to bound across the compartment.

I barreled into the pirate guarding Martin, driving my sword up into his chest and out his back. Yanking the sword free, I dropped the laser pistol in Megan's lap.

"Free Martin. I'm going to need his help real soon."

Shouts of rage echoed around the bridge as the pirates drew their swords and converged on me. At least one of my gambles had paid off. The bridge was so packed with vital instruments that the pirates weren't willing to use their lasers. I knew I could take any of them in a straight fight, but the pirates outnumbered me five to one. With Boost available, there would be no doubt of the outcome. But you can't have everything and, in this fight, I couldn't have Boost.

I leapt toward one of the pirates and away from Martin and Megan, drawing the attention of all of the pirates along with me. Two of them came at me together, one from the right and one from ahead of me. My sword flashed as I parried their thrusts. I tried every feint and trick I knew, but without the added speed of Boost I couldn't mount an attack against either man. Then a third pirate joined the fight and their combined attacks overwhelmed my defense. Within seconds, I felt cold steel plunge into my left shoulder.

Pain exploded as the pirate's sword grated against my shoulder blade and my left arm dropped to my side, useless. My balance thrown off, I swung my sword wildly across the attacks of the other two pirates. As much by luck as skill, I beat aside both attacks with the single parry. But my wild swing also left me open to attacks from all three of the pirates.

The man who had stabbed me grinned and leaned into his blade, still sticking into my shoulder. Then, when the pirate had me pinned and vulnerable to attacks from his fellows, the pirate pulled his sword from my shoulder. A second later I realized the pirate was no less surprised than me. He rose off the deck and flew across the bridge, crashing into the two pirates not yet in the fight.

Moving almost too fast to see clearly, Martin Bane flowed past me, his mouth stretched in a feral grin. "Megan, David is hurt worse than he knows. Help him sit down before he falls down."

The other two pirates fighting with me brought their swords to bear on me, each looking for a killing blow. In an instant, they forgot all about me as this new, deadly threat came at them. They attempted a defense but Martin moved too fast for them. Sliding in between the two men, he slammed their heads together. With a dull crack, both men collapsed to the floor, senseless.

Scooping up their two swords, Martin advanced on the remaining pirates. The three of them struggled to their feet as Martin's swords flashed in a dizzying pattern. The swords moved so fast you could actually hear them cutting through the air.

The pirates' eyes widened and Martin said, "I can kill or capture. It matters not to me, but maybe it does to you three."

Their swords clattered to the deck.

In the sudden silence that followed, I heard lots of feet pounding down the corridor toward the bridge.

The just-surrendered pirates grinned at the sound of what they knew could only be reinforcements. Believing the approaching men had diverted Martin's attention, one of the three reached for his sword. One of Martin's swords changed direction. With a howl of pain, the pirate pulled his hand back—minus the tip of its middle finger.

"Help me get back up," I said to Megan, who had just helped me sit down. "I need to be ready to fight."

"You can't fight with that wound, David. But maybe we could shut the door. Do you know how to do that?"

"No. I've got some allies who have taken over the door controls. They'd have to-" I stopped speaking as a thought struck me.

"They'd have to what?"

"They can see the passageway and control the door," I mused. "Why haven't they already shut the door?"

"You're asking the wrong person," Megan said.

Megan was absolutely right. Raising my voice, I shouted in Mordanian, "This is Captain Rice. Who approaches?"

The reply came clear and strong and, most importantly, in Mordanian. "We're marines from Her Highness's flagship, sir."

The pirates' grins vanished at the sound of the unfamiliar

language. Seconds later, a dozen Mordanian marines crowded into the bridge while several dozen more stood in the passage. Beside the marine commander, looking woefully out of place among the heavily armed men, stood the petite blonde woman from the room down the passageway.

The commander saluted. "We couldn't understand a word this young woman said, but she was most adamant we follow her."

"I'm glad you did. And your timing is most excellent. Now that you're here, I've got to go aft. Rupor and his men charged off in that direction and may require our help."

"Oh hell no, David! You are in no shape to lead these men anywhere," Martin said. "You have to see a medic. I will go with the marines."

"I'd not have chosen those exact words, sir," the marine commander said, "but I must agree with Captain Bane. Your wound must receive attention."

The commander detached four marines to help me out to the medic station, then he and Martin led the Marines aft in search of Rupor. I could do nothing more but wait for news.

INCORRECT CONCLUSIONS

"Let's get you outside to the medic, sir," one of the marines said, pointing at my shoulder.

"Of course, private," I said. "Sorry I'm keeping you from all the fun."

"Your health is more important than another notch on my blade, sir."

"Callan will appreciate your concern." I pushed off from the bulkhead I'd been leaning against. To my surprise, I pitched right past 'upright' and fell toward a face-first landing on the deck. Megan and the blonde reacted quickly, catching and steadying me. I'd lost more blood than I'd thought.

"Thank you, Megan." I turned to the blonde and switched to gal base, "And thank you, um-?"

"Laura."

"Thank you, Laura. Are the rest of the women still in your compartment?" At Laura's nod, I continued, "If you don't mind, I'm going to assign a squad of marines to guard your compartment until we finish dealing with the pirates. Can you turn on the translator so my people can talk to you?"

"Thank you for the marines." Laura motioned for one of the

marines to help her. "They're the kind of men you told us abounded on this world?"

"Each one is honorable to a fault. My oath on it."

"There's no need for an oath. I trust you." Laura handed me off to the marine she summoned. Then she stepped over to the communications station and flipped some switches. "That should do it."

A second later, a translation came from the ship's intercom.

I switched to Mordanian. "Megan, this is Laura. Are you willing to act as a liaison between my men and Laura's women?"

"She and her friends are the allies who helped you?" When I nodded, she continued, "That ought to make an interesting verse in my song. What will Her Highness think?"

Laura smiled at the translation. "You can assure the princess that her... Oh, what's the word they used? Ah, yes, assure the princess that her paramour has been a perfect gentleman."

Megan frowned. "David is Princess Callan's husband, not her paramour."

Laura's eyebrows shot up. "Husband? But Caudill-"

"Jumped to an incorrect conclusion," I interrupted. "One Rupor and Callan played along with so they could get Orrons off my chest. And I mean that quite literally."

We reached the hatch to the ladies' compartment. I assigned one of the marines with me to guard the hatch. "I'll send more men and more...appropriate...clothing as soon as possible."

When we neared the airlock, we met more Mordanian marines boarding the ship. I selected a squad to help guard the women's hatch and directed the rest toward the fighting. Exiting into dazzling late afternoon sunlight had all of us squinting and blinking.

Apparently, it's a medical emergency when the prince consort is bleeding. Rather than wait for the marines to carry me to him, the medic rushed toward me. Right on his heels ran a very concerned Callan.

I gritted my teeth as the medic poked and prodded around my

wound. After a moment, he said, "He needs a surgeon, Your Highness, not a medic. I'm afraid the sword nicked an artery."

Callan's face paled at the medic's pronouncement, but she kept her composure. "David, can that thing in your head do anything to fix the wound?"

"My implant? Nothing it hasn't already done. If we had medical nanites, it could direct repairs, but we don't have any of those."

Ignoring the confused look the medic gave us, Callan asked, "Could there be some of those nan-whatevers on this spaceship? I'd think pirates would want a whole lot of them."

"I'm sure you're right about the pirates, but I think the nanites were destroyed in the crash. I can't think of any other reason why Caudill needed Tristan to tend to his wounded," I said. "But maybe the women who helped me hid some nanites. You should send someone to ask Laura."

"Who is Laura? No, tell me later." She turned to one of the marines who had brought me out. "Private, do you know who Laura is and where to find her?"

"Yes, Your Highness, I do."

"Good. I want you to take Milo and go find her."

I'd almost forgotten Milo was with us before he stepped up to Callan's side.

"Milo," she said to him, "ask this Laura it they have..." Callan got a faraway look in her eyes as she searched for the right phrasing. "Any tiny medical machines. Tell her about David's wound, if it it helps."

Milo looked as pale as Callan and twice as serious. I hated to see his spirit weighed down worrying about me. Fortunately, sixteen year old boys are easily distracted.

"And Milo," I added. "Look Laura in the eyes when you talk to her."

"What?" he and Callan both asked.

"The pirates chose the clothes the ladies are wearing. Their attire leaves a lot to be desired, starting with sufficient fabric to cover them decently. Strive to be a gentleman, Milo. Don't let your eyes wander too much."

A hint of Milo's impish smile returned. "I'll try, David."

The private and Milo bounded into the spaceship and disappeared from view. While they were gone, I told Callan everything that happened after Rupor, the marines, and I set off for the ship. Just as I got to Martin's heroics on the bridge, Laura and Milo dashed through the airlock.

Ignoring all the marines ogling at her, Laura came straight to Callan, "I hate to say it, but we don't have any medical nanites. But that's not the worst of it. I'm afraid the pirates overwhelmed Prince Rupor's marines and captured the prince. They're holding both the prince and the doctor hostage."

PROMOTE SOMEONE ELSE

Callan frowned in concentration as she listened to the computerized translation of Laura's words. As the computer finished speaking, she assumed her court face. "Private, give this woman your shirt."

Laura's eyebrows climbed as the private removed his shirt.

Callan allowed a smile to light her face briefly. "Laura, you have traveled with these pirates and know them better than anyone else I know. I will need your advice during my negotiations with them. At the same time, I can't have my marines distracted by the pretty, half-naked woman I've brought into their midst."

Obviously relieved to have the shirt to wear, Laura replied, "You realize there's no chance your marines will pay any attention to me with you standing right beside me."

I said, "Sure they will, Laura. After all, Callan isn't half-naked."

Callan and Laura glared at me.

I wilted under their gazes. "Um, blood loss makes me say stupid things?" The glares didn't break. "So, why don't I just lay here and listen to you over the radio?"

"I think that's a good idea," Laura said.

Turning toward the airlock, Callan added, "And make sure you don't die."

Callan, Laura, and an escort of marines vanished into the pirate ship. I listened as Laura told Callan about the remaining pirate officers and answered Callan's incisive questions. Otherwise, I concentrated hard on not dying. Callan had better appreciate how seriously I was taking her last order to me.

At the end of Laura's briefing, I heard Callan call out, "I am Princess Callan of Mordan. I wish to speak to the pirate commander."

After translation lag, one of the pirates yelled, "Captain Caudill is our commander. You can talk to him."

"No, I can't. Caudill is dead." Callan let that sink in for a few seconds. "It appears someone just got a promotion."

The pirates were silent for several seconds before the same pirate spoke. "My name is Artin. If you're telling the truth, I guess I'm in command."

"I most assuredly am telling the truth. Now, Captain Artin, I've been told you are holding my doctor and the crown prince from our neighboring kingdom."

"That's right, lady," Artin sounded more confident of himself on the topic of hostages. "Here's a list of our demands. We-"

"I am here to accept your peaceful surrender, Captain Artin. I will not listen to, much less accede to, any demands."

Callan's response caught Artin off guard. "Well, um...Maybe we'll start cutting up that prince. Yeah, if you don't start satisfying our demands, that's exactly what we'll do."

"Captain Artin, sometime in the near future you and your crew *will* end up as my prisoners. Any atrocity visited upon your hostages will, in turn, be visited on each one of you tenfold."

"You can't do that!" Artin sounded like he was trying to convince himself more than he was Callan. "Torture and mistreatment of prisoners is against Terran Federation law."

"You do not seem to grasp the situation, Captain Artin. My country is not a member of this Terran Federation, nor are we bound by its laws. Furthermore, in Mordan my word *is* law." Callan blew out her breath in irritation. "I grow tired of this,

Captain Artin. The choice is yours. Surrender peacefully or I swear that you and every single one of your men will die slowly and in unspeakable agony, begging for the merciful release of death."

Silence stretched for several seconds. I could only imagine the looks of disbelief plastered over the pirates' faces at Callan's response to their demands. Artin's next words confirmed the accuracy of my mental image.

"Look, princess, is there a king or another prince I can talk to, because I don't think you get the picture. We have your prince and your doctor. *We* hold all the cards."

"No, Captain Artin. You hold nothing more than a single compartment in a crashed spaceship. *I* hold everything else. That includes all the food, all the medical care, and hundreds of men-at-arms who want nothing more than my permission to come in there and carve you scum into little pieces." Callan spoke slowly, as if explaining this to a child. Alas, the sarcasm in her voice was lost in the mechanical translation.

"Can you believe this, men?" From the tone of his voice, Artin obviously couldn't believe it. "You don't even care what happens to our hostages, do you princess?"

"I care more deeply than a vile and violent man such as you could ever hope to understand. That is why I am giving you one last chance to surrender peacefully." She paused for several seconds but Artin didn't take the hint. "The rest of you pirates, is there someone I can speak with in that room who *isn't* stupid?"

"The captain speaks for the crew, lady. Seeing as you're the one who promoted me by killing Caudill, you're just going to have to deal with me."

Callan sighed then spoke quietly. "Sergeant, who is your best marksman?"

"That would be Corporal Dobbs, Your Highness."

"Corporal, I am tired of speaking to this idiot. Would you please promote someone else."

"Hey!" Artin called. "What are you muttering–"

There was the snap of a crossbow firing and Artin's voice cut off with a gurgle. Pirate voices rose in shocked surprise.

"I do hope your new captain is more intelligent than your previous one," Callan called over the hubbub. "Whom do I congratulate on their promotion?"

More muttering among the pirates was followed by a tentative voice. "Um, this is Captain Rondle?"

"Are you asking me or telling me, captain?"

"I... Uh..."

Martin's voice cut in. "May I speak to the pirates, Your Highness?"

"Oh God yes, Martin. Please be my guest."

Switching to galactic basic, Martin said, "Princess Callan represents the most enlightened monarchy on this planet. If you surrender peacefully, she will take that into consideration when dealing with the rest of you. Unfortunately, her tolerance for fools was sorely tried by Artin. She won't be as patient with you, Rondle. If you want to come out of this alive, *don't* be another Artin."

Rondle responded with remarkable alacrity. "I see your point. We surrender!"

Minutes later, Callan and her escort of marines swept out of the airlock and came my way. My wife was in full princess mode. She assumed this bearing as easily as she put on a new dress—easier, when I considered how many ladies-in-waiting were required to help her change clothes. Most of the time, Callan only went into princess mode while presiding in court or during official royal appearances. Today, she used it as armor to hold her worry for me at bay.

"Private?" Callan smiled at the private who gave his shirt to Laura. "I'm afraid we have twenty-two more women in need of proper clothing. On my authority, please gather a shirt for each of them. My page, Milo, will be along shortly to guide you to them."

She turned to the medic. "Corporal, please prepare to move my husband. Tristan will be operating in a surgery on board the pirate ship."

Callan's princess armor cracked a bit when she knelt beside me. I wiped a single tear from her cheek as she said, "I see you're still alive. Thank you for following my orders."

"I strive to please, Your Wifeness."

Callan gave a bark of laughter, quickly smothering it into a quiet fit of giggles.

"I've been saving that one for just the right moment," I said.

Through her giggles, Callan replied, "How very thoughtful of you."

"Your Highness, we're ready," the medic said.

Once again, the princess armor snapped shut around Callan as she rose to her feet. "Follow me."

She led the way to the surgery. Inside, we found Tristan staring goggle-eyed at what I considered a somewhat outdated ship's surgery. Once I arrived, Tristan's attention focused entirely on me. His face grew serious as he examined my wound.

"He's lost a lot of blood and is losing more by the second. Let's get started while there's still a chance to save him."

SABOTEURS

Tristan's pronouncement hung in the air for a second, then people bustled all around me. One of Laura's women—a med tech, I assumed—hooked me up to one of the machines in the surgery.

"Are you ready for me to put him under, Doctor?" she asked.

"Yes, Pamela."

As Pamela fiddled with her machine, Callan lifted my right hand to her lips. "I'll be here waiting for you when you wake up, darling."

I squeezed her hand. "That's good, because I can't think of anyone else I'd rather see."

Then Pamela's machine did its job and everything faded to black.

Despite the anesthesia, some small part of me remained aware of what happened around me. Or maybe what I think I remember is simply sounds my implant picked up and then leaked into my dreams.

"*There's the cut in the artery. Now, let's see if- Damn! Clamp the artery! Now!*"

"*His blood pressure is dropping, Doctor.*"

"*Pamela, we need to try that blood transfusion thing you told me about.*"

"Tristan, what's happening to David?"

"Martin, get her out of here and find me some blood donors. At least three, preferably more."

"Martin, don't you dare try to take me away from David!"

"Callan, you're distracting Tristan and neither he nor David can afford the distraction. You've got to leave."

"Hang on just a little longer, lad!"

I woke up. Callan, dry eyed and calm, sat next to me, holding my hand. Tristan stood on the other side of me, watching Pamela take readings from her machines. Laura was at the foot of the bed, along with four other women. All of them wore marine shirts and, to a woman, looked quite fetching in them.

I grinned at my wife. "We have *got* to get you one of those shirts, Callan."

Callan rolled her eyes. "You nearly died and *that's* the first thing you think of? Maybe you should try thanking those women for donating their blood instead of ogling at them."

"Or, even better," Laura said, "you could thank us by keeping your promise."

"David has my full support, but don't you need a working spaceship before David could hope to lead a mission to rescue your husbands?" Callan asked. "As I understand it, this one is rather badly broken."

"Oh, it's not broken, Your Highness," Laura said. "Merely sabotaged."

"Who sabotaged the ship?" I asked.

Laura grinned. "We did."

"You women committed sabotage without Caudill or his men discovering it?" I asked.

Laura nodded. Her grin grew wider, as did the matching grins of my blood donors.

"Is that why the pirates didn't simply threaten to blast our airships out of the sky with their lasers?"

"Yep. The external lasers were the second system on our list."

I considered Laura's comment for a moment. "Let me guess, the aft inertial dampener was the first system on the list?"

"Got it in one," Laura said. "A bunch of Caudill's men, including most of his best officers, manned the aft laser banks during wormhole exits. We knew killing the inertial dampener would also kill half the crew."

"You and David have talked about inertial dampeners a lot lately. Could you please explain what one is?" Callan asked.

"Sure..." Laura's brow furrowed as she thought through something. "You know how you sway back when an airship speeds up and sway forward-" Laura began.

"I know what inertia is, Laura," Callan interrupted with a smile. "I don't know why you need to dampen it for space travel."

Laura reddened. "Oh, right, sorry. So anyway, inertia is the big problem entering and exiting wormholes because a spaceship instantly accelerates to well over the speed of light going in and does just the opposite coming out."

"Ah, that explains a lot," Callan nodded. "So these dampeners keep everything inside the ship from being crushed against the ship's walls when it accelerates or decelerates."

"Such strong forces generally just cause everything to disintegrate, but you've got the gist of it," I said, then turned to Laura. "From what you're telling me, I'd guess you and your husbands weren't just a random bunch of tourists on a space liner?"

"Right. We were supposed to be part of a second colonist wave." At Callan's quizzical expression, Laura added, "The first wave is mostly agronomists and farmers. They get the farms working so future colonists don't starve. The second wave is mostly engineers and technicians to build the infrastructure for future waves of colonists."

"So, you're all engineers and technicians? And, what, Caudill kept your husbands at the base to repair ships? So, you women were..." I trailed off, unwilling to bring up such a painful subject.

Laura was less squeamish than I was. "My friends and I repaired Caudill's ship, served as hostages against our husbands' good behavior, and served as...entertainment...for the crew in our spare time."

Staying well away from that last 'duty,' I said, "So you had plenty of opportunity to insert backup controls into ship's systems and then bided your time. But why did you choose this wormhole for your sabotage?"

Laura smiled. "Because we knew we'd find you at the other end."

Callan turned to me. "Are you famous in the star-spanning civilization you've told me about, darling? Some kind of galactic hero?"

"No, I'm just a Scout."

"Just a Scout?" Laura interjected. "Your Highness, the Scout Corps are a rare breed among a complacent and unadventurous people. They blaze trails, discover new planets, and find lost civilizations. Scouts are the last heroes in a civilization desperately in need of them.

"When we discovered the pirates were following a Scout's emergency drone," Laura continued, "we knew the Scout would find a way to help us."

"That's a lot of faith based on an emergency drone," I said.

"You're here. The pirates are dead or captured. We're free," Laura said, ticking each item off on her fingers. "I'd call that faith well placed."

"Don't laud me too much, Laura. I had a lot of help capturing this ship and freeing you. Beyond that, all I did was my duty. It's nothing more than any man would have done."

Laura and Callan exchanged glances. "He believes that to his core, Laura."

"You married a remarkable man, Your Highness. A most remarkable man, indeed."

Callan leaned over and kissed me. "I know."

"And if I have anything to say about it, David *will* be a famous galactic hero," Laura said. "Milo told us tales of your adventures. Even discounting his exaggerations, it's an amazing story."

"What exaggerations?" Callan asked. "Milo is usually quite truthful."

"Let's see, the most unbelievable one had David Boosting for over ten minutes while single-handedly defending a trapdoor from creatures Milo called trogs."

"Milo first heard that story from me, Laura." Callan leaned her head on my shoulder. "I was in that cellar and saw it all. It really happened."

Laura's eyes went wide and her jaw went slack. Finding this whole conversation embarrassing, I took advantage of the brief silence to change the subject.

"Now that you're free, how long will it take you to repair the ship and train a crew?"

Laura closed her mouth and pondered for a moment. "I'd say it'll take three weeks to repair the ship. Training a crew is an iffier proposition. Considering the tech level we've seen here, I *think* we can train a crew to handle the less technical jobs in six months."

"Then I think you'd better get started," I said. "We've got a pirate base to take and your husbands to rescue."

AASHLA'S HOPE

Six months to train a crew sounded optimistic in the extreme to me, but Laura's approach didn't occur to me. Training astrogators and engineers was impossible to do in six years, much less six months. The educational foundation just didn't exist to support teaching such advanced skills. But Martin and I already knew astrogation and the women's combined knowledge formed the foundation for a good engineering crew. A true emergency would run our small technical crew ragged, but we could handle the load long enough to reach the pirate base and, assuming a successful rescue and escape, the nearest naval base.

We'd train Aashlanders in laser gunnery and missile control. And, if we found anyone with the right mindset, we'd train one or two helmsmen as backups for Martin and me. Our training was well short of what you would find on a naval vessel—or a pirate ship, for that matter—but if we found ourselves fighting a ship-to-ship battle with the pirates we were in deep trouble anyway.

My bigger concern centered around training helmsmen, a misplaced concern as it turned out. Once he learned the control layout, Nist proved himself just as talented flying a spaceship as he was flying an airship. The real surprise was our second best helmsman. Perhaps it was youthful reflexes or his absolute dedication to making sure he got to come with us, but Milo was almost as good as Nist.

Rupor worked with Tartegian and Mordanian marines, forming a shipboard force split equally between the two services. The marines chosen to accompany us split their training time between shipboard tactics and unit cohesion drills, which Rupor insisted Martin and I perform, also.

Every crew member and marine received intensive language lessons from Heidi, Laura's communication specialist. Our crew would hold a huge advantage over the pirates if they understood the pirates' language. Fortunately, a designed language such as galactic basic is easy to learn. All the crew were fluent weeks before launch. Megan, of course, disapproved of the language. She declared gal base a soulless language bereft of poetry and emotion and claimed she'd never compose a song in the language. Despite her displeasure with gal base, she spoke it better than anyone else on the crew.

Preparing a crew for a single voyage was easy compared to what Callan and Rupor went through. Every country and city-state on the planet clamored to be included. Alliances formed and dissolved daily as politicians maneuvered to secure a spot for their representatives. Callan squashed three attempts to make us renege on my promise to rescue the women's husbands. Her father, King Edwar, fought against nobles intent on traveling with huge retinues. Laura's team repaired the ship and trained the crew weeks before the diplomatic wrangling ended.

Six and a half months after it crashed, the newly christened spaceship *Aashla's Hope* rose into the sky. After nearly three planet-bound years, I finally returned to space.

WHO ARE YOU?

As the *Aashla's Hope* cleared the atmosphere, everyone not busy at a work station rushed to the view ports. Gasps rose as the crew got their first look at their planet from space. Fortunately, Martin and I had seen this coming and had a work schedule setup that allowed everyone to get a look at the planet within the first hour.

We had plenty of time to enjoy the sights while the nav computer scanned the area of the planetary ring close to the wormhole entrance. The computer began plotting the movement of every rock large enough to threaten our spaceship. Martin and I watched the process for a while, verifying everything was proceeding as expected.

Martin turned to me. "I'll take the first bridge watch. Why don't you go find Callan and relax for an hour or two."

"You don't want to spend some time with Megan doing the same? It's been a lot longer since you saw the view from space."

"She'll be busy staring out the view port and strumming on her guitar. I will just be a hinderance until she finds the right melody. And I can live without a space view for a couple of hours." Martin waved me toward the hatch. "Now, get out of here. Go kiss your wife or something."

I found Callan sitting next to Megan, who *was* experimenting with melodies as she gazed out a view port.

"You know, our cabin has a view port, too," I said, wrapping my arms around Callan.

Callan smiled and, without a word, took my hand and led me back to our cabin. Taking Martin's advice a step further, I kissed my wife *and* something.

Eight hours later, the nav computer displayed a winding course to the wormhole entrance. Martin and I took one look at the twists and turns required and summoned Nist.

"Do you think you can follow this?" I asked, showing him the course projection.

Nist nodded. "Sure. It doesn't look that complicated."

"Well, it looks like a hopeless tangle of spaghetti to me." Martin waved Nist toward the helm. "Take us in, Nist."

Seventeen nerve wracking minutes crawled past. The bridge crew gasped at close brushes and even ducked instinctively when one asteroid barely slipped over the ship. Only one person on the bridge remained calm. In truth, Nist looked like he was having the time of his life. Finally, the *Aashla's Hope* slipped past the last asteroid and plunged into the wormhole.

In the early days of space exploration, wormhole travel proved deadly. The invention of the inertial dampener fifteen hundred years ago changed all that. Now travel through a wormhole is deadly dull. To combat boredom, Martin and I kept the crew on their toes with simulations and exercises. Rupor kept the marines busy with shipboard drills. Laura and the women with her kept an eye on the spaceship's systems and struggled to quell their rising anticipation. No one aboard begrudged them their excitement since they'd be seeing their husbands for the first time in over a year.

Everyone had some job to do except for the diplomats, Callan, and Megan. The two young women—already fast friends before we lifted off—spent many more hours together. Megan asked for Callan's opinion on various songs she was working on, including one that was shaping up to be an epic ballad about Callan and me. Megan's lyrics did not exaggerate our adventures, but listening to it embarrassed me all the same. Callan loved it, though, and requested it often. In fairness to Megan, the song was exciting and moving. The verse where Rob died always brought a lump to my throat and Callan openly cried. The verse where Martin and his fleet arrived over Faroon just in time to save me always had my heart hammering.

Between wormhole jumps, Martin and I plotted courses past small asteroid fields. The gunnery crews gained hours of invaluable live-fire experience during those passes. Sometimes Milo and I went out in the pinnace, as well, allowing the gunners to practice firing—simulated, of course—against an evasive, human-controlled target. It had the added benefit of giving Milo hours of piloting experience. By the time the ship entered the wormhole to the pirate base, the crew's rate of fire and accuracy had tripled and Milo's skill flying the pinnace rivaled Nist's.

The final wormhole jump seemed interminable, as was the slow crawl through real space from the wormhole exit to the asteroid field concealing the pirate base. We approached to within five light seconds of the field before we received the pirate's recognition challenge. Martin keyed the response code Rupor's interrogators had...coaxed...from the pirates and we waited.

"We're being hailed," called Heidi from the communications console.

Martin rose from the command chair. "It's about time. Put it on screen."

A lean, hard face filled the view screen. "Ya took yer sweet time returning, Cau-"

The pirate's eyes locked on Martin. "Who are you and where is Captain Caudill?"

NOT INTERESTED?

"I regret to inform you that Captain Caudill was killed after his spaceship crashed onto a lost colony world. Most of his crew were also killed in the crash." Martin inclined his head. "I am Martin Bane, new captain of this ship."

On the view screen, the pirate's lips compressed. "Caudill had himself an experienced crew and a top o' the line ship—something you look to have figgered out fer yerself. Would ya care to be explainin' to me how that ship and that crew managed ta crash?"

"They crashed the same way *I* crashed on the planet eighteen years ago." Martin took a couple of steps toward the view screen. "The wormhole exits into the middle of a planetary ring. The collection of great big rocks flying all around that exit tend to take care of the rest. It didn't help that Caudill's aft inertial dampener failed on exit."

The face on the view screen winced, the first sign of actual emotion from the pirate. "Ya got logs that back up yer story?"

"Of course. Only a fool would approach this location without them. Name a comm channel and I'll send them to you."

"Channel four three one." The head tilted to one side. "Now lad, you say Caudill was killed *after* his ship crashed. I sure would like a mite more details than that."

Martin shrugged. "Caudill was under the impression a few laser pistols and a crashed spaceship made him king of the world. I showed him just how wrong he was."

"Yer saying ya killed Caudill and then had the gall ta come to this here base and stake a claim on his spot?" A mirthless grin split the face. "You sure you ain't a big ol' idiot?"

"No, I am a pirate. Based on Caudill's logs, I've been a member of the brotherhood longer than he was. The difference is I was stuck flying airships in an atmosphere while Caudill had this space-ship." Martin smiled. "*Had* is the operative word."

"Ain't you jest a laugh riot." The compressed lips were back. "Gimme one good reason not ta blast you into little bitty pieces and maybe I'll let ya live."

"I come bearing gifts, ones you won't get if you blast me out of space," Martin replied.

"Well don't that beat all. And what gifts could a backward, lost colony have that we'd give a tinker's damn about?" sneered the pirate.

"My gift doesn't come from the planet." Martin leaned toward the screen as if sharing a secret. "My gift comes from Caudill's personal files."

The sneer vanished from the face. "I be listening."

"As you might guess, it took me a long time to break the encryption, but I had plenty of time while my crew repaired the ship." Martin returned to the command chair and lounged in it. "I know where Caudill hid his treasure."

I struggled to keep my face impassive. Was Martin out of his mind? We found no heavily encrypted files on Caudill's computer. We found no treasure maps, either. Besides, the myth of buried pirate treasure is millennia old, dating back to the days of wind-powered ships plying the oceans of Terra. Did Martin expect an actual pirate to fall for such a silly story?

Given my train of thought, I almost missed it when the glow of avarice lit the pirate's eyes. The pirate blinked it away a second later, but I knew what I had seen.

"If Caudill had a hidden treasure trove, *I* never heard of it," the pirate spat.

"Yes, no doubt you and Caudill were like brothers," Martin drawled. "I'm sure you and he shared all your deepest secrets. Why, I bet you can tell me all about Caudill's childhood, his parents, the object of his first schoolboy crush, and what drew him into this piratical life. We pirates are such trusting folk. Yep, we're just one big happy family."

Martin and pirate on the view screen stared at each other for several seconds.

"Not interested? Very well." Martin looked at Nist. "Helmsman, plot a course for–"

"What's yer offer, Bane?" the pirate growled.

"Equal shares of Caudill's treasure, split between me and all the captains who use this base. In return, you allow me to join your brotherhood on an equal footing with the other captains. I won't accept status as a junior captain or some such."

"I'll go tell the other captains o' yer petition. You jest hold yer position. We'll holler when we's made a decision."

The view screen cleared.

"Signal terminated," Heidi announced.

"What were you thinking, Martin?" I didn't yell, but it was close. "Buried pirate treasure is one of the oldest stories in the book."

"It's old because people believe it, David." Martin maintained his calm in the face of my fury. "Even pirates believe it. They're sure the big, famous raiders hold far more wealth than they display. Raiders being an untrustworthy lot, they assume men like me have all of that excess hidden away somewhere remote. I know of three groups currently searching the desert for *my* buried treasure. All three of the expeditions are led by men who served under me." Martin dazzled me with a smile. "I know how pirates think. Trust me."

Thirty-eight minutes later, the pirate was back on the view screen.

"We be grantin' ye docking permission. Will ye be takin' a piratical name?"

"I've gone by Martin Bane for eighteen years and see no reason to change that now."

"Very well. Welcome ta the brotherhood, Capt'n Bane."

"I'm looking forward to a profitable relationship," Martin replied. "Now that I'm one of you, perhaps you'd care to introduce yourself?"

"Where be me manners? You can call me Captain Quint."

Martin's eyebrows rose and he sketched a half bow. "I am most honored to meet a living legend such as yourself."

"Scorch the honor, Bane. I be plenty satisfied if'n you git us to Caudill's treasure and then do yer part ta support the Brotherhood."

Martin smiled. "I foresee exciting and profitable times ahead for us, Quint."

"Buoy channel eight one three be today's safe course ta the base. T'other captains an' me will meet ya in the docking bay."

"I look forward to it," Martin said. "Oh, I do have one other request. In order to repair the ship, I required the cooperation of the women Caudill had on board. I offered them time with their husbands in return for their help."

"Ya done got their help or ya'd still be stuck on that there planet. Ya be a pirate, Bane. Ya ain't got ta keep yer end o' the bargain."

"And you'll happily accept that explanation if I choose to keep Caudill's treasure to myself?"

Quint's eyes narrowed. "Tain't the same thing, Bane. We be yer partners. Them women be jest useful playthings."

"I've been a pirate for a long time, Quint, and having a reputation for keeping my word has been very profitable." Martin's face hardened, transforming from my genial friend into a ruthless pirate in the blink of an eye. "Do not presume to tell me how to run my ship. We will work within your current repair schedules, but my women *will* have time with their husbands."

Quint glared at Martin before giving an abrupt nod. "All right, Bane, ya gets yer way this time. I'll give the repair bay manager the word."

Martin's face relaxed and my friend was back. "It's been a pleasure negotiating with you, Captain Quint."

"Transmission terminated," Heidi said. "And thank you for standing up to him. I haven't seen my husband in over a year."

"Soon you'll be able to spend all the time you want with him," Martin smiled. "Nist, we have families to reunite. Take us in."

DOCKING BAY

A s Nist wove the ship through the asteroids, following the course laid out by the buoys, Martin and I called a final meeting of our command staff. Callan and Rupor, along with their respective marine commanders, represented the Aashlanders. Laura and Heidi represented the women whose husbands were held in the base.

Tristan invited himself. "Someone has to be around to speak common sense and rein in you impetuous young people."

"In a few minutes, we'll be docking at the pirate base," Martin said. "We've had to work around a lot of unknowns formulating our plan. We don't know how many pirate ships are docked at the base nor the crew complement carried by the ships."

"One of those unknowns turned out to be your story of buried treasure," Rupor said.

"An inspired bit of improvisation, don't you think?" Martin grinned.

"Perhaps you could explain why that is so, Martin?" Tristan asked.

"First, it got us access to the base. Quint looked more like he was ready to have the base defenses open fire rather than allow us to dock," Martin said. "But the story will also sow discord among the captains. They'll debate and argue and discuss who will come with me to fetch the treasure. In the end, all of the captains will come with me. That will create a power vacuum at the top, hampering the pirates' response when you make your move."

"What if they return in time to lead their men?" Laura asked.

"I'm not planning on bringing any of them back with me," Martin replied.

Laura gasped and Heidi's hand flew to her mouth. In contrast, the Aashlanders just nodded.

The intercom buzzed and Nist reported, "We're on our final approach to the base."

I looked around the table. "Everything we've done for the last six months has led to this point. Our success will not only free those held by the pirates, it will save countless thousands of lives that would have been lost to these pirates in the future. Today, Aashla emerges from galactic obscurity. Today, we write her name into galactic history!"

Heading back to the bridge, Martin spoke quietly. "That was a very inspiring little speech you gave at the end of the meeting, but you know it's complete bunk. It's a big galaxy and news of our raid against the pirates—no matter how daring—won't hold the public's attention for more than a few hours."

"I don't know, Martin, you're the one talking about the pervasive mythology surrounding pirates. There's something about piracy that sparks our imagination and it includes those who fight it." Martin still looked skeptical, so I said, "Let's test it. How many pirates can you name from Earth's ancient days of salt water sailing ships?"

Without thinking, Martin replied, "Blackbeard, Long John Silver, and Captain Jack Sparrow. I could name a few more if I gave it some thought."

"I'm pretty sure Blackbeard wasn't real—the stories have his headless body swimming around his ship, you know—but you've still proven my point. It's been thousands of years since any of those men hoisted the black flag, but you know their names because humans find piracy fascinating. A thousand years from now, someone will probably still tell stories of the infamous pirate Captains Caudill and Quint and how they were brought low by a bunch of Lost Colonists flying a captured pirate ship and led by a reformed air pirate."

"Well, when you put it *that* way, there is something rather mythical about this whole venture," Martin mused. "If you want to take it even deeper into mythology, our tale even has overtones of the Trojan Horse."

I clapped Martin on the back. "Now you're getting into the spirit of the adventure."

The hatch opened before us and we strode onto the bridge, Martin taking the command chair with me taking a computer station.

"Nist, report."

"We are just about to round the last buoy, Martin."

"Good." Martin turned toward me. "David, has the course through the asteroid field been uploaded into your old messenger drone?"

I began verifying the upload right after we entered the bridge. Heidi suggested using the old drone I'd fired off when I first exited the wormhole over Aashla as our insurance policy. The idea met with universal support. The drone led Caudill right to our planet and caused me some problems when Caudill's crew cracked the encryption and figured out who I was, but now it might save our lives.

"Yes, this course is recorded, another course is set for the nearest naval base, and our cry for help is intact. The thruster burn timer is set to thirty minutes," I said.

"Good. Release the drone."

The drone drifted free, then we rounded the last buoy and a huge opening yawned in the large asteroid before us. Beyond the opening, we saw a well-lit, well-equipped docking bay. Within, I counted six ships with space marked for one more.

"Oh joy. It looks like all the pirates are at home right now," I said.

"Of course," Martin sighed. "The rescue would be too easy if half the ships were out prowling."

"Oh mighty pirate captain?" Nist sang out. "The big hole in the bigger rock is glowing."

"Hm? Oh, that. Don't worry about it, Nist. That's an atmospheric energy shield. It keeps the air in the docking bay from leaking out. We'll pass right through it."

I went to the communications console. "Heidi, can you give me a ship-wide channel?"

Her fingers flew across the console. "You're on, fearless leader."

"All hands, this is David Rice. We are entering the pirate base as I speak. Everyone knows the plan and their part in it, but I want to remind you all of a few things. All of you now speak galactic basic well enough to understand what the pirates are saying. I cannot stress how important it is for us to hide that knowledge for as long as possible. There's no telling what we can learn if the pirates believe we can't understand them.

"With that said, don't wander far from the ship, do not go out alone, and check your honor at the airlock. Reacting to an insult will give away our language advantage and put the pirates on alert.

"Finally, all of the pirate ships using this base are docked. The bad news is we're more heavily outnumbered than anticipated. The good news is we can take out half a dozen of the galaxy's worst criminals all at once. Keep a clear head and stick to the plan. Failure is not an option. Rice out."

"David?" Martin said. "We may have to modify that plan a bit."

"What do you mean?"

Martin pointed at a dozen locations in the docking bay. "Those are military-grade automated defense lasers. If we take off without sending the proper pass code, the lasers will cut this ship to pieces."

YOU DON'T TRUST US?

Martin and I stared through the view screen at the automated defense lasers.

"We can't leave the docking bay with those in place and the navy will get sliced to ribbons if the lasers are active when they come to our rescue." Martin turned to me. "Have you got any bright ideas?"

I shrugged. "We'll have to find a way to disable them, obviously."

Laura, who had been on the bridge observing, stepped up to Martin and me. "Let me guess, you're scrapping the carefully laid plan"

"*Bad* plans are scrapped at the last minute, my good woman," Martin said. "*Good* plans simply require a few revisions."

"Well, my good man, when you put it that way I feel so much better," Laura replied.

I couldn't tell if this was stress-relieving banter or if nerves were stretched to the breaking point. Before I could think of something to say to defuse the situation, Callan stepped in.

"Laura, to protect their wives, your husbands are forced to perform maintenance for the base, right?" When Laura nodded, Callan continued. "You and the other ladies on this ship were in the same position with Caudill. You used your positions to sabotage his ship."

Martin and Laura flashed grins at each other.

"I told you we had a good plan, Laura."

"And the simple revision is our husbands disabling the lasers."

"While David and I are leading the captains on the wild treasure chase, yes."

"And when the two of you get back, we can just power up and leave."

Callan frowned. "You hadn't mentioned David going with you, Martin."

"We'll need a pilot and I can't trust anyone the captains choose. And six against one is much worse odds than six against two." Martin gave her a smile. "Consider it one last adventure for David. Something he can tell your grandchildren about when he's a doddering old man."

Callan sighed and slipped her arm around my waist. Anything she might have said was cut off when Nist spoke.

"We've docked, Cap'n. All engines stopped."

Through the view screen, we saw men entering the docking bay.

"Time to go meet the Brotherhood," Martin said.

A moment later, the airlock cycled and we stepped off the ship. Arrayed before us were the six pirate captains.

Footsteps rang on the ramp behind us as Rupor ran out to join Martin, Laura, Callan, and me. The pirates didn't so much as glance at the prince. They were much too busy leering at Callan. It appeared women were as rare among pirates as the stories said, because the six pirates acted like they hadn't seen a woman in ages.

Speaking his native language, Rupor said, "I have half a dozen men armed with lasers stationed just inside the airlock. I doubt we'll need them, but I prefer to err on the side of caution."

It was a good idea, one I wish I had considered. Rupor's military training proved useful months ago when we captured the ship and it was proving useful again.

Quint grimaced at Rupor and growled, "What's the elsie sayin'?"

"Elsie?" Martin asked.

"El Cee. Lost Colonist," Quint said. "How long you been on that planet, Bane?"

"Eighteen years."

The pirates all nodded as if that explained everything. "There been a spate o' lost colonies being found in the last few years. Newsies called 'em Lost Colonists but most folks just shortened it to elsie," Quint said. "So, what's the elsie sayin'?"

"He said he stationed six men with lasers inside our airlock as a precaution against treachery."

The pirates muttered and exchanged glances before Quint scowled and said, "You don't trust us, Bane?"

"Ah, how utterly foolish of me," Martin replied. "I thought I had joined a *pirate* Brotherhood, not the Fractured Feelings Fraternity of Fragile Flowers."

Quint's scowl deepened and the other five pirates cast hard glares at Martin. Martin folded his arms and met the glares with the mocking smile he does so well. Quint barked a laugh, quickly followed by the other five captains.

"I believe you'll do right fine, Bane," he said.

The light patter of feet on the ramp sounded behind me. I didn't even need to hear her speak to know who it was.

"What did I miss?" Megan asked.

Megan's arrival did draw some open stares away from Callan, at least.

"Well now, seems t' me you found yourself a secret source o' fine lookin' women, Bane." Quint was back to growling. "The rules of the Brotherhood say share and share alike."

The other five captains muttered "Yeah" and "Tha's right" while their eyes darted back and forth between Callan and Megan. They were almost drooling after Quint's pronouncement. I wanted to step between the pirates and Callan in the worst way. Callan laid a hand lightly on my arm, so I stayed put.

Martin's voice cut through the building tension. "You don't have any kind of stupid 'sharing' rule, Quint."

"I been part o' this Brotherhood fer nigh on thirty years, Bane. You been part o' it fer ten minutes. Who do you think knows more 'bout the Brotherhood?"

"Caudill's files had a copy of the captain's agreement for the Brotherhood. If I'd found anything so idiotic as a sharing agreement in the articles, I'd never have contacted you."

One of the other captains piped up, "It's an unwritten rule."

The other four captains nodded. Quint kept his gaze steady on Martin, watching and, I expect, evaluating him.

"Is that so?" Martin asked. Martin pointed at Laura. "Then perhaps one of you gentlemen could explain why Caudill had all of the wives on his ship?"

More muttering from the five, then one said, "Caudill was different. And you ain't Caudill."

"No, I'm not. Caudill is *dead*. His ship is *my* ship now." The captains stopped nodding. "One of your *written* rules provides very detailed rules for settling disagreements between captains. Quint, the next time you or your little Greek Chorus make another ridiculous claim, I will follow those rules to the letter and deprive one of these six ships of its captain."

Martin's glare swept across the six captains. "Are we clear, gentlemen?"

For the second time since we exited the ship, Quint burst out laughing. "Caudill was a good captain, but I think we be trading up with you." Quint pretended to wipe tears of laughter from ice cold eyes. "Now, 'bout Caudill's treasure-"

"We'll talk treasure after Laura and her friends see their husbands."

"I told you we'd work that out, Bane."

"And I'm telling you we'll work it out first, Quint."

"You puttin' pleasure slaves ahead o' treasure?"

"No, I'm putting my crew ahead of a treasure that isn't going anywhere."

"Yer crew?" one of the Greek Chorus said. "But Caudill-"

"For the last time, I. Am. Not. Caudill." Martin turned back to Quint. "Well?"

Quint raised a wrist comm to his mouth. "Send 'em in."

The docking bay hatch slid open and a crowd of men hesitated before walking forward. Laura gave a small gasp and went flying across the bay. Behind us, dozens of feet rang on the boarding ramp as the rest of the women followed her.

Martin watched for a few seconds then said, "Now we can talk about treasure."

THEIR INSIDE MAN

Martin turned to me and spoke in Mordanian. "I'm off to discuss treasure with these lovely gentlemen. You're in charge until I return."

Martin's lines were for the recordings the pirates were bound to be making. In the short time we expected to be with the pirates, we doubted they would record a large enough sampling of Mordanian for their computers to complete a translation. Even so, we saw no reason to take chances.

"Yes, sir, Cap'n," I replied.

Martin turned back to Quint, switching back to galactic basic. "Lead on, Captain Quint."

Quint cocked an eyebrow as Laura and the man I assumed was her husband strolled, arm-in-arm, toward the boarding ramp to our ship. "And where do you think you be goin', Mister Barrages?"

Laura's husband stiffened and I heard a tremor in his voice when he replied. "I'm going to spend time with my wife, Captain Quint, as you promised I could."

Other couples trailing along behind Laura and her husband stopped to watch. I saw fear written on the faces of the men and uncertainty on the faces of their wives.

"I know what be promised and what ain't promised," Quint

growled. "You got a big ol' room where all of y'all sleep. Git on along back there."

Martin stepped between Quint and the couple. "I told you, Quint, I take care of my crew. That includes a little privacy for family reunions." Martin turned to the couple. "You may carry on, Laura."

Laura started toward the boarding ramp, pulling on her husband's arm.

Martin looked at the other couples. "That applies to the rest of you, as well. Enjoy yourselves."

Quint and the other captains scowled but said nothing as the couples streamed past them.

"You made a bunch o' pleasure girls part o' your crew, Bane?" Quint asked after the last couple had entered our ship.

"No, I made skilled techs my engineering staff," Martin replied. "If I hadn't done that, I'd still be on that lost colony and you wouldn't be about to discuss the division of Caudill's treasure." Martin motioned toward the docking bay doors. "Shall we have that discussion, gentlemen?"

Watching Martin and the captains walk away, Megan said, "Those men are *not* happy with Martin."

"Tell me something I don't know," I replied.

Typical of Megan, she took it as a challenge.

"Those husbands are all terrified of their captors," she said. "All of them except Heidi's husband."

As Megan's words sank in, I nodded my head toward our ship. "Let's go inside and discuss this further."

Switching from observant to obstinate, Megan asked, "Why? It's not like any of the pirates can understand us."

"Is 'because I asked politely' sufficient?"

"Oh, wait," she said, comprehension dawning. "It's because of those 'recording' things you've told us about, right?"

A few pirates looked up at Megan's words. Well, at one of her words. There is no Mordanian word for 'recording,' so we'd simply used the gal base word. Hearing a familiar word from people who aren't supposed to speak his language might make a pirate suspicious.

I looked at the men around us and didn't see any narrowing of the eyes or anyone hurrying off to report the verbal slip to a superior. Callan was already speaking before I turned back to Megan.

"That's exactly right, Megan." Turning toward the boarding ramp, my wife added, "Come on."

I entered the ship in time to catch the tail end of Callan's admonishment to Megan. All I can say is that Callan took a more gentle tone than I'd have done—*far* more gentle. Nodding and biting her lower lip, Megan listened attentively to my wife. I left her to it, since Callan's approach was working.

"Your impetuous nature is one of your most endearing qualities," Callan wrapped up, "but for the next few hours you must keep a tight rein on it."

I put a smile on my face and carefully kept my tone neutral as I asked, "Could you tell us what you observed concerning Heidi's husband?"

"When that old, scary pirate spoke, all of the men reacted like whipped dogs," Megan said. "They looked down and scrubbed all expression from their faces. Heidi's husband kept his head up, looking at the other men and smirking. It's like he thinks he's above them or something."

I thoroughly disliked the sound of that. "Do you think he's working for the pirates—like he's acting as their inside man among their hostage tech crew?"

Megan gave my question careful thought before nodding. "It's possible there's something else behind his expression, an indomitable will or something heroic like that, but I don't think so. He's nothing like you."

"Thank you for that assessment, Megan. And for the compliment." I turned to one of the guards Rupor had stationed inside the airlock. "Please bring Heidi and her husband to me."

Moments later the guard returned—alone.

He snapped off a salute and reported, "Sir, they're gone."

A CHALLENGE

"Check with the guards at the forward airlock," I said. "Have them seal the exit if Heidi and her husband haven't gone out that way."

The guard saluted and ran off. I strode off toward the bridge. Callan, Megan, and Rupor fell in behind me.

"Does anyone know why Heidi's husband would even bother boarding the ship if he only planned to stay for a few minutes?" Callan asked.

"There could be any number of reasons," Rupor said. "Once aboard, it's likely Heidi told her husband of our plan to sabotage the lasers—that is an integral part of the plan, after all. If he's working for the pirates, he'll want to report our plan as soon as possible. It's also possible he just wants to show off his beautiful wife. After all, the pirates have quite a severe shortage of women here. It's a petty and foolish thing for a prisoner to do, but men do foolish things when women are involved."

As we approached the bridge, the guard I'd sent to the forward airlock returned.

"The woman and her husband left the ship no more than a minute before I reached the airlock," he reported. "The guards say the woman appeared reluctant but left voluntarily."

Nodding to the guard, I strode onto the bridge. "Give me a video sweep of the docking bay. Stop and zoom in if you see Heidi out there."

Seconds later, Heidi and her husband filled our view screen. The pair stood less than a hundred yards from our ship. A gang of grinning pirates had them surrounded and one of their number laughed and talked with Heidi's husband. Heidi pressed close beside her husband, fear written on her face. Her husband, fear building on his face, argued vehemently with the pirate.

"The man may be working with the pirates, but they sure don't seem to like him much," I said. "I've got to get out there and defuse this situation."

"I'll come with you," Rupor said.

"You're our military commander, Rupor. You need to stay here with your command," Callan said. "Megan, do you mind going with David? You can be his translator."

"Why would she speak gal base and not the ship's second in command?" I asked.

"Captain Bane taught me," Megan answered. "He would want his woman to speak his language, wouldn't he?"

"It sounds reasonable to me," I said. "Let's go."

A moment later, Megan and I approached the outer edge of the pirates gathered around Heidi and her husband.

"I'm getting tired of arguing with you, Chapman," the pirate said. "If you won't share your woman with us, there's only one thing I can do. Erwin Chapman, I challenge you to a duel. If you win, you get my rights within the Brotherhood. If I win, I get your woman."

As if our situation weren't complicated enough, Heidi's husband had managed to find a way to make things more precarious. If Chapman was the only one involved, I'd have left him to his own devices. But I couldn't just stand by and let Heidi suffer through this.

I turned an expectant look on Megan and tilted my head

toward Heidi and her husband. Catching on, Megan gave a Mordanian translation of what had just transpired.

Over the excited talk from the pirates, I called out in Mordanian, "Megan, tell them Heidi is a member of our crew and not a prize to be fought over."

The chatter around the two men died down at the sound of my voice. Curious, the pirates turned their attention our way. Megan took advantage of the lull in conversation and spoke in exaggeratedly careful gal base. "Commander Rice says you can do what you want with the spy but the woman is ours!"

In Mordanian, I said, "Um, Megan, that's not exactly what I said."

"I know, David, but if I repeat what you say exactly won't that make it easier for the machines to translate our language?"

She made a very good point. "That's a very smart move, but that means you're in charge of these negotiations. I'll try to offer advice if it's needed, but that's the best I can do."

"Words and reading crowds are my business, David. You have to trust me."

"I do. Carry on as you see fit. If the situation really goes downhill, we can always switch to you directly translating my words."

By now the pirate arguing with Chapman had gotten over his surprise. "How did an elsie woman learn gal base?"

"I speak five languages native to my planet. Learning your soulless language didn't pose much of a challenge," Megan replied. "Now, Heidi is coming with us."

The pirate suddenly remembered the original discussion. "Wait just a minute. What do you mean the woman is yours?"

Maintaining the act, I said to Megan, "Just nod your head as if I guessed the gist of the pirate's question."

Megan nodded, then I muttered a bunch of unassociated Mordanian strung together.

Megan turned back to the pirates and switched to gal base. "Heidi is a full member of our crew. Our captain is a member of this Brotherhood. That means you can *challenge* her to a duel but you cannot *win* her in a duel—especially not a duel with a hostage who's wormed his way into Quint's good graces by spying on his fellow hostages."

The pirates exchanged glances. "What are you talking about? Who said he's a spy for the captains?"

Megan looked my way and switched to Mordanian. "Blah blah blather pretend to translate."

I suppressed the urge to laugh. "Don't do that! It would ruin the scene if I started laughing in the middle of the negotiation."

Megan turned back to the pirate. "All of the men other than Chapman were terrified when Quint ordered them away. Chapman just smirked. It wasn't hard to figure out the rest."

"Erwin, that's not true, is it?" Heidi asked, her eyes wide and pleading.

"It's...complicated," Chapman said.

The pirate laughed. "Yeah, it's complicated. But I'm going to uncomplicate it for you, honey. Chapman, the challenge still stands, only now I'm going to kill you just for the fun of it."

Chapman paled at the pirate's words. "B-but I'm useful to you. Captain Quint said so!"

"You *were* useful, Chapman," his challenger said, "but we got those other men toeing the line right nice like. Your tech skills aren't real good. And your other skills are—what was the word the captain used, boys? Oh yeah—redundant."

Another pirate got into Chapman's face. "Do you know what that means? It means we can live without you, Chapman."

As raucous laughter rose from the other pirates, Heidi turned an imploring look on me. I sighed and nodded to her. Relief spread across her face.

Megan eyed me with an appraising look. "You're going to save Chapman's sorry hide, aren't you?"

"I'm doing it for Heidi, not Chapman. But yes, unless we can find a way out of this duel, I'm going to try to save his sorry hide. See if you can find an angle that will let us buy these guys off or something."

Megan raised her voice and switched back to gal base. "You can't kill Chapman."

"Yeah I can, lady. And you can watch me," the challenger called back.

"Chapman is married to a member of our crew. That means he belongs to her. You may only challenge him if she grants him permission to duel."

Hope flared in Chapman's face.

"Nice try, woman, but Chapman is just *married* to her." The pirate jerked a thumb at Heidi. "That don't mean he *belongs* to her."

"Tell that to my ex-wife!" one of the other pirates quipped, drawing more laughter from the pirates.

As the light of hope faded from Chapman's eyes, the challenger continued, "I'll grant you had a point about the woman, but not about her husband. Chapman is ours."

"It was a valiant try, Megan," I said, "but these pirates want blood. It's time to get me involved in the duel."

"You know Callan won't approve of this," she replied in Mordanian. Switching back to gal base, she said, "Commander Rice says he is disappointed in his fellows in the Brotherhood."

The challenger turned mocking, wide eyes my way. "Gosh, I don't want to disappoint *Commander Rice* none. Please tell me how we disappointed him so we can fix it right up."

"He and I are both displeased to learn what cowards you lot are."

The mocking expression vanished, replaced by a hot glare. "Who you calling a coward, lady?"

"You, obviously. Who but a coward would challenge a man wholly incapable of defending himself?" Megan's voice dripped with disdain. "Your cowardice disgusts him so much that Commander Rice issues challenge to you. Should you defeat our commander in a fair fight, Chapman is yours to do with as you wish. Should you lose, well, you won't care about anything ever again, will you?"

One of the other pirates spoke quietly to the challenger. A grin spread across the challenger's face as he listened.

"Well now, this is more like it. We got us a new challenge, boys!" he called. Putting a hand on the other pirate's shoulder, the challenger said, "Simmons and me are going to meet Chapman and Rice together. A two-on-two challenge to the death."

A cheer rose from the pirates, Chapman's face went white, and Heidi buried her face in her hands.

Megan hung her head. "I'm sorry, David. All I've done is make things worse."

"Don't blame yourself. You did a lot better than I could have, Megan. Like I said, the pirates want blood."

A gruff voice cut through the commotion. "What be the meanin' o' all this, then?"

Martin and the other pirate captains were already back. The negotiations must have gone smoothly. Seeing the captains, hope returned to Chapman's face.

"Captain Quint! These men challenged me to a duel," he cried. "Me! Your inside man."

"An' why should that matter to me?" Quint asked.

The response shook Chapman, but he tried another appeal to Quint. "But what if I've learned something important?"

"I s'pose there be a first time fer everything," Quint spat.

Chapman tried one more time. "But Captain Quint-"

Quint spun around, a blaster materializing in his hand. "Shut up, Chapman, or I'll kill you m'self."

Chapman backpedaled, his hands held out in supplication.

Turning away and holstering his blaster, Quint added, "Have a good time killin' him, boys."

HE'S RUNNING

Martin stayed behind as Quint and the other five captains walked away. Taking in the scene around me, he spoke to me in Mordanian. "You're involved in this fight, aren't you David?"

"He's doing it for Heidi. After all she went through to get back to her husband, David couldn't just let the pirates kill her man in front of her. It's all quite gallant on David's part." Megan turned a level stare on me. "I prefer heroic songs with happy endings, so don't get yourself killed."

"At long last, I have a good reason to survive a fight," I grinned just in case Megan didn't figure out I was kidding.

Megan grinned in return. "I'll make sure to tell Callan of your good fortune."

"Bane!" Quint and his pirate chorus stopped about fifty feet away. "Come on. We got us a treasure to find."

"I'd love to join you, Quint," Martin replied, switching back to gal base. "Unfortunately, your men dragged my pilot into this fight. We'll have to wait until the duel is finished."

"I gots plenty o' pilots. I'll have one git out here," Quint said.

"I am not getting into a pinnace outnumbered seven to one," Bane said.

"We be headin' out for the treasure now. If'n my pilot ain't ta yer likin' you can get another one o' yours. You do got another pilot, don't you?"

"Of course I have another pilot, Quint." Martin looked at me and shrugged. "I'll go get him."

"Are you taking Nist?" I asked in Mordanian

"No, I'll take Milo." Martin switched back to Mordanian. "His size and age won't alarm them and, as much as I like Nist, Milo will be more useful if it comes to a fight." Turning toward the pirate captains, he added, "Try not to get yourself killed, David."

As he walked away, I turned to Megan. "Find out the details of this challenge. What weapons we can use, where we fight, who can watch, that sort of thing."

Moments later, we were back on our ship as the pirates made preparations for the duel. Laura and some of the other women consoled Heidi. Chapman sat alone, ostracized and avoided. Rupor watched Chapman with unconcealed disgust.

"How could a woman as courageous and intelligent as Heidi marry a cur such as him?" Rupor hissed in a low voice.

"In normal circumstances, he may be a fine, upstanding man," I said.

"You're excusing him?" Rupor asked.

"No, I was answering your question, Rupor. Adversity doesn't always bring out the best in a man, but the man only finds that out when adversity strikes." I eyed Chapman. "I suspect life on a colony would have broken Chapman, but it would have taken longer."

Callan slid in beside me. "Everyone's here, David."

I switched to gal base so everyone could understand me. "You all know that Chapman and I are fighting a couple of pirates. The duel is held in a zero gravity room surrounded by viewing plat-forms. Most of the other pirates will be there to watch, so that's when you and your men," I pointed to Laura's husband, "will disable all of the defense lasers in the docking bay. We'll draw the fight out as long as we can, but don't waste any time. Come back to the ship as soon as you're done. We'll leave once Chapman and I get back. Questions?"

There were none.

"Keep your composure, do your job, and we'll be safe on a naval base this time tomorrow." I turned to Chapman. "Let's get this over with."

Chapman and I stepped out of the ship and then red lights began flashing all around the docking bay. The pirates took note of the flashing lights but simply returned to their tasks. Was this some kind of test or a minor warning? I wanted to stop one of the nearby pirates and ask what was going on, but I wasn't supposed to understand gal base. I couldn't ask Chapman for the same reason.

Looking back to the airlock, I called, "Could someone please send Megan out here?"

As the marine guard in the airlock headed into the ship, I turned back to the docking bay. Chapman was thirty feet away, running for the hatch out of the docking bay and into the main base. Cursing, I took off after him. If Chapman got into the base proper, he might be as good as gone.

The pirates watched him dash past, laughing. One or two tried to trip him, but most just settled in to watch the fun.

"Twenty credits says the elsie catches him," one pirate called.

"Done," called another. "But the bet is off if someone trips Chapman."

More bets were called and accepted and, within seconds, all attention in the docking bay focused on Chapman and me.

Behind me, I heard Megan call, "David, what are you doing?"

"Chapman's running away."

Megan used language quite fitting for a pirate base and, based on the catcalls from the pirates, joined the chase.

"Go back to the ship, Megan," I yelled without turning.

"I won't," she yelled back. "You can't run around the base without having a translator."

There were good reasons behind the decision to pretend ignorance of gal base, but I really regretted that decision now. If I caught Chapman before he got out of the airlock, though, it wouldn't matter. And that looked to be the likely result before Megan cried out behind me.

"Get your hands off me!"

One of the pirates cried out in pain and more harsh laughter erupted from the other pirates.

"That ain't no way for a pretty plaything to act," a pirate said.

"Let me go!" Megan shouted.

I risked a look over my shoulder. A handful of pirates clutched at Megan, trying to pull her into a rough embrace. I found myself torn between my desire to help Megan and the absolute necessity of catching Chapman.

"Unhand that woman, you miserable pirates," demanded a strong voice.

The pirates didn't understand the command as it was in Mordanian—or Tartegian, from the speaker's point of view—but the meaning was clear. The pirates backed away as Rupor charged across the bay, two squads of marines backing him up.

Relieved of a difficult decision, I turned back to the chase— just in time to see a cargo boom swinging toward my head. I dropped and slid under the boom, losing precious time as a result. As I rolled to my feet, Chapman ducked through the hatch and disappeared into the main base.

CHASING CHAPMAN

I rushed to the hatch out of the docking bay. The docking bay wasn't in vacuum nor was there any imminent threat of decompression, so I should have just been able to yank the hatch open and move on. Instead, the hatch held firm. Two blinking lights caught my eye—a green light showing the airlock was cycling and a red one showing someone had manually switched the airlock to operate under vacuum conditions. Chapman had plenty of time to get lost in the base while I waited for the airlock to recycle.

I looked back toward Megan. Rupor and the marines had safely removed her from the clutching pirates. Rupor's face contorted in righteous rage while Megan's displayed offended anger. The pirates muttered among themselves and eyed the marines arrayed between them and Megan. The situation looked volatile, to say the least, but it would become explosive if Chapman found anyone to listen to him.

That's why, when the airlock finished recycling, I switched off the vacuum conditions override and left Rupor and Megan to handle the situation. With a last glance back to the docking bay, I saw Callan descending from our ship. Perhaps she would ensure cooler heads prevailed.

Beyond the airlock, I found corridors leading left, right, and straight ahead. I didn't see Chapman anywhere. A couple of pirates lounged against the wall, grinning at me.

"I bet you wish you could speak civilized, elsie," one said.

I looked at him and shrugged then peered down the corridor straight ahead as if looking for something.

"Chapman didn't go that way, moron," the other pirate said.

I whipped my head back to the pirate. Maybe I could get them to tell where he went. Speaking slowly, I said, "Chapman?"

"Send him the wrong way," the first pirate said.

The other pirate pointed down the corridor to my right. Could he be telling the truth? It wasn't likely.

Swinging my head to the left, I pretended to spot something and yelled, "Chapman!" Then I dashed down the corridor to my left.

I dodged around pirates who mostly ignored me. A few tried to trip me up or get in my way. After I 'accidentally' knocked a couple of pirates down, the rest stayed out of my way. Seconds later, I rounded a bend in the passage and saw Chapman. He sauntered along fifty or sixty feet ahead of me, acting as if he hadn't a care. I hid behind a pirate just as Chapman looked over his shoulder. Somehow, he didn't see me. I trailed behind him for close to a minute, managing to avoid being spotted. The pirates just went about their business, ignoring both of us.

Chapman turned a corner and I took the chance to sprint closer. I peeked around the corner and spied Chapman just twenty feet ahead. A chill settled over me as I spotted his destination.

Chapman's path led straight to the base's communications center.

What could Chapman do from the base's communications facility that he couldn't already do? He didn't need a radio to reveal our identities and our plans. Then it dawned on me that Chapman's plan went beyond getting out of the duel. He hoped to gain prestige at the same time. That was far less likely to happen if he spilled everything to just any pirate in the base. No, he'd need to get the attention of people with rank. Everyone of sufficient rank was aboard our pinnace and not due back until after the duel.

Twenty feet ahead of me, Chapman entered the communications room. When I followed, he stood before the pirate officer on watch, an earnest expression on his face..

"Go away, Chapman. I ain't callin' the captains fer ya," the officer said.

"Why not? It's extremely important," Chapman whined.

The officer gave Chapman a nasty grin. "I got a hundred credits bet on you dyin' in the first minute o' that duel. You ain't gonna talk yer way out of fightin' them two fine lads o' the Brotherhood."

"But I won't even mention the duel. I swear. Please, just thirty seconds!"

"Even if'n I wanted to let ya speak to the captains, ya know we gotta go silent right after one of the wormholes opens up."

So, the pirates had detected the wormhole opening for the messenger drone we launched before docking. That explained why the flashing lights didn't seem to alarm anyone. I saw the sense in the pirates' approach, too. They shut down communications until they discovered what triggered the wormhole. No doubt they extended communication blackout if they detected ships traversing the system. Barring naval patrols, those ships were likely easy pickings. But the one place where the pirates did *not* want ships disappearing was the system where their base was hidden.

The pirate officer crossed his arms. "You gots somethin' to say, you say it to me."

Chapman's shoulders sagged. "Yeah, okay, I'll tell-"

I grabbed Chapman's shoulder and spun him around to face me. Alarm registered on his face as I drove my fist into Chapman's gut with all my strength. He doubled over, the wind whooshing out of him. I stepped into my next blow, putting all of my weight and strength into an uppercut to Chapman's chin. He rose a foot off the floor and flew back four or five feet before sprawling, unconscious, at the feet of one of the other pirates.

The officer of the watch stared at me, his mouth hanging open. I grinned and made a show of dusting my hands off. The pirate officer laughed at my little act. Still grinning, he drew his laser pistol and leveled it at me.

EXCELLENT TIMING

Staring down the muzzle of a laser pistol, I half raised my hands. Once the pirate understood I had no plans to do anything stupid, I mimed pointing the gun at Chapman.

The pirate shook his head. "I got no idea what Chapman wanted ta tell me, but I figger you clobbered him to shut him up. Suddenly, I'm right curious what he aimed to say."

I shrugged as if I didn't understand what the pirate had said. Inspiration struck and I continued with my pantomime. I pointed to Chapman then wove my hands in the curving motion that has meant 'woman' to every man since before recorded history.

The pirate leered. "Yeah, Chapman's got himself a hot wife. Wish I knew how that gutless wonder hooked a babe like her."

Keeping a hand held out, as if on the shoulder of the woman, I threw a fist at what would have been the woman's head.

"Chapman punched the babe, huh?" the pirate said. "That ain't against the rules 'round here."

"And to think you call *us* uncivilized," Megan's voice sounded behind me. She strode up beside me, five marines trailing in her wake. The marines carried lasers but kept them pointed at the floor.

"I heard one of ya spoke gal base," the pirate said. "That'll make this easier. We're gonna hold yer boy here till Captain Quint gets back."

"No, I'm taking David and Chapman back to our ship. You're going to stand aside and not interfere."

"And why would I do that?"

"Because David didn't break any of *your* rules, but Chapman broke one of *our* rules."

"Okay, we don't got rules against a bit of fightin' as long as the work gets done. So you can take yer boy, but yer rules don't count on the base. Chapman stays here."

"Chapman hit Heidi while aboard our ship," Megan countered. "Our ship, our rules, our punishment."

The pirate shrugged. "Seems like a lotta trouble just 'cause he punched his wife."

"Oh, it does? Let me tell you something about our planet." Megan's voice dropped an octave and she leaned forward. "One of our greatest heroes is a man who spent his life challenging abusive men to duels. When he left a town, he left behind fresh graves, new widows, and a far more polite population. So you see, we uncivilized lost colonists take this kind of behavior very seriously."

Megan ordered one of the marines to carry Chapman, spun on her heel, and led us out of the room. The pirates in the hallway gave us a wide berth as we marched back toward the ship.

Keeping my voice low, I said, "You have excellent timing, Megan. How did you come up with that story about the duelist so quickly?"

Megan gave me a meaningful look.

"Wait, do you mean you didn't make that up?" I asked.

"If you like, I'll sing the song for you sometime. Make sure you've got a couple of hours to spare," she smiled. "The full version has eighty-six verses."

Moments later, we returned to the docking bay—just in time to see Milo landing our pinnace next to the ship.

"Why is the pinnace back so soon?" Megan asked.

"It's probably because one of the system's wormholes opened,"

I replied. "It's the same reason the base is operating under radio silence. The pirates don't want to risk giving away their position to passing spaceships."

I turned to the marine carrying Chapman. "Sergeant, we're going to delay the pirates long enough for you to get Chapman into the ship. Stuff him in a room with only one door and keep a guard on that door at all times. If he causes any problems, just hit him until he stops."

"Yes, sir," the marine replied. Speaking to his second-in-command, he added, "Corporal, you and the men stay with the Prince Consort and the young lady."

As the corporal acknowledged the order, I spoke to Megan. "Make a big show of kissing Martin when we get to him."

A devilish smile lit Megan's face. "With all these people watching? How scandalous! Of course, it does sound like fun, but please explain why I am doing it?"

"You're the only one of us known to speak gal base. You may have to wander the base a lot more than I'd prefer and you're an extremely attractive woman."

Megan batted her eyes. "Why, David, I do believe you've been letting your gaze linger on women other than your wife. What would Callan say about that?"

"She'd say that I'm married, not blind. The point is, you've got to show these pirates that you're Martin's woman. They *must* believe that messing with you will draw the ire of a pirate captain. That belief may be your only protection away from the ship."

Megan heaved a theatrical sigh. "Very well, David, I shall do my best to display some modicum of attraction to Martin."

When Martin exited the pinnace a few seconds later, Megan's eyes lit up, she flashed a dazzling smile, ran lightly forward, and threw herself upon him. Arms wrapped around Martin's neck, she locked her lips on his and gave him quite the hero's welcome. After a startled second, Martin returned her greeting with obvious enthusiasm. Either he was a better actor than I believed possible or he held deeper feelings for Megan than I'd ever realized.

When the two finally came up for air, Megan asked, "Did you bring me something from the treasure? You promised me a pretty jewel."

Martin played his part to the hilt, playfully tapping Megan on the nose with a finger. "We didn't get to the treasure, my dear. The wormhole opened up and the other captains insisted we return to base."

Rolling his eyes, Quint turned to me. "I saw Chapman's body being carried aboard your ship. I guess the duel be over?"

Megan slipped from Martin's arms. "Excuse me, Martin, I've got to go translate for your lunkhead first officer."

As I stood there with a look of incomprehension, she told Quint, "Chapman is unconscious, not dead. We've taken him on board our ship to face punishment for striking a woman. The duel will have to wait."

"Wrong, woman. The duel be first. The challenge be given and accepted afore Chapman hit his wife." Quint turned to the other captains. "I don't rightly see why hittin' yer wife is a crime, no how."

Megan's voice chilled considerably. "What makes you think Chapman didn't hit his wife before the challenge was made?"

"Ain't no way yer 'lunkhead' here woulda stepped in ta help Chapman if'n he'd already done smacked the woman. So the fight be on—and there ain't no time like the present, I say," Quint raised his voice until it echoed through the docking bay. "Stop workin' boys. It be time fer the duel!"

YOUR BEST IS EXCEEDINGLY GOOD

Quint gave us five minutes to gather Chapman and report to the dueling arena. That left us little time to modify our plans to fit this ever-changing situation.

"Our top priority is still disabling those sentry lasers in the docking bay," I told our hastily gathered command staff. "Laura, has your husband briefed all the other men? Are they ready to go?"

She nodded. "They know what to do and one of the men had a suggestion for speeding up the process. Instead of spending ten minutes disabling each laser, they're going to disable the four control clusters for the docking bay. Each one will take about fifteen minutes, but they'll be able to work on all four simultaneously."

"Good. Wait until the docking bay clears for the fight before sending them out. The fewer pirates they run into, the better." I turned to Rupor. "Have you got squads of marines assigned to guard each of the sabotage teams?"

"Yes, Rice," Rupor replied. "But I strongly disagree with your plan to simply 'run for the docking bay' after this duel. That might have been acceptable when none of the pirate captains were here, but it will not work now."

"Rupor's right," Callan said. "The captains will expect Martin and Megan to sit with them. As Martin's royal benefactors, Rupor and I will be expected to be there, too."

I hadn't considered that. "None of you will be able to just slip away from the captains. Okay, Rupor, what did you have in mind?"

Rupor outlined a plan for a fighting withdrawal, with the marines bearing the brunt of the fighting. "The plan is short on details and will require considerable initiative from the officers, but they're well-trained men. They can handle it."

"How will we get away from the captains?" Megan asked.

Martin answered, "For the most part, we'll make it up as we go. We don't know enough about the arena setup to do any real planning." He looked at Rupor. "I suggest we wait for the first serious wound and then make our move while the pirates are distracted by the blood."

Rupor nodded agreement and I added, "That just leaves one question. What do we do about Chapman? He's proven we can't trust him. If he has the chance, he's sure to try to alert the pirates from inside the arena."

Rupor said what was on everyone's mind. "Get him killed early in the fight or, if you have to, find a way to kill him yourself."

"I'm afraid you're probably right. We can't risk the lives of hundreds of people over the life of a man who is actively trying to get us killed." I looked around the room. "Do we all agree?"

One by one, everyone nodded.

"Then let's get this over."

Tristan gave me smelling salts to revive Chapman. "Remember, he'll be groggy for a minute or two after he wakes up."

"I'll keep that in mind," I said.

Throwing Chapman over my shoulder, I joined Martin, Megan, Rupor, and Callan at the airlock. One of Quint's pirates waited for us at the foot of the ramp.

"Cap'n Quint sent me to lead the way."

Together, we set off for the arena.

As the pirate led us away, Heidi dashed up. Her eyes were red and swollen, though any tear tracks had been scrubbed from her face.

"I'm coming with you," she declared in accented Mordanian. "Erwin is my husband and I should be there."

Laura ran out of the airlock, her face creased with concern, as we turned to face Heidi. I expected Callan would be the first to speak, but Rupor surprised me.

Stepping in front of Heidi, he gently took her hands in his and looked her in the eye. "No good can come of this, m'lady. Regardless of Chapman's current deeds, he is a man you have held in your heart for many years. The anguish you feel now will be as nothing to that which you would feel watching him fight in the arena. I implore you to stay on the ship and draw strength from the love of your friends. Leave this harsh business to those of us who have less gentle souls than you."

"But the princess will be watching her husband fight."

"She accompanies us as the royal benefactor to Captain Bane. Were she not required to play that role, she would remain with the ship, as well."

Laura placed an arm around Heidi and steered her back toward the ship. "Prince Rupor is right, Heidi. Come back to the ship with me."

The lovely redhead allowed herself to be guided back to the ship. Everyone turned to follow the pirate so only I noticed Rupor's gaze linger on Heidi for a second. He realized I was watching and gave a parade ground about-face.

Quietly, so only I could hear, he said, "If you can find some way to save her husband's worthless life, you will have my support. She must have the opportunity to break her marriage voluntarily or I fear she will carry guilt for the rest of her life."

I regarded Rupor for a few seconds, realizing for the first time just how deeply his feelings ran for Heidi. Considering his behavior over the previous six months from this light, I wondered that I hadn't figured it out much earlier. I'm sure Callan and Megan would shake their heads and mutter about clueless men. On the other hand, I expect comprehension was just dawning on Martin, too.

"I'll do my best, Rupor."

"That's all I can ask, Ri- David." A friendly grin crossed Rupor's face. "And in all honesty, your best is exceedingly good. If any man can find a way to bring Chapman out of this alive *and* keep him from alerting the pirates to our intentions, it's you."

A busy couple of hours loomed ahead of me. I had to find a way to draw out the duel so the control systems could be sabotaged, kill two pirates without giving away my identity as a scout, join the fighting withdrawal to our ship, and somehow keep Chapman alive in the bargain. No pressure. Just another typical day at the office.

I spent the next ten minutes making and rejecting plans and then the time for planning was at an end. Our guide pirate showed me into a room, telling me to come out the other side when the bell sounded. As soon as we were alone, I waved the smelling salts under Chapman's nose. He awoke, looking about wildly. He moaned as he recognized the room.

"Chapman-"

I was interrupted before I could say more.

Ding.

KILL 'EM

Cheering swelled from the arena, making Chapman even more frantic than the ringing of the bell had done. As Tristan warned, the man was also groggy after returning to consciousness. I had to grab him by the shoulders and hold him still.

"There's no time to explain my plan." Because I didn't *have* a plan, not that he needed to know that. "Do as I tell you to do and you will get out of this alive. Do you understand?"

Chapman nodded and I reached for the handle to open the door. Catching Chapman's eye, I let my true opinion of him shine through. He quailed at my expression.

"But if you even *think* about warning the pirates of our plans, I will cheerfully kill you myself."

I felt the brief disorientation that comes from stepping through a gravity field then pulled Chapman along behind me. We hung, weightless, in a big cube of a room measuring about a hundred feet on a side. Half a dozen spheres moved lazily within the arena, serving as cover and objects to use for changes of direction.

All but the two walls opposite each other—I chose to call them the floor and ceiling—held seats. Wide-spaced bars gave the combatants something to push off from, but the pirates filling the seats were also free to reach into the arena and interfere with anyone who got too close to them. With the exception of the pirates who had bet on Chapman and me, I knew we had no friends in the stands.

To my left, in the center of the wall, was the captains' chamber. Rank had its privilege, as walls separated the officers from the common pirates. Quint and the other five captains sat with Martin, Megan, Rupor, and Callan. The six captains leaned forward in their seats, faces lit with the same anticipation shown by their men.

The door swung shut behind us—no retreat for those in the arena, obviously—revealing a small weapons locker bolted to the back of the door. I found two big, wicked knives inside the locker. Taking one for myself, I handed the other to Chapman.

A cheer rose from the pirates as our two opponents pushed off from their side of the room, each heading for a different sphere within the arena. Grabbing Chapman's collar, I pushed off toward a different sphere, one closer to the pirate on my right.

"What are you doing?" wailed Chapman.

"They're planning to come at us from two sides, probably so one can keep me busy while the other deals with you. If we're in position and closer to one than the other, I'll have an easier time disrupting their plan. All you have to do is stay with me and cover my back if one of the pirates gets close. I'll handle the rest."

I brought us to a stop against my chosen sphere. Seconds later, the pirates worked their way around their spheres to face us. The pirate farther away prepared to push off from his sphere toward us, but held his position. I turned back to the other pirate and crouched, ready to take the attack to him if he moved first. He suddenly grinned and shoved off hard toward the door Chapman and I had come through. Looking back, I realized why the man was so happy.

Chapman had panicked and fled back the way we had come. He floated slowly toward the door, a sitting duck for the grinning pirate. The pirate, obviously experienced in zero G, flew as straight as a well-aimed crossbow bolt toward Chapman. Their paths would cross in a few seconds and I held no illusions as to the end result. I could already picture crimson spheres of Chapman's blood floating around the arena. Would Chapman's body become some sort of macabre version of the beach ball sports crowds bat around for fun?

Shaking off that gruesome image, I glanced at the other pirate. The look dashed my hope that he would launch himself at me or Chapman. The man hung onto his sphere, watching me like a hawk. Once I committed myself, he'd be free to choose the best counter to my move. I fought a strong temptation to leave Chapman to his fate, but I also believed Rupor was right. If Chapman died in this duel, Heidi might spend her life wondering what she could have done to save her husband. Painful as it would be for her, she needed to see him for the low-life he was and then make a break from him on her own terms and of her own accord.

Without another thought, I launched myself toward the grinning pirate. I pushed off *hard* from the sphere, planning to overtake the pirate before he reached the panic-stricken Chapman. The other pirate shouted a warning to his friend. A quick glance backward showed the second pirate following me. He moved more slowly than me, though, having put less muscle into his launch. Was that because he felt a twinge of cowardice or simply a tinge of caution? Whatever the reason, it meant I'd have a few seconds to deal with the grinning pirate before his partner reached us.

Warned by the shout, the grinning pirate spun around to face me. Then he opened himself into a knife-fighter's stance. In full gravity, it would have been a good move. In zero gravity, not so much. The grinning pirate held his knife low, ready for a thrust to my gut, with his other arm held high to block my knife. Holding my arrow-straight posture, I raised my knife above my head as if preparing for an overhand slash. The pirate's grin widened as he waited for my unprotected chest to get within knife range.

At the last second, I tucked and spun one hundred and eighty degrees. Then I kicked out at the pirate with my feet. The pirate's knife slashed the bottom of my boot just before my kick connected with his chest. The pirate's knife spun away and the man tumbled backward toward the seats. I, on the other hand, now flew straight back toward the second pirate.

Caught unprepared, the trailing pirate did the same thing his fellow had done. Had no one ever bothered to teach zero gravity martial arts to these pirates? Everything I'd done so far had been covered in the first few weeks of basic training at the academy. I went for a backward spin this time, planting my feet in the pirate's groin and shoving hard away from him. The pirate howled in pain as I shot away from him and toward Chapman.

Catching Chapman, I spun us about and prepared to use the bars in front of the crowd to propel us back toward the center of the arena. With howls of glee, the watching pirates reached through the bars and grabbed our feet.

"We got 'em, boys," a voice called from the crowd. "Now git over here and kill 'em!"

SURRENDER OR DIE

Before the pirates grabbed our feet, I thought Chapman was as panicked as a man could possibly be. It turns out I was wrong about that. His breath coming in short gasps and pants, Chapman gyrated and flailed and kicked, struggling to free himself. The only thing he accomplished was to make the pirates laugh all the harder.

Straining to break myself free, I only looked Chapman's way when his left arm smacked me on the side of my head. I saw his right hand, knuckles white as they gripped the knife, swinging my way. Training and instinct took over. I blocked his swing with my right arm, grabbed his wrist with my left hand, and twisted the knife free. Being disarmed by his 'partner' so surprised Chapman that he went still.

Around us, the pirates went still, too. Arms still reached through the bars to hold onto us, but they directed all of their attention toward the center of the arena. Looking over my shoulder, I saw our two opponents twenty feet away and gliding slowly toward us. Both of them played up to the crowd, making flashy slashes and jabs to show how they planned to deal with us.

Through the comparative silence, Quint's voice rang out. "Looks like yer boy be done fer, Bane."

"Ten thousand credits says my second-in-command gets away safely *and* takes Chapman with him."

Quint barked a laugh. "Done!"

Well, that settled it. I couldn't let Martin lose a small fortune betting on me. Bending over, a knife gripped in each hand, I slashed hard and fast at the arms stretching through the bars to grasp Chapman and me. Cries of pain and anger broke out from the pirates below me. They snatched their arms back from my blades and backed away from the bars.

With our feet free, I wrapped an arm around Chapman and launched us away from the bars and just out of reach of the two pirates floating toward us. By the time the two pirates finished their slow drift to the side of the arena, I had the two of us safely hanging onto one of the spheres in the middle of the arena.

The crowd of pirates went deadly quiet. They'd gotten the bloodshed they wanted, but the wrong bodies had shed the blood.

"My oh my," Martin said. "It seems my 'boy' left quite a mess in his wake. And, I might add, you owe me ten thousand credits, Quint."

"Yer boy were clever, Bane, I'll grant ya that," Quint growled. "But them what's watchin' ain't part of the duel."

"The second those men reached through the bars, they made themselves part of the duel. But I think your real worry is the money you just lost. I'm feeling rather generous at the moment, Quint, so how about another bet? Double or nothing."

"Name it."

"I bet my lad can stay alive in the arena for another five minutes without killing his opponents."

"*And* he's gotta keep Chapman alive fer the same five minutes."

"I'll agree to that, Quint."

"Then the bet be on, Bane."

If everything was going according to plan, the docking bay lasers would be disabled in five more minutes. Bane's bet gave me free reign to lead the two pirates on a merry chase without drawing suspicion from the captains. It was a good idea, but we'd barely been in the arena for a minute and it was nothing short of a miracle Chapman was still alive.

Of course, Chapman heard everything Bane and Quint said. His reaction was entirely predictable. Chapman panicked. Eyes wide with terror, Chapman flung himself toward Quint and the other pirate captains.

I lunged for Chapman, trying to catch his feet and keep him with me. My hands hit the bottom of his boots but had nothing to grab onto. My near miss sent Chapman tumbling, but he was still heading straight for the captains' box. Meanwhile, I lost contact with the sphere and drifted just out of reach of it. I found myself stranded in midair and an easy target for the pirates.

Our two opponents grinned at our predicament while the watching pirates roared in laughter. The two pirates exchanged a glance and then they both launched themselves at me. I'd have done the same thing in their situation. Unarmed and panicking, Chapman posed no threat. They could kill him at their leisure once they didn't have to worry about me. And here I was, just hanging around and inviting them to attack me.

Spinning back toward the sphere, I tried swimming in its direction. Given time, I could stop my slow drift away from the sphere and begin drifting toward it. But that was time I didn't have. The pirates arrowed in on me, each with one arm in front to block any attacks and one arm ready to slash or stab with the knife. My strokes grew more frantic as I tried to get back to the safety of a solid surface.

At least, that's what I *hoped* it looked like. I had very little going for me. The illusion of panic might yield a split second of advantage just as the pirates reached me. I also prepared for the one thing I hadn't expected would be of any use to me in this duel —Boost. Working and fighting in zero gravity is all about finesse and control. Boost is just the opposite, being all about strength and speed. In almost every zero G situation, Boost hinders far more than it helps. With a bit of luck, I could create that rare situation where it helped far more than it hurt.

With the pirates almost upon me, I stopped thrashing and pulled my knees up. Just before they were close enough for me to reach, I kicked at them. The two pirates laughed aloud at what they took to be mistimed kicks. Reaching out with their free hand, each pirate grabbed onto one of my legs. I flung my legs wide as if trying to throw them off. In response, each pirate wrapped his arm tightly around the leg he held. And *that* was what I'd been waiting for.

Boost!

Adrenaline flooded my bloodstream and time slowed. I had just enough time to see the pirates' grins begin to fade as I brought my legs back together with all of my Boosted strength.

Crack! The pirates' heads slammed together. Stunned, the two men lost their grips on my legs and one of them lost his grip on his knife. I pulled my knees up and kicked them again. This time they tumbled away toward the far wall and I floated back to my sphere.

Dropping Boost, I looked for Chapman. He was still tumbling, but had begun shouting something as he neared the captains' box. The crowd noise remained too loud for anyone to hear what he was saying, but I could read his lips.

He was shouting, "Captain Quint! They're not pirates. It's a trap!"

I wanted to grab the knife floating close by—it would have given me three of the four in the arena—but shutting Chapman up was far more important. Tensing my legs beneath me, I shoved off hard toward Chapman. I was tired of dealing with this loathsome excuse for a man and his cowardly attempts to ingratiate himself with the pirates.

With anger written on my face and a knife clutched in each hand, I must have looked like death incarnate falling toward Chapman. His voice rose to such a shrill tone that it pierced the roar of the crowd. But he no longer cried his warning to Quint. Instead, he squealed, "He's going to kill me! Help!"

The pirate captains heard his cries, as did most of the pirates watching. To a man, they all roared with laughter at this unexpected addition to the drama of the arena.

I glanced at the others in the captains' box. Megan, remembering our script, was shouting in Mordanian about Martin's most recent bet. Callan stepped to the back wall of the box, out of the way if a fight broke out, and pulled Megan along with her. Hand lightly resting on his sword hilt, Martin moved close to Quint. Rupor met my gaze and slowly shook his head; tacit agreement that Chapman could not be saved from himself. Then Rupor stepped as far from Martin as the box would allow.

Turning my attention back to Chapman, I was surprised to see he'd managed to stop tumbling and was now mere feet from the captains' box. He still screeched in a higher pitch than a man his size should ever be able to reach, but he had changed his tune yet again.

"Captain Quint! They're not pirates. They're Scouts. It's a trap!"

This time, Chapman was too close and his voice was too piercing to be ignored. As the words got through to Quint, his laughter faded. Concentration sharpened his features and Quint's eyes shot about the box, noting everyone's position. The other captains were just starting to take notice of Chapman's words when I caught up with the coward.

Putting a knife-wielding hand on the back of Chapman's head, I smashed it hard into one of the bars in front of the captains' box. Chapman went limp as his head bounced off the bar.

I swung my arms up and caught a cross bar with bent wrists. Tucking, I swung around the cross bar and between the two side bars. Gravity returned as I landed inside the captains' box.

Knives held ready, I straightened before the startled captains. The watching pirates fell silent at yet another unexpected development in their entertainment. When I spoke, my voice carried throughout the arena.

"I am David Rice, Scout First Class of the Terran Exploration Corps. Surrender or die."

THE BLOOD SINGS

From Chapman's warning, Quint already knew something was amiss and the other captains were starting to figure it out. Once we attacked the captains, the pirates around the arena would come to the same conclusion. So, my ultimatum gave away nothing the pirates weren't going to discover in the next second or two. It did achieve the effect I hoped for—it gave the captains pause. It lasted only a second, but when you're outnumbered every little bit helps.

Steel rasped against leather as Martin and Rupor drew their swords. At the same time, Quint broke for the zero gravity arena. With a bound, he dove between the bars, kicking off from them to launch himself toward one of the spheres.

Once he was clear of us, Quint bellowed, "Take 'em afore they git away, lads."

That broke the spell. With a roar, pirates surged through the bars and into the arena. In the box with us, the pirate captains went for their swords.

With a flick of my wrist, one of my knives flew across the box and buried itself in the throat of a pirate captain. Gurgling, blood fountaining from his neck, the man stumbled into another pirate.

Off balance, that pirate made an easy target for Rupor's flashing blade.

I wish the remaining three pirate captains got unnerved by the sudden violence and the rapidly shifting situation, but it didn't happen. Violence and chaos are part and parcel of the life of a pirate. Drawing their swords, the pirates advanced to meet us. The box rang as steel met steel.

No one rose to the position of pirate captain without being skilled with a blade. These men were no exceptions. They knew hundreds of pirates were swarming their way. If they fought defensively, they could hold us off until their men arrived and overwhelmed us.

Martin and Rupor pushed their pirates' defenses to the limit, but I only had a knife. Fighting at such a disadvantage, there was no chance I could finish off my opponent quickly without Boosting. I hated the idea of using Boost so early in what could become a running fight, but I saw no other option. Then I saw six inches of bloody steel push out of my opponent's chest.

The pirate fell forward, revealing Callan holding my blood-coated sword.

"The pirates don't allow lasers within the base, darling, only blades," she said, reversing the sword and handing it to me. "So I brought yours."

"Remind me to kiss you when we have the time," I said, slashing the back of the pirate fighting Martin.

As Martin thrust his sword through the wounded pirate, I spun and ran my blade through the pirate facing Rupor. The prince sketched a salute with his sword.

Megan opened the door out of the captains' box and ran through. The rest of us followed. The first pirate had just reached the bars of the captains' box as I slipped through the door. In the corridor, Mordanian and Tartegian marines fought shoulder to shoulder against more pirates. Our escape route was blocked.

"Martin, find us a way out of here," I called, spinning to guard the door I'd just stepped through.

"Already on it," Martin replied over the clash of weapons.

"Marines, withdraw from your position slowly until the door Captain Rice is guarding is in front of you," Rupor ordered. "We'll be surrounded, otherwise."

Sword at the ready, Rupor joined me at the door into the captains' box. He lunged as the door swung open and was rewarded by a cry of pain from inside.

"Takes you back to when we stormed the pirate spaceship a few months ago, eh what?" he grinned.

I slashed an extending sword arm and the blade dropped to the floor. "What, being heavily outnumbered and too close to the dark edge of death?"

"Exactly, my friend," Rupor enthused, parrying a hastily jabbed pirate sword. "A man is never more alive than when he's defying death. It makes the blood sing!"

"Last time my blood sang, it also leaked in large quantities. And I recall that you were captured." I lunged at a face inside the door. The face disappeared as the pirate jumped back and tripped over someone behind him.

"True, but we have your friend Captain Bane with us this time," Rupor said, pulling his sword from the belly of a pirate.

As if on cue, Martin called, "I've found something. Keep up the fighting withdrawal while I get the ladies into the air duct."

Air ducts? Not bad, and they might even get us quickly and safely behind our own lines—assuming we didn't get hopelessly lost in them, instead. But I could see one problem with that escape route.

"How are we all going to get into the ducts without leaving some marines behind to die?"

The sergeant leading the marines replied, "That's our job, sir, and we're damned good at it. The pirates will pay heavily before they get past us."

The marines' fighting withdrawal reached Rupor and me. I fell in beside a young private who couldn't be more than a couple of years older than Milo.

"Martin, there's got to be something we can do to give all of us a fighting chance."

Rupor fell in beside me as we backed down the corridor and away from the door. Overeager, the pirates inside the captains' box rushed into the corridor and smashed into the other pirates' front line. It was a golden opportunity and the marines took full advantage of the confusion. Swords flashed and men screamed. Seconds later, nine pirates lay dead or dying and the pirates paused to regroup.

In the comparative silence, Martin didn't have to shout. "I've got an idea for getting all of us away from here."

Martin's tone was as casual as possible under the circumstances, but there must have been something in his look that gave Callan pause.

"What kind of idea?" she demanded.

"It's simple. We take advantage of the confusion and everyone retreats into the duct."

Before us, the pirates were already regrouping. Their confusion hadn't lasted nearly long enough for Martin's plan to succeed.

"And what, exactly, is going to cause this confusion?" Megan asked.

"David and I will," he replied. "When we attack the pirates while Boosted."

THE CRIMSON BALL

The advance of the pirates slowed as the pirates argued over who would be on the front line. It appeared everyone wanted the first crack at us. That gave Callan and Megan time to express their opinions of Martin's plan.

"Isn't that *always* the plan?" Callan asked. "Danger looms, David Boosts, and his life gets shortened because Boost abuses his body. I didn't marry the man just to watch him Boost himself into an early grave."

"And, speaking as the expedition's bard, do you have any idea how hard it is to find rhymes for Boost?" Megan added.

"There's always loosed," Martin said. "As in 'The men did Boost, and death was loosed.'"

"Dearest, I'd have starved years ago if I had your way with words," Megan replied.

"That's it!" Callan exclaimed. "Megan, words and images are your livelihood. Why not tell the pirates exactly what will happen to them if they attack us again. Be as colorful and graphic as you like."

Megan grinned, grabbed Martin and me by the arm, and stepped toward what would soon be the line of battle. "Come on, boys, let's put on a show."

Facing the pirates across ten feet of corridor, she began singing in gal base. Seriously, Megan sang to a blood-thirsty gang of pirates.

Come one, come all
To the crimson ball!
I've a Scout to my left,
And a Scout to my right,
And Boosted they'll be,
When they join in the fight!
With a wink and a glance
They'll ask you to dance.
Then their blades will flash,
They will cut and slash!
Then your heads will fly,
And you each will die,
As we paint the hall red
With the blood of your dead!
So come one, come all
To the crimson ball!

I found the grisly song all the more jarring for the spritely tone Megan used. But she abandoned that tune for the last two lines. Those were delivered in a tone so menacing I felt a shiver run up my spine.

"All fun aside, boys," Megan said into the silence, "you will end up looking just like a girl's dolls after her spiteful little brother finishes playing with them—heads and arms scattered everywhere. Look at the bodies you just dragged aside. Hacked and slashed as they are, those are *pretty* corpses compared to what David and Martin will leave behind if they Boost."

Turning toward the air duct, Megan looked back over her shoulder. "Or you could just say we slipped away when you eager lads from the arena crashed out into the stalwart fellows in the corridor. It's such an easy story to remember and who could say otherwise?"

With a parting smile, Megan began walking away.

"Let's go, everyone," she hissed. "They're non-plussed right now, but I don't know how long that can last."

While Megan sang, two marines had pulled the grating up from the air duct. One by one, we jumped into the duct. Dropping down last, I yanked the grating back in place. Bending double, we hurried through the duct, unsure where it would lead.

The hubbub surrounding the arena faded as we rushed away from it. Martin slipped around everyone to take the lead while I stayed at the back to guard against pursuers.

"That was nicely done back there, my love," he said to Megan. "When did you have time to come up with that song?"

"I just made it up as I sang it."

"Callan," Martin said, "could I suggest you have Megan appointed as the official bard of the Mordanian Court when we get home?"

"Please ignore Martin," Megan said to Callan. "My songs are meant to be sung in taverns, on trails, and on street corners, not cooped up in a stuffy palace filled with stuffy nobles."

Megan suddenly remembered she was talking to a noble who lived in the palace. "Um, no offense, Your Highness."

Callan laughed. "None taken, Megan. I hope you'll agree to perform at the palace someday, but you have too much wanderlust to be happy stuck in one place. How fortunate for you that Martin shares your love of the itinerant lifestyle. You'll give us enough advance notice to catch up with the two of you for the big day, won't you?"

"What big day?" Megan asked.

"Your Highness, has anyone told you that you are much too observant?" Martin said.

"I *am* sorry, Martin," Callan said, contrition creeping into her voice. "You've always been one to act once you made up your mind, I just assumed..."

"Would someone mind letting me in on this big secret?" Megan said, her voice rising.

"I'd hoped to be on one knee rather than bent double running through an air duct, but it seems the universe had other plans." Martin looked over his shoulder. "Megan, will you marry me?"

"Oh, is that what this is all about?" Megan asked. "Sure, I'll marry you."

"Until we have more time, please consider yourself thoroughly kissed, my dear."

"Consider my heart to be all aflutter and me near to swooning, dear heart."

"You've made me the happiest man in the air duct."

"My congratulations to the both of you," I called. "But can you see a way out of this duct, Martin? My back is killing me."

"David, you'll be my best man, of course," Martin called back. "And I see a grating about fifty feet ahead."

"I'd be honored," I said. "Do you hear any sounds from ahead?"

"Excellent," Martin called. "I don't hear anything. We can assume there isn't any fighting above the grate, at least."

"We might as well complete the wedding party while we're down here," Megan said. "Callan, would you be my matron of honor?"

"Matron makes me sound so old. I'm only twenty-three, you know."

It was Megan's turn to laugh. "There is a specific connotation to the term 'maid.' Unless you're saying David and you have not-"

"Matron it is," Callan interrupted. "And, like David, I'd be honored."

"My compliments to the happy couple," growled the marine sergeant, "but could I suggest you hold off setting a wedding date until we're back aboard the ship?"

"Good idea, Sergeant," Martin said. "The corridor above sounds empty. This is as good an opportunity to get out of this duct as any."

At a nod from me, Martin lifted the grate and climbed out. Two marines followed him before Chapman's voice rang out.

"There they are, Captain Quint. Just like I told you."

I DON'T KNOW WHAT I WAS THINKING

Rupor, who was about to ascend into the corridor, sighed. "My apologies, David. I shouldn't have suggested you try to save that snake Chapman. I don't know what I was thinking."

"You were thinking about the woman you love, Rupor," I said.

Rupor's eyebrows shot up. "Is it so obvious?"

Moving up next to Rupor, I pulled myself up into the corridor. "I'd wager all of the women on the ship have probably figured it out. The men are probably as clueless as I was before you sent Heidi back to the ship."

Rupor rose from the air duct to join us in the corridor. "Then, if the chance presents itself, you know why I must be the one to kill Chapman."

"He knows nothing of the sort, Rupor," Callan called from below. "David, don't let Rupor kill that slime unless there is absolutely no other choice."

"Martin, I expect you to help David with that," Megan sang out.

"But I-" Rupor began.

"Your Highness," growled the sergeant, "a wise man listens to what women have to say concerning affairs of the heart."

Rupor stared at the marine for a second.

"I've been married nearly as long as you've been alive, Prince Rupor," the sergeant said. "After that many years, a man either learns a few things about women or spends a lot of cold nights on the couch. I've never slept on the couch. Now, gentlemen, could I suggest we turn our attention to these pirates?"

Our section of the corridor got quite crowded as two more marines climbed up to join us. One more marine, the young private I'd fought next to only a few minutes ago, prepared to join us.

"Stay down there, Harris," the sergeant ordered. "If we can't break through the pirate lines, it's your responsibility to get the women back to our ship."

"Yes, sir!" Harris replied.

We turned our attention back to the pirates. Two groups stood to either side of us, blocking all exits except the air duct. Despite having the numerical advantage, the pirates just milled about. Quint, arms folded, glared at us from behind one group. Chapman, eyes bright and looking all the world like a weasel, stood next to Quint.

"Why aren't they attacking?" one of the marines asked.

"Quint's probably waiting for even more men to arrive so he can overwhelm us," Martin said.

"Then let's not wait for them to attack us," I said. "Marines, stand aside and give Martin and me clear paths to the pirates."

Stepping forward, I looked in the eye of each pirate on the front line. Switching to gal base, I said, "There's a warlike indigenous race living on my adopted planet. Do you know what their name for me is?"

The pirates exchanged confused glances before one responded, "Um, no?"

"Pay him no never mind, boys," Quint called. "We got 'em outnumbered."

"Then why aren't you attacking, Quint?" I said. I turned my attention back to the front line. "They call me the Hand of Death. If you don't stand down, my hand will deal your death."

The four on the front line exchanged nervous glances.

"Ignore his yammerin'," Quint commanded. "He be outnumbered. Ain't no way he attacks."

Sword raised, I charged.

The eyes of every pirate watched me. None of them saw Quint's face go slack and his eyes go wide when I attacked. Slowly, he backed away from his men, opening his mouth twice before finding his voice.

"Ha!" It sounded more like a cough than a laugh. "I goaded him right good. Twenty thousand credits to the man what deals the death blow."

The gleam of greed replaced fear in many of the pirates' eyes. They stopped backing away and readied their blades. Over their heads, I saw Quint and Chapman turn and run back down the corridor. I wanted to Boost, jump over the men, and chase Quint. But there were too many men to leap and the ceiling was much too low. I'd have to settle for Boosting and taking my frustration out on the pirates standing before me.

"Boarding party discipline, sir," called the sergeant from close behind me.

That made me pull up short of the pirates' line. A second later, Rupor, the sergeant, and a private stood beside me.

"Hold to the drill, gentlemen," Rupor said, "and we'll set this rabble on their heels."

The sudden change in tactics sent the pirates edging back again. With Rupor calling the cadence, the four of us stepped forward in unison and engaged the pirates.

The popular image of pirates is one of vicious bands of cutthroats swarming throughout a ship, cutting down all who dare to stand in their way. For once, the popular image matched reality. But 'vicious' is nothing more than an attitude and 'swarm' is a tactic long abandoned by military-minded men. Pirates never fight trained military units unless they're cornered or can overwhelm them through sheer numbers.

The pirates outnumbered us five or six to one, but the confines of the corridor kept the number of men actually fighting us to four. We advanced, slashing and stabbing with coordination and an economy of motion strange to the pirates. Unsure how to react, the pirates fell back on their preferred fighting styles. They hacked and slashed with big, strong strokes that were as likely to get in each other's way as they were to force one of us to block the blow.

Within seconds of the first clash of steel, blood dripped from our swords and four new pirates stood before us. Rupor blocked a pirate's attack and immobilized the blade.

"Bind!" he snapped.

The private's blade stabbed into Rupor's pirate as the sergeant and I shifted into defensive mode, covering the two men dealing with the immobilized pirate.

"Clear!" Rupor called as the pirate fell away from him.

Five more pirates fell before the rest of them realized they didn't have the skill or tactics to win against four blades working as one. Our opponents turned and ran, abandoning the three men still engaged with us.

"Your fellows have left you," Rupor said. "Be smart chaps and drop your swords. If you do, I give you my word we won't kill you."

Three swords clattered to the deck.

"That's the first smart move I've seen all day," I said. "When you see your fellow pirates, tell them we simply want to get back to our ship, nothing more. If they don't get in our way, we won't kill them. Now, scram."

Pirate footfalls faded quickly and we headed back to the air duct. Martin and his marines finished routing their pirates as the sergeant called to his man.

"Harris? It's safe to come up now."

Harris didn't answer. Heart leaping to my throat, I rushed to the opening. A dead pirate lay below in the air duct. There was no sign of Harris, Megan, or Callan.

INTO THE AIRLOCK

A fraid of what I'd see, I leapt into the air duct. Martin was right behind me. A quick look around told the story well enough.

Up toward the arena, a new opening yawned in the side of the duct. If I looked through the opening, I was certain I'd find a metal plate and a maintenance tunnel. I assumed Chapman told Quint about the tunnel and Quint sent men through it to either cut us off or attack us from behind. The plan would have worked, too, except the pirates found easier, more tempting prey waiting for them in the air duct.

"Looks like Harris killed one of the pirates and then took off with Megan and Callan," Martin said.

"And the pirates chased after them instead of attacking us," I added.

Bent double, I set off down the duct as fast as the cramped conditions would allow. Martin was right behind me.

"Keep up with them, lads," the sergeant ordered. "Our captains won't be thinking clearly 'till their women are safe."

Part of my brain—a very small, very remote part—knew the sergeant was right. The animal part of my brain and the husband part of my brain already pictured me hacking every last pirate into very small pieces for what I feared they'd done to my wife.

"Harris is a smart lad, sir," the sergeant called, perhaps trying to convince Martin and me to show more caution. "He'll run if he can and fight if he has to. He'll keep the ladies safe."

It was a good try and might have worked if we hadn't come across the blood stain. It wasn't much, a smear of blood on the side of the duct. It might not even have been Harris's blood. Even if it wasn't, it was evidence of more fighting.

Rounding a bend, we saw the duct end in the side wall of a hallway. As we drew closer, I saw the grating leaning crookedly against the far wall of the corridor, red blood shining from a spot in the middle of the grate. Harris must have barreled into it without slowing down, clearing an exit for Callan and Megan. It also told us Harris was wounded.

Exiting the duct, Martin and I rose to our full height and looked both ways down the corridor.

"There!" I shouted and set off running to the right.

A knot of pirates hacked and slashed at Harris, who stood resolutely between the pirates and the two women. With every stroke he exchanged with a pirate, Harris and the women retreated a step. The marine bled from half a dozen minor cuts and a wound to his left shoulder.

We were fifty yards away, shouting to draw the pirates' attention and running as fast as our feet could carry us. The sounds of their own battle must have drowned out our voices, because none of the pirates turned our way. Then Callan and Megan ran out of room to retreat and Harris was forced to stand and fight. The pirates pressed the attack for a couple of seconds then suddenly pulled back. One of the pirates hit a control on the wall and a heavy door slid between the pirates and the trio.

The pirates had driven the three of them into an airlock!

Harris obviously realized it, too. Through the window in the airlock door, I saw him spring forward. He was too late. Steel hit steel as the door finished closing. Without taking his eyes from the airlock window, a pirate slapped the control to open the airlock to the void of space.

A RED HAZE

Through the small window in the sliding airlock door, Callan caught sight of me racing down the corridor. For a second, hope flared in her lovely face. But as Harris lunged toward the closing door, she realized there was no way I could reach her in time. Hope gave way to despair before my view of her was blocked by pirates crowding around the window to watch the three meet their doom.

I felt as if my heart had burst inside my chest. A red haze fell across everything before me and my vision narrowed until I could see nothing but the closest pirate. From far away, I heard myself vent a howl of inarticulate rage and remorse. Beside me, Martin did the same.

Boost!

The pirate at the end of my tunnel vision was just turning around when my sword cut him in two.

As the pieces of the pirate fell away, another pirate appeared at the end of my red tunnel. His sword came up in slow motion then fell away as I severed his arm at the elbow. Terror etched itself on the man's face as I drove my sword into his chest, stopping only when the hilt hit his breast bone. With a heave, I flung the body over my head, yanking my sword free as the dying man fell to the corridor behind me.

On the edge of my narrowed vision, I saw a pirate trying to sidle around me. My left fist shot out and crushed the man's throat. The gurgling, gagging man slid down the wall, doomed to a slow death by asphyxiation.

The next pirate tried to back away, both hands held before him imploring me to spare him. Pirates behind him shoved him back toward me. I swung and my sword sliced his throat wide open.

With no hope of escape, two pirates charged at me. I stepped forward to meet them. With a broad sweep of my sword, their heads bounced off the corridor wall.

Finally, I came to the man who had closed the airlock door. The man who had pressed the button and consigned my wife, my reason for life, to the cold void of space. He huddled against the wall, hands raised in supplication. Tears streamed down his face and his mouth moved frantically as he begged for his life.

I was not in a forgiving mood.

Sword raised to give the man a faster death than he deserved, I stepped toward him.

"David! No!"

Oh, God, I could almost hear Callan's voice calling to me.

"Darling, stop! For me, for us, stop!"

Green eyes appeared at the end of my red tunnel. Soft, loving hands wrapped around my neck and pulled me toward the eyes. I dropped my sword and, not daring to hope, reached toward the vision before me. My hands met warm, live flesh and I pulled Callan into my embrace.

My vision cleared. Hearing returned. I was vaguely aware Martin and Megan were similarly entwined. Covering my wife's face with kisses, I rejoiced.

Callan was alive!

IT'S THE LAW

At last convinced that this wasn't a dream from which I would awaken, that Callan truly was alive, I stopped smothering her with kisses and simply held her close.

"How?" I asked. "I saw the airlock door close. I saw the pirate cycle the airlock. How did you survive?"

"Ask Private Harris," Callan said. "He's the one who saved us."

Martin and I both turned to the private, who looked uncomfortable under our gazes.

"Go on, Harris," the sergeant encouraged. "Tell them what you were telling me."

"Well, sir, I realized we were in an airlock as soon as Her Highness and Miss Megan," and here Harris turned to Megan, "I'm sorry ma'am, I don't know your family name."

"It's Tuttle, but you're more than welcome to call me Megan."

"Like I was saying, I figured out it was an airlock when we ran out of room to retreat. I mean, it would be stupid to make a corridor that didn't go anywhere. Then when those bast- uh, pirates jumped back, I figured out their plan. I remembered all that spaceship safety training we got from those ladies who used to be prisoners of the pirates, especially how airlock doors won't open if the other door isn't fully shut and sealed."

Harris held up a mangled sword. "I jumped forward and stuck my sword between the door and the wall. The door looked like it shut and it sounded like it shut, but it didn't shut. Of course, we'd have been in real trouble if you and Captain Bane hadn't shown up, sir."

"That was quick thinking, lad," the sergeant said. Turning to me, he added, "Like I told you, he's a smart one."

I grasped Harris's hand. "Thank you. Those words are inadequate, but they're all I have."

Martin followed suit. Then Callan and Megan surrounded Harris. He blushed a deep scarlet when they both hugged him and kissed him on the cheek. Finally, Rupor pumped the private's hand, offering a hearty, "Good show, lad."

"I hate to interrupt, sir," the sergeant said. Pointing at the lone surviving pirate, the one who had tried to cycle the airlock, he added, "But we need to decide what we're going to do with him and then get out of this corridor before some other pirates trap us down here."

The pirate sat huddled on the deck, staring at me with wide, wild eyes.

"He's guilty of the attempted murder of a member of the royal family of Mordan," I said.

The pirate started shaking his head violently. "I can't be guilty unless I have a trial! It's the law! I've got to have a trial!"

"What a staunch defender of law and order you are all of a sudden," I sneered. "What due process did you follow before attempting to murder my wife?"

"I didn't know who she was!"

"Well, ignorance won't be a problem for you much longer. There is only one penalty for your crime—death by beheading."

"You can't do that! You're a sworn officer of the Terran Federation. You have to follow the law."

"Damn me, but the man is right," I said. "Neither Martin nor I can carry out the sentence."

"My planet is not a member of this federation," Rupor said. "Perhaps you would allow me the honor?"

"By all means," I replied. "Does anyone have anything to say in this pirate's defense?"

My companions all shook their heads. The marines dragged the pirate to his feet and down the hallway a dozen yards. The man blubbered and pleaded for his life, something I felt certain would draw harsh laughter from the pirate if our positions were reversed. Then Rupor's sword flashed and pleading stopped.

"They- they just executed him! Chopped off his head." The voice came from down the corridor.

Pirates crowded into the corridor from the same air duct we'd come through moments earlier.

Just as the sergeant feared, we were trapped.

OUT THE AIRLOCK

The pirates continued to pile into the corridor fifty yards away. Silence fell over them as each pirate took in the scene before the airlock. Bodies and pieces of bodies lay scattered around us, with splashes of crimson breaking the monotonous gray of the rock from which the pirate base had been carved. One of the pirates said something to his fellows. The distance reduced his words to an indistinct murmur, but his fellow pirates heard him clearly enough—including the one in charge.

"Shut yer trap, Benson," Quint ordered. "This ain't no ball, crimson or t'otherwise. Now git down there and take 'em, men."

"Martin," I asked, "any bright ideas?"

"Actually, yes. See if you can delay them for a minute or two."

Turning my attention back to the pirates, who started a slow shuffle in our direction, I called, "Hey, Quint, if you want someone to 'git' us, why don't you step to the front and lead by example. Bring my old pal Chapman with you." I held up my blood-stained sword. "I've got a few pointed remarks to make to him."

Some of the pirates laughed.

"Stop yer laughin' and git moving," Quint bellowed.

Once again, a few pirates took a few steps in my direction.

"I've got to say, Quint, you do seem to have a way with commanding men," I yelled. "How do you manage to get them to go to their deaths while you stay in the rear, ready to run if the battle goes against you?"

The pirates who had shuffled forward stopped and looked behind them.

"Did Quint tell you what he did just a few minutes ago, when we met in a different corridor?"

"Pay him no never mind and charge," Quint commanded.

"Maybe you could ask Chapman about it. He was right by Quint's side throughout the fight." All the pirates looked back at the pirate captain, uncertainty written on their faces. "Quint, they all know Chapman for the coward he is. What does it say about you that you've been shoulder to shoulder with him every time we've met in battle?"

Quint's face went so brightly red I thought he might pop an artery. Grabbing Chapman by the arm, he dragged the hapless turncoat through the crowd to the front.

"Ain't nobody gonna git away with callin' me no coward, Rice," he yelled. Turning back to his men, he shouted, "Like I said, let's git 'em!"

Sword in one hand and dragging Chapman with the other, Quint led the charge. Their faith in Captain Quint restored, the pirates roared and charged after him.

"Martin, how's that idea coming?"

"Surprisingly well, David," he said. "You did such a good job distracting them, I don't think any of the pirates noticed me rummaging around in the storage locker at the end of the corridor. It held more vacuum harnesses than we need. Once you put on your harness, we can get out of here."

I sprinted back to the airlock. Martin tossed a harness to me and started closing the airlock door to the corridor. I slipped into the harness quickly and was ready by the time the door closed. As the door cut off the pirates' shouts, I grabbed the safety strap looped along the wall and wrapped an arm around Callan.

"Ready."

Martin pressed the emergency release. There was a brief rush of air escaping as the outer door opened. Then I led the way out onto the airless surface of the pirate's asteroid base.

ON THE SURFACE

Callan glowed in the nimbus of the air-preserving forcefield her vacuum harness projected around her body. I would have loved nothing more than to admire her heavenly form, but we had to get away from the horde of pirates bearing down on our position. Martin finished showing the others how to activate their comm units, so I stepped through the base's gravity field and into the almost-nonexistent gravity on the surface of the asteroid.

"Keep your movements controlled and gentle after coming through the gravity field," I warned. "One wrong step could send you spinning off into the asteroid field. In fact, it's best if we all clasp hands. It will slow our progress but we will all be anchored to each other."

Taking my hand, Callan grinned with excitement and stepped through the gravity field. Her grin faded and she turned a slight green.

"Oh, I feel like I'm going to hurl," she moaned. "What's wrong with me?"

"It's just a touch of space sickness," I explained. "Most people suffer from it the first time they experience low or no gravity."

And, indeed, the rest of the Aashlanders also suffered from it, though none quite so badly as my wife.

"You usually look lovely in green, my dear," I said, trying for a light tone, "but that shade just doesn't suit you."

"Ha, ha. Maybe I'll throw up on you and see if green suits *you*."

"Perhaps a change of subject is in order."

"Good idea, husband." Callan still looked sick, but at least there was a bit of humor reflected in her eyes.

"Martin, how many harnesses are left in the locker outside the airlock?" I asked. "We need to prepare for pursuit."

"No pursuit is coming from that airlock, David," Martin replied.

"Our good Captain Bane had each of us grab extra harnesses," Rupor said. "We piled then next to the airlock exit and they blew into space when the air rushed out."

I gave Martin a thumbs up. "Very clever."

"I think 'very obvious' is the more appropriate phrase—at least to anyone familiar with vacuum and pirates," Martin said.

"Okay, since you insist we'll go with 'very obviously clever,'" I said. "The upshot is the pirates have to find another airlock before they can come out here after us. With luck, we'll reach another airlock or the docking bay before they find us."

"Sir?" Harris asked. "How do you know where to go without a sun to guide your direction?"

"My implant has a fairly accurate idea of where we are in relation to the docking bay. I'm just following the map it has constructed of the asteroid—both inside and out."

"So our lives are in the hands—figuratively speaking—of that tiny machine you tell us is in your head?" Rupor asked.

"Welcome to my world, Rupor," Callan said.

I recognized Rupor's and Callan's words for what they were— banter meant to keep everyone's minds off their roiling stomachs. I was about to answer in kind when a bright light flashed across my vision. Looking to my left, I spied a squad of pirates about a hundred yard away. They moved with easy familiarity on the surface of the asteroid. Far worse, they all carried laser pistols.

DON'T GET YOURSELF KILLED

"We've got to get under cover before their aim improves," I shouted.

"David, let's split into two groups," Martin called. "Once everyone else is under cover, we can figure out what to do."

Doubling the potential targets while making those targets half the size struck me as a very good idea. "Sergeant, Rupor, let go of each other."

Our low gravity conga line broke in two, leaving me with Callan, Harris, Megan, and Rupor. Fortunately, the asteroid was pockmarked with craters and rubble from countless collisions with smaller asteroids. It should only take a few seconds to get under cover.

Bright light flashed at my feet and another light blazed past Harris's head, reminding me that we might not have a few seconds. The pirates were getting the range and it was only a matter of time —a very short time—before they scored a hit. I had to put rock between us and the pirates *now*.

I was leading my group toward a very low ridge only a few feet away. Our slow pace meant it would take too long to get us all behind the ridge. Then I had an idea.

Wedging my foot under a tiny outcropping, I said, "All of you, hold onto each other as tight as possible. Those of you at the end of the line brace yourselves."

Wrapping both hands around Callan's wrist, I pulled her up and over my head. In the light gravity, five full grown adults had a combined weight less than a child's weight in normal gravity. Callan arched up and over me with the other three trailing like a whip cord. My foot pressed against the underside of the outcropping as the line of men and women pivoted about that one spot. My wife came down on the uncovered side of the ridge, but the rest came down just over the crest.

Slipping my foot free, I said, "Harris, pull us over to you."

The young guard's hard yank brought Callan and me barreling into him. The three of us flew past Rupor and Megan. I feared we might spin off the surface of the asteroid and out into space when, with a hard jerk, we came to a stop and slammed down onto the rocky surface. Glancing to the other end of our line, I saw Rupor hugging a small spire like a lover.

Next to me, Callan's weak stomach gave way and she retched miserably. Megan reeled Callan in, wrapped my poor wife in a sisterly hug, and tried to comfort her. I longed to do the same but our lives were at stake.

"Martin?" I called over the comm.

"That was quite a show you put on over there," he replied. "Is everyone okay?"

"Scrapes and scratches, but we'll live. Do you think we have piratical eavesdroppers?"

"There's no doubt about it. All the harnesses were set to the same channel." Martin was silent for a couple of seconds. "Were the seniors still playing the search and rescue prank on plebes when you were at the academy?"

"Of course they were. Traditions die hard at the academy. Switch now."

Every plebe in the Scout academy spent one night in a two man ship, monitoring channel five sixteen for orders to move in on a pirate ring. It was the space-based equivalent of a snipe hunt. I changed my channel, showing the others how to do it at the same time.

"Do you read me, Martin?"

"Loud and clear. Now that we can have a private conversation, have you had any bright ideas?"

"Yes. I think you and I ought to go for a swim."

Megan asked the question that was on the mind of every Aash-lander. "How are you going swimming when there's no water? Is this some kind of Scout thing?"

"Asteroid miners developed it and named it, but they do teach it in the Scout Academy," I answered. "It's a fast way of moving across uneven surfaces in very low gravity. You lay down and pull yourself along with your hands and feet, pushing off the surface just enough to stay a few inches above it. The miners called it swimming because it looks more like someone swimming underwater."

"So we're all going for a swim?" Callan asked.

"More or less. Martin and I are going to use it to get close enough to attack the pirates," I said. "The rest of you will use it as best you can to get closer to the docking bay."

"David, what makes you think your fellow fighting men would not follow you into battle?" Rupor asked, bristling just a bit. "Leave a man or two to guard the women, of course, but do not presume that we are unworthy to join you."

"Rupor, would you take an untrained soldier into battle? One who had listened to a very brief description of the principles of swordsmanship but had never held a sword?"

"Of course not, but swordsmanship is a complex science while this swimming you describe sounds quite simple."

I pointed to a high outcropping about twenty yards away. "Tell you what, Rupor, if any of you reach that rock before Martin and I reach the pirates, I'll withdraw my objections and you're welcome to join us fighting the pirates."

Rupor nodded, both satisfied and more thoughtful.

Callan kissed my lips. "Don't get yourself killed."

Megan scooted up next to me and kissed my cheek. "Don't let Martin get himself killed."

Rupor pulled himself past me. "I'm not going to kiss you, but would appreciate it if the two of you came back alive. Your deaths would put quite the damper on my courtship of Heidi."

"I wouldn't want my death to inconvenience you, Rupor. You have my solemn vow that I will endeavor to stay alive," I replied. Turning to Harris, I said, "You've got good instincts, Harris. Pay attention to them and I know you'll get the women safely back to the ship."

"If you're quite finished kissing your wife and being kissed by my wife-to-be," Martin said, "perhaps we could get on with this?"

"Yes, O Jealous One. You go northwest and I'll go northeast."

"Got it. Last one to the fight buys the drinks when we get back to civilization."

With that, I swam quickly away from my group. Swimming across the surface of an asteroid looks easy and sounds easier, but it takes a lot of practice to achieve a balance of upward push and forward pull. I hadn't gone asteroid swimming in close to four years, but I was quite accomplished at it before crashing on Aashla. The rhythm came back to me within seconds and I flowed across the asteroid's surface faster than I could have run in full gravity.

A couple of laser shots flashed around me, but neither one was close. I was too low to present a good target and too fast for accurate aiming with a hand weapon. Meanwhile, the shots told me where to find the pirates. I slithered and swam around rocks and craters and ridges until I got behind the pirates' position. Then I headed straight in, hoping to catch them by surprise.

I came upon a band of four pirates moving and shooting toward the ridge we had hidden behind. With a grin, I pulled myself forward at top speed. Then luck turned against me. One of the pirates looked down at his belt to get a fresh energy pack for his pistol and saw me out of the corner of his eye. We were on different comm channels, so I didn't hear his shout, His friends most definitely did.

I was twenty feet from the pirates when they spun about, pistols raised to burn me to a crisp.

ARE EITHER OF YOU DEAD?

Three pirates brought their lasers to bear on me while the fourth pirate fumbled to replace his discharged energy pack. I had no cover available and the pirates could easily burn me before I covered the twenty feet separating us. That left only one option.

Instead of reaching forward for my next swimming stroke, I planted my right hand at my side then pushed hard to the left. Laser blasts flashed where I had been a split second before, but I was five feet to the left now. As the pirates swung their aim in my direction, I pushed off a lump of rock with my left hand and passed just under the pirates' aim before they realized what was happening.

After missing me twice, I doubted the pirates would overreact to my movement again. But I thought they would expect more of the same from me. Rather than zigging back to my left, I pulled my knees in tight and then kicked out and down. Pushing off that hard and at any kind of upward angle should have sent me flying off the asteroid and into empty space. But I'd closed in on the pirates, so crashed into three of the pirates instead.

Two of the men tumbled backward with arms windmilling and legs kicking. Both lost hold of their lasers, which went spinning off to who knows where. The third staggered back and tripped over the fourth pirate, who still crouched trying to reload his pistol. The tripping pirate smacked his head against the rock the pirates had been using for cover and dropped his laser.

That left me standing over the fourth man. Made clumsy by his haste to replace his laser's energy pack, the man dropped both of them. I grabbed the straps of his vacuum harness and heaved him straight up. The pirate's mouth opened in a scream I could not hear as he flew off into the void.

The pirate who had hit his head was groggy and unresisting as I stripped off his spare energy packs and sent him up to join his fellow. I picked up both lasers, reloading the empty one.

"Martin?" I called on the comm. "I've got a couple of lasers. Two of the pirates are out of the fight and two more have been disarmed. Where are you?"

"Having less success than you, it appears," Martin replied. "Assuming you're responsible for the two pirates heading into space, I'm about forty feet west of you, pinned down by laser fire."

Now that I knew what to look for, I spotted laser flashes to the west.

"I'll be there in a few seconds. In the meantime, do as Megan instructed and don't get yourself killed."

"Thank you for that advice, David. It would never have occurred to me."

I was already swimming in the direction of the laser flashes when I replied. "Don't thank me. I'm just relaying Megan's orders. But if you like *that* advice, just wait till you're married."

"I heard that," Megan said over the comm.

"So did I," Callan added dryly.

"Um, the stress of combat makes men say things they don't really mean?" I offered as I came up behind the two pirates firing at Martin.

"Yeah, what he said," Martin added.

My first shot burned a hole right through the pirate on the left. The pirate on the right reacted as if he was in normal gravity, spinning and jumping so fast he lost his footing and rose off the ground. Martin swam up, grappled the laser from the floating pirate, then shoved him up to join the other two in orbit.

"Are either of you dead?" Megan asked.

"No, sweetheart," Martin replied. "And thank you for the invaluable advice on dying, which I shall always endeavor to follow to the letter."

"You'd better, dearest," Megan growled.

Martin looked at me. "As a reformed pirate, it pains me to admit that I don't really like pirates any more. Let's finish this."

Without another word, Martin and I slithered off toward the remaining pirates.

"Far be it from me to interfere with such bold battlefield heroics," Rupor said, "but this might not be the best time to engage in a full assault on the rest of the pirates."

Martin and I exchanged glances and slowed our advance on the pirate's position. It was hardly the sort of comment either of us expected from Rupor, so it caught our attention.

"We're listening," I said.

"You've rather suddenly and spectacularly shot or scattered half a dozen of the pirates. We may not have heard the cries of those six men, but the other pirates will be sharing the same comm channel. They heard everything."

"And why does that mean we shouldn't continue attacking?"

"You attacked their superior numbers, overcame their superior weaponry, and took six of their number out of the fight. Now is the time for us to make a tactical retreat while the pirates are still back on their heels and reluctant to engage us."

The sergeant added, "His Highness has a point, sirs."

"In case there is any doubt, I fully support Rupor's suggestion, also," Callan said.

"Do I need to add my vote to the tally?" Megan asked.

"I believe we're outvoted, David," Martin said. "The rest of you keep moving toward the docking bay. We'll catch you up."

Without another word, we changed directions and swam back

toward our family and friends. A couple of minutes later, we caught up with them. They had gotten beyond the large rock I'd pointed out to Rupor before Martin and I went on the offensive, but not by much.

"Yes, David, you were right," Rupor said. "Swimming on an asteroid is far more difficult than I imagined."

"I didn't say anything about your progress."

"No, but you were thinking it."

What can I say, he was right. Were my thoughts really that plainly written on my face?

"Yes, love, anyone who knows you well can see your thoughts clearly written on your face," Callan said.

"To your credit, your words and actions always match your thoughts," Megan added.

"Enough with the fawning over Honest David," Martin growled. "I've been thinking how best to get us moving faster. David's game of crack the whip, when he flung four of you behind the ridge, gave me an idea. We'll split into two groups again, line up head-to-foot, and David and I will each tow a group behind us. The rest of you just have to use your free hand and foot to keep yourself a few inches off the ground."

"Just like a train," I exclaimed. I got blank stares from everyone but Martin. "But I guess most of you have never heard of trains..."

It was the work of but a moment to create the two line ups. For simplicity, we went with the two groups we'd split into earlier. That left me towing Callan, Megan, Rupor, and Harris. Rupor suggested Martin and the marines serve as our rearguard, just in case the pirates went on the offensive sooner rather than later. With that decided, I towed my four passengers in the direction of the docking bay. It took a few minutes for everyone to get into a rhythm, but once they did we made good time across the asteroid.

"How long will it take to reach the docking bay?" Callan asked.

"At the rate we're going, we should reach the entrance in another five minutes," I replied. "In fact, the ship should be within range of our comms about now. Heidi is monitoring channel ten seventeen. Switch to that channel after your next push off from the ground."

Since I didn't have to hold onto anyone's foot, I went ahead and changed channels with one hand while keeping us moving with the other. The signal had some static, but I had no trouble hearing Heidi's voice.

"*Aashla's Hope* to the captain. Do you copy?"

"Loud and clear, Heidi."

"Oh, thank God. We've been worried sick, David. Where are you and who's with you?"

"I've got their Highnesses, Martin, Megan, and a squad of marines. We're swimming across the surface of the asteroid toward you. We should be there in-"

"Get under cover, now!" Heidi cried. "Quint just sent an armed pinnace out to find and destroy you."

FLYING BODIES

We were surrounded by all sorts of good cover against an attack from the ground, none of which would do any good against an attack from above. I scanned all around us hoping to spot something close by, but came up empty.

"David, look to your right and back a bit," Rupor called.

I immediately swung to my right, trusting Rupor to know what he was talking about. A jumble of boulders lay scattered across the surface, just thirty yards away from us. The rocks were far enough apart for us to wriggle in between them but close enough to give cover from every direction except directly overhead. In truth, it was better cover than I'd hoped to find.

"Martin, do you see the cover Rupor found?"

"It looks great," Martin said. "Get the ladies and His Highness wedged in there as fast as you can."

"What about you? Aren't you coming?" Megan asked.

"No ma'am," the sergeant answered. "We're going to keep heading straight."

"What?" Megan cried. "You'll be an easy target out there."

"Yes, they will, miss," Harris said. "It's a marine's duty to protect civilians from the enemy, even at the cost of his life."

Megan stifled a cry but, to my relief, she didn't break our train.

"Don't worry, Megan," Martin added, "we won't be quite the sitting ducks you imagine. The pinnace will come upon us suddenly and probably be past us before they even realize we're here. I think we can reach that overhang ahead of us before they can get back to us."

"*Aashla's Hope*," I called, "how long before you can come after us?"

"We began the startup procedure as soon as the marines retreated back to the docking bay," Heidi said, "but the reactor won't be online for another seven minutes."

"Do *not* cut any corners to get to us sooner," Martin ordered. "A reactor containment breach would be far worse than the eleven of us being forced to hide for a few minutes."

"Heidi is piping your conversation throughout the ship," Laura said. "As chief engineer of this ship, I acknowledge and accept your order, sir."

I reached the edge of the boulder field and pulled up. Catching Callan's hand, I guided her in between two of the larger ones.

"Keep moving, Callan. Megan is coming in right behind you."

As Callan slipped from my sight, I sent Megan in after her.

"You're next, Harris," I said. "Whatever happens, stay with the women and guard them with your life. The prince and I will be just inside the edge of the field, keeping an eye out for pirates."

It was a tighter fit for Harris, but he managed to pull himself in after Megan. Before Rupor and I could get under cover, the pirate pinnace swept up from the direction of the docking bay.

As Martin predicted, the little ship overflew our positions, but the pilot really knew his business. Braking thrusters fired and the pilot threw the ship into a flat spin. The pinnace was still moving away from Martin and the marines, but the gunner got off one shot before the pinnace passed beyond the horizon. The bright beam cast the bleak landscape into sharp relief for a fraction of a second. And, in terrible silence, the laser struck the ground and bodies went flying.

THEY COULD BE DEAD

B lasted bits of rock spun off into space as I struggled to see through the afterimage of the bright laser beam. I saw two bodies tumbling across the surface of the asteroid and out of sight. A third body pin wheeled into space. I had no idea what had happened to the remaining two men.

"Martin?" I called. "Sergeant?"

Over the comm I heard a gasp and the sound of someone trying to stifle crying. I received no reply to my call.

"David?" Callan's voice was quiet, calm, and controlled. "What happened?"

"The pirate gunner took a shot at Martin's group before the pinnace passed over the horizon. It appears to have been a hit or a very close miss."

"What of Martin and the marines?" she asked.

"I...don't know. They aren't answering their comms, but they could be unconscious or the comm could be damaged."

"Or they could be dead," a small, shaking voice added.

"We don't know that yet, Megan," Callan said, her voice stronger and more commanding than before. In that voice, I recognized her switch to princess mode. The situation demanded decisiveness, not emotions. If Martin was dead, she'd cry later.

"David, swim over there and find out what happened to the men. Go as fast as you can, but also be careful. That pinnace will be back soon."

"What will the rest of you do?" I asked.

"Stay here where we have some cover. Now go."

I swam off as fast as I could go, terrified of what I might find but even more terrified of the uncertainty I felt.

"Heidi," Callan called, "how many casualties do we have under Tristan's care right now?"

"My latest report shows fourteen dead, six in critical condition, and dozens of wounds ranging from serious to minor," Heidi replied. "According to Tristan, none of the injuries in the last group are life-threatening."

I zipped over the ground, swimming faster than I'd done since academy relay races. The laser had scorched a three-foot line in the asteroid. Even if the shot was a direct hit, no more than two of the men could have been struck by the beam.

"Those casualties are lighter than I'd feared, but heavier than I'd hoped," Callan said.

"According to reports, as long as our men were withdrawing, the pirates only fought hard enough to keep them moving backward," Heidi replied.

"Odd," Callan said. "Why wouldn't the pirates fight harder? If they *wanted* us to escape, they could have just let us go."

"Callan, the pinnace is returning," Rupor interrupted.

"They could have transmission scanners," Heidi said. "Maintain comm silence for your own safety."

At the scorch mark, I'd turned toward the docking bay. Martin was towing the marines in that direction. If the blast struck behind him, it was likely he'd be thrown in the direction he was already going.

I risked a quick look over my shoulder, hoping to spot the pinnace. It was easy to find. The pilot flew back to us slowly, the canopy of the little ship facing down toward the asteroid.

"Maintain comm silence," I said. "The crew is trying to spot us visually."

I heard an exhalation of breath. Callan did that when she was exasperated with me.

"Yes, dear, I know I'm not maintaining comm silence," I said. "If the crew of the pinnace is going to find anyone, I'm going to make sure it's me."

I got my wish. The pinnace rolled over to bring its belly gun to bear on my position. I zigged to the right then zagged to the left. A hurried laser blast struck a good ten yards from my position. All I needed was another couple of seconds and I could reach some form of cover.

I put my hand into a dark depression, planning to push off the side of it. Instead of rock, my hand touched clothing. Instinctively, I grabbed a fistful of fabric. My momentum pulled the man out of the shadows. He was covered in burns and blood, but a scar stood out on his cheek.

I'd found Martin.

I'M COMING TO HELP

I couldn't tell if Martin was dead or alive and wouldn't be able to find out until I could put some cover between the pinnace and me. As if to drive that home, the landscape was lit by the flash of another laser shot. The ground boiled not more than three yards from where I would have been if grabbing Martin hadn't checked my speed.

"I found Martin."

The pirates already knew where I was, so there was no reason not to give Megan some hopeful news. I slung Martin over my back in a miner's carry, another thing included in the low-gravity vacuum training at the academy. I wouldn't be as fast or maneuverable as before—something that might get me killed—but at least I knew how to carry a wounded man.

"Is he alive?" Megan asked.

I wished she hadn't made even a short broadcast over the comm, but I understood why she did it. Meanwhile, I was swimming again, trying my best to move fast and change directions even faster.

"You know Martin," I said. "He's hard to kill."

Another laser blast flashed. That one hit so close the heat

conducted by the rocky surface burned my hand. Bits of blasted rock pelted Martin and me, giving both of us new cuts and bruises.

"Heidi, please tell me you're about to pull out of the docking bay and blow this pinnace out of the sky," I called.

"I'm sorry, David, but the startup sequence still has-"

"Hang on, David! I'm coming to help."

"Milo? What do you mean?"

Instead of zigging or zagging, I came to a complete halt. The next laser blast hit even closer than the one before it. This time, I lifted my hand off the ground before it could burn, but my toes got uncomfortably warm through my boots.

"He took the pinnace," Heidi replied. "We assume he's coming to pick you up."

"You were all just sitting around in the ship hoping David and Callan weren't going to get killed," Milo said. "When I lived on the street, hoping never got me anything. And it's not going to save my friends now."

With each shot, the pirate gunner got closer and closer to burning Martin and me. No matter how random I tried to make my movements, some pattern must be emerging. Maybe I was too slow. Or maybe it was time for a complete change in evasion tactics. I pushed my upper body off the ground with my hand and pulled my legs up tight against my chest. When I was pointing a bit above the distant ridge I'd been trying to reach, I kicked hard off the surface of the asteroid. Martin and I arrowed toward the ridge, moving faster than I could swim across the ground. But now I was going in a straight line course—one I could not change for several seconds.

The move took the gunner by surprise. His next shot hit well to the left of where I had stopped, as if he had guessed I would head off in that direction. I would have gone that way, too.

"Milo," Heidi called, "what are you planning to do?"

"I'm going to save the only people besides my sister who have ever cared about me."

"We're going to be fine, Milo," I said.

"No, you're not," Milo said. "Not without help. I can see you and the pirate pinnace. The laser is already tracking your path."

It looked like my gamble had only bought me a few more seconds of life.

"Callan, Megan," I called. "I'm sorry."

"No! You're not dying if I can help it!" Milo shouted, drowning out the cries from Callan and Megan.

Milo's pinnace sped past me, mere meters above my head. The pirate laser flashed but the pinnace blocked the shot.

"Take care of Kim for me," Milo said.

The pirate pilot didn't realize what Milo was doing until it was too late. Milo crashed his pinnace into the pirate ship and they both disintegrated in a ball of flame.

HE'S ALIVE

In the vacuum of space, the fiery explosion lasted less than a second, but it seemed as if it went on for years to me. The image seared into my brain as I passed over the ridge I'd hoped to hide behind. The image consumed my attention as I landed, instinctively cradling Martin to protect him from further injury. The image remained clear and horrible even as my vision blurred from the tears filling my eyes.

"No, Milo!" Callan wailed, far too late for Milo to hear her or heed her.

Megan's quiet crying for Martin gave way to sobs as the loss of Milo and her dread for Martin overwhelmed her.

In a quiet, controlled voice, Rupor recited a prayer for the dead.

And the mild jolt of our landing caused Martin to moan in pain. *He was alive!*

"What's going on?" Heidi called. "What happened to Milo?"

"Martin is alive, Megan. Concentrate on that. He's *alive!*" I forced as much hope and joy as I could muster into my voice. I didn't feel any of it—I didn't feel anything, at the moment—but Megan and Callan needed *something* hopeful to cling to.

Megan's sobs eased a bit. "A-alive? Are you sure?"

"Yes, Megan, I'm sure. I told you Martin was hard to kill."

Rupor flowed straight from the prayer for the dead to a prayer for Martin to remain among the living.

"Is someone going to tell us what's going on out there?" It was Laura this time. I'd forgotten Heidi was broadcasting to the whole ship.

"Milo is dead." Callan was back in princess mode, using it as armor to protect herself from the pain. "He rammed the pirate pinnace, sacrificing himself so the rest of us could live."

Gasps and cries sounded over the comm as Callan's words hit home.

"We will have time for our grief later, after we're away from this God-forsaken rock." Callan's voice grew stronger as she spoke. "But I will *not* allow Milo's death to be in vain. We *will* leave this place. We *will* bring these pirates to justice. And we *will* make Quint and Chapman pay for all they have done!"

"This is all my fault," Heidi's cry was full of anger and sorrow. "If I hadn't married-"

"There's no time for that, Heidi," Callan cut in. "I understand why you blame yourself. I blame myself for Milo's death, as well. But none of us can afford the luxury of guilt or self-pity. Can you put those feelings aside and handle communications for me?"

"Yes." There was a sniffle after the word, but Heidi's voice was firm again.

"Good. David, do you think it's safe to move Martin?"

I gave Martin a very fast check over. His worst injuries appeared to be burns. If we got him to a modern medical bay—like the one on the *Aashla's Hope*—his wounds weren't life threatening. "Yes, he can be moved."

"Good. You're closer to the docking bay, so we'll come to you. We won't be as fast as you, but we'll get there."

"As you wish, Callan. Permission to search for the rest of Martin's team?"

"Of course, David. We'll call when we reach Martin."

Ten minutes later, we were all together behind the ridge. There was no sign of the pirates who'd been on the surface chasing us. Maybe they were scared off after the loss of their pinnace. They left us alone, which was all I cared about. I'd found the bodies of the sergeant and one of the other marines. A third marine still lived, though with worse burns than Martin. I remembered the fourth man flying off into space and resigned myself to never finding his body.

With Harris carrying the wounded marine, we swam to the docking bay entrance. I slid carefully up to the spaceship entrance to the bay and peered inside. Hundreds of pirates milled about under the watchful eye of Quint. Chapman stood just behind Quint. But I spotted something else that made my blood run cold.

Without the crew of the *Aashla's Hope* realizing it, the pirates had fastened docking clamps to the landing gear. The ship and all aboard her were trapped in the docking bay.

BLOW THE CLAMPS

"A*shla's Hope*, the pirates have locked you in place with docking clamps," I said.

"Oh." Laura's single-word exhalation carried more feeling, more frustration, and more defeat than the loudest, most profane rant imaginable.

"David, most of us were raised with airships rather than starships," Callan said. "Please explain what you're talking about."

"Docking clamps are a safety device designed to hold a ship in place during repairs. They're like the ones holding the pinnace-" My voice broke, my vision blurred, and once again I saw the awful explosion that had taken the life of a young man I loved like the little brother I never had. Knowing this was not the time to mourn Milo, I took control of my voice. "In a large, immobile bay like this one, docking clamps allow engineers to perform engine test burns at high thrust without worrying about balancing thrust vectors."

There was silence for a few seconds before Megan said, "So, the clamps keep the ship from moving no matter how hard you run the engines?"

"Right. That's what I said."

"No, darling, that's what you *meant*," Callan said. "Megan, thank you for the translation."

"Now that we all understand the situation," Laura said, "what are we going to do about it?"

"Once the ship is fully...online? Is that the right word?" Rupor asked.

"Yes, Rupor."

"Good. Once the ship is online, why not use the ship's laser batteries to burn all the pirates in the docking bay? Then we can release the clamps and be on our way."

It was a reasonable question from someone unfamiliar with ship-mounted laser batteries, but I could imagine Laura's mouth working as her brain tried to find just the right words to convey her horror at the thought. I jumped in to answer before she found her voice.

"Rupor, firing the lasers in such a confined space would be deadly to all of us. The reflected heat, alone, would melt the ship's skin. And rock blasted from the docking bay walls would only have one place to go—back on the ship."

"What he said," Laura confirmed.

"Ah," Rupor mused. "Remind me to study up on these modern weapons after we're done dealing with this pirate rabble."

"I wish I had his confidence," someone murmured over the comm.

"Come now, people," Rupor said. "This is a puzzler, certainly, but we have as fine a collection of people as I have ever had the pleasure to serve with. There *is* a solution. We *will* find it."

"At the very worst, we can just sit tight until the navy sends a task force," someone said. "They're bound to have gotten that messenger drone by now."

"No, I'm afraid we can't just wait," Laura's husband spoke up. "These pirates hit planetary settlements as well as shipping. They've got mobile laser batteries that *can* be fired in the docking bay. Quint has probably already sent for them."

The comm was silent again as everyone digested this latest news.

"Use shaped explosive charges to blow the ship free." The voice was weak and rasping.

"Martin!" Megan cried. "You're awake."

"Indeed, dear heart," Martin gasped. "I've been awake for a minute or so, but couldn't quite find my voice until just now."

"I'm glad you're speaking again, my friend," I said, "but your suggestion won't work. Anyone leaving the ship to place explosives on the docking clamps would be an easy target for the pirates."

"I'm disappointed in you, David. Don't you claim to have watched every adventure vid in existence?" Martin replied. "Haven't you seen *Star Ranger and the Space Pirates*?"

"I said I watched the *good* vids, Martin."

"You're insulting a classic, Wonder Boy."

"Would you boys quit arguing about vids and enlighten the rest of us?" Callan demanded.

"Star Ranger faced just this situation in that vid. His solution can be our solution." Martin paused, perhaps to gather strength or perhaps for dramatic effect. "We don't blow the docking clamps. We blow the landing gear it's clamped to."

THE MADNESS OF MEN

There was another silence as everyone considered Martin's idea. The crew had access to the landing gear without getting out of the ship. And flying without landing gear was a lot better than not flying with landing gear. I couldn't find any obvious flaws.

"Laura, you're our engineer. What do you think?" I asked.

"Well, we're going to be in for one heck of a jolt when the ship drops two meters to the deck after we blow the landing gear," she said, "but the ship can take it. Give me a minute to check the specs for the landing struts."

"I might be able to keep the ship from dropping to the floor," Nist offered. "We can bring the repulsers online just before the explosives go off. If we time it right, the repulser's hum won't alert the pirates and the ship won't hit the floor."

"Good idea, Nist. Figure out what you'll need to do to pull it off," I said. "And Martin? Not a bad suggestion for an old man."

"I attribute my brilliance to a misspent youth and a weakness for Star Ranger adventures. So, did I miss anything while I was out?"

"I'll tell him," Megan said.

I watched her turn off both of their comms and lean in close so their atmosphere shields overlapped. Seconds later, Martin's face screwed up in pain that had nothing to do with the burns covering his body. Despite those burns, he pulled Megan into a hug with one arm and reached the other out to clasp Callan's hand. A moment later, he thumbed on his comm.

"I'm sorry, David." Martin's voice was quiet, the emotion he felt over Milo's death evident.

"I know, Martin. We all are."

Laura chose that moment to check back in.

"David, I've checked the specs for the landing gear and Martin's idea will work. We'll need a shaped charge attached to the right spot on each of the six struts."

"I sense a 'but' in that explanation, Laura," I said.

"You're right. The weak spot in the landing struts is about a foot below the well the gear retracts into after liftoff."

"Will you have to leave the ship to place the charges?" I asked.

"No, we can get into the well and place the charges without leaving the ship," Laura replied, "but if any of the pirates notice what we're doing, it won't be hard for them to stop us."

"It sounds like we need to make sure the pirates aren't paying any attention to the ship while you're placing the charges," I said.

"Well, yes, a distraction would help." Weary sarcasm tinged Laura's voice. "I suppose I could open the ship's airlock, point to the other side of the docking bay, and shout 'Oh my God, what is that?' But I don't really think that will work, David."

"It might work if she was naked," Martin said.

"It's going to take my teams at least a minute to place the charges," Laura said. "Maybe Callan could hold their attention that long. I know I couldn't."

"No one is getting naked in front of the pirates, least of all my wife," I said. "How long will it take to prepare the charges?"

"They're ready now. Pirates keep plenty of explosives on hand to blow the airlocks of ships they're attacking."

"Good enough. Arm a squad of marines with laser rifles and get them to the ship's airlock," I said. "I expect I'm going to need some covering fire."

"You're planning something dangerous, David," Callan said. "What is it?"

"I'm going to walk into the docking bay and arrest Quint and Chapman."

"That's not dangerous, David," Martin said, "that's suicidal."

"Listen to Martin and don't do this," Callan pleaded. "It's bad enough that Milo is gone. Don't make it worse by sacrificing yourself, too."

"My soon-to-be ex-husband isn't worth it," Heidi added, her voice quiet but forceful. "Cowards like him and snakes like Quint aren't worth your life, David."

"I am not planning on dying, people," I said. "But I am also not planning on letting those responsible for so much death—Milo's and countless others across the galaxy—escape justice. I owe this to all the dead whose souls cry out for a reckoning. By God, I am David Rice, Scout First Class of the Terran Exploration Corps. It is my *duty* to follow this through."

"Aw hell, you had to go and drag duty into it, didn't you?" Martin muttered. "Could someone loan me a sword?"

"*What?*" Megan cried. "Don't be stupid, Martin, you're half covered in burns! You can't be thinking of joining in this madness."

"He can and he is, Megan," Callan said. "There is no talking to David once he starts going on about a Scout's duty. I can only assume the Scout Academy inflicted the same madness on Martin."

"You are quite correct, Your Highness," Martin said. "I managed to forget that madness for a long time—until your husband reminded me of who I had been and who I could be again. Where David leads, I *will* follow."

"As will I," Rupor said.

"You're all mad!" Heidi cried.

"Mad we may be, Heidi," Rupor replied, "but ours is the glorious madness of honor, of oath, and of duty. It is the madness of men. It is this madness that draws the love of the best and brightest women the galaxy has to offer. And it is this madness that will bring down that most loathsome pirate, Captain Quint."

"If only..." Heidi whispered. I doubt she meant it to be heard, but it fell into the silence that followed Rupor's speech.

In the most gentle voice I'd ever heard Rupor use, he said, "You do yourself a disservice, Heidi. You are not responsible for your husband's actions."

"But I'm the one who fell in love with a coward instead of one of you mad warriors. How can that not be my fault? How can I ever show my face around any of you again?"

"Perhaps you had to marry Chapman so you could meet your rightful madman," Rupor said. In a lighter tone, he added, "Have you ever considered just how beautiful you would look in Tartegian black and gold?"

A collective gasp sounded over the comm before Laura's husband asked, "Am I imagining things, or did Rupor just propose to Heidi?"

"Rupor of Tarteg," Heidi said, her voice more full of life than it had been since we reached the pirate base, "you had better survive this mad scheme of David's and make your intentions clear in person. *Do you understand me?*"

"Of course, my dear," Rupor said. His voice was even, but he wore the biggest grin I'd ever seen on his face. "It should be easy enough. After all, there are three of us."

"Begging the prince's pardon, but he has miscounted," the marine commander said, "There are *one hundred and sixty-three* of us. The men are already gathering at the airlocks, ready to sally forth on Captain Rice's command."

"One hundred and sixty-four," Harris said.

"I appreciate your fervor, Harris," I said, "but you will stay here and guard the women."

"That's what I'll be doing, sir," Harris replied. "I believe I can best protect Her Highness and Megan by keeping you and Captain Bane alive. I realize I risk court martial for disobeying your order, but I am coming with you."

"I like this one, David," Callan said. "He reminds me of you."

I sighed. "Martin, have you got a sword?"

"Yes. The wounded guard's sword was still buckled about his waist."

"Very well, gentlemen, it's time to let madness reign."

BAD AT MATH

I pulled Callan to me and kissed her. "I'll be back for you soon."

Her cheek tight against mine, she whispered fiercely, "You'd better be."

Martin and Megan broke apart at the same time Callan and I did. Then the four of us swam off toward the lip of the docking bay.

"Laura," I called over the comm, "are your teams ready to go?"

"It took some persuasion on my part to keep them from taking up swords and joining you in your glorious charge into the docking bay," Laura replied, "but they've got the charges and are in their positions now."

"Good. Blow the charges as soon as all your teams have gotten to safety. Pick up Callan, Megan, and the wounded marine before you do anything else. After that, you're in command until Martin or I get back on board. You've got good instincts. Follow them."

"Aye aye, Captain Rice!" Laura said.

There was something in the way she snapped off her response that made me ask, "Are you saluting, Laura?"

Laughter erupted over the comm. "Um, yes, sir."

"At ease, Chief Engineer."

We reached our position just below the lip of the docking bay. I pulled myself up enough to see over the lip of the bay floor. There were at least four hundred pirates gathered in various places throughout the docking bay. Half of the pirates were formed up around the *Aashla's Hope*. Their swords were sheathed but close at hand. All but a handful of the rest manned various positions close to vital controls. That left a dozen formed up around Quint as his personal guard. Chapman stood just behind Quint, subservient but readily available in case Quint needed to speak to him.

I looked at my companions. Rupor wore a grin of suppressed excitement. Martin wore a grimace of suppressed pain. Harris wore a smile of suppressed nervousness. I could only imagine the faces of the marines on board the *Aashla's Hope*. I felt as if I should say something before we charged out against such superior numbers—something to settle the men's nerves and channel their excitement. I drew a blank until I remembered something from ancient Terran history. Without a hint of shame, I stole it.

"Gentlemen, Tarteg and Mordan expect all men to do their duty."

Next to me, Martin spoke but his voice was drowned out by a roar from the men echoing over the comm. Martin stopped trying to speak and just gave me a thumbs up. Then we pulled ourselves up and into the docking bay.

The pirates glanced about, nerves set on edge by the roar they'd heard from inside our ship. Heads turned toward Quint, looking for guidance. Irritation crossed Quint's face and he prepared to speak. That was just what I'd been waiting for.

"Heidi, broadcast my comm outside the ship so everyone can hear me," I said. "And crank the volume."

"You're on, David."

"Git yerselves under–" Quint began before I drowned him out.

"To all pirates within this base—in the name of the Terran Federation, I order you to lay down your arms and surrender!" I stalked forward, flipping my sword in the casual manner of one who has had to live by the blade. Martin, Rupor, and Harris matched me stride for stride, all three flipping their blades in unison with mine.

A few pirates spotted us and pointed. Within seconds, every pair of eyes in the docking bay turned upon us.

"Yer an idiot, Rice," Quint shouted, but his voice was still weak compared to my amplified one. "We got you outnumbered four hunnert to four."

Rupor chose that moment to bark, "Marines, form up!"

With a whoosh, every airlock in the *Aashla's Hope* opened and the marines poured out of the ship. As our marines took up their positions around the ship, the pirates surrounding the ship stirred nervously.

"Were you always this bad at math, Quint, or is it a recent thing?" I raised a hand in salute to the marines. "Either way, you've seriously miscalculated the odds."

"Maybe so, but we still got more than twice yer numbers," he shouted back.

"That you do. And if your men faced their typical prey—a bunch of merchant spacers or the crew of a space liner—your numbers would make a difference." I waved my arm toward the marines. "Take a long, hard look at our marines. Do those men look like they're afraid of you? You pirates are used to being the foxes rampaging through the hen house. But today your fox den has been invaded by wolves—and one wolf is worth five of you little foxes."

I pointed my sword at Quint. "You can stop the slaughter, Quint. Surrender or we'll destroy you, just like we destroyed Caudill and his crew."

Quint glared across the docking bay at me. "I'd rather die first."

"So be it." I raised my sword above my head and cried, "For Milo!"

With a roar, I charged into battle.

QUINT'S GETTING AWAY

Charging with me, my three companions joined in my battle cry. "For Milo!"

At a barked command from their commander, one hundred and sixty marines raised their voices as one. "For Mordan! For Tarteg! For Milo!"

The marines charged the encircling pirates. Unnerved by the marines' precision, both in maneuvers and in voice, the pirates fell back before the onslaught. I must remember to congratulate the marine commander's choice of battle cry later.

"Heidi?" My voice boomed out across the docking bay. "Route me back to the ship's channel and cancel the broadcast."

"Done, sir."

The four of us engaged half a dozen pirates, steel clashing against steel. We pushed the pirates back a couple of steps before they found a rhythm of their own. Precious seconds ticked away as we traded blows. They were seconds Laura's teams would use to place the charges on the landing struts. They were seconds Quint or Chapman might use to disappear into the base. They were seconds I could not afford to waste on these men.

"I'm going to Boost in ten seconds. Be smart and get out of my way." The pirate in front of me looked at me in disbelief. "Yes, I'm talking to you and your friends. I don't care about you but if you don't surrender now I will cut you down where you stand."

"Believe him lads." Martin's voice still sounded rough, but the pain from his burns was driven away by the excitement of combat. "David takes duty very seriously and you're standing between him and Quint."

Comprehension dawned on the pirates' faces. They dropped their swords and moved aside. As pirates rushed to join those fighting the marines, hardly any pirates stood between me and Quint. The opportunity was too good to waste.

Boost!

Adrenaline poured into my system. Time slowed. Fatigue faded. Vision sharpened. Muscles surged. I flew across the docking bay, an arrow aimed at Quint and Chapman. My focus was so tight on Quint that I was halfway across the bay before I realized I was not alone. I looked to my left. Martin ran with me, stride for stride, lips stretched wide in a savage grin. Footsteps pounded behind me and I risked a look over my shoulder. Rupor and Harris sprinted for all they were worth, almost keeping up with us.

At Quint's shouted command, a squad of his pirate guards blocked our path. They held their swords raised, ready to defend their captain. I lowered my shoulder and Martin did the same.

I switched from gal base to Mordanian. "I'm going to tuck and roll low past the first row and come up in the middle of them."

"Good idea. Make sure to swing your sword to the right. I'll be on your left."

As one, Martin and I dropped and rolled between startled defenders. We rose to face pirates unprepared for immediate combat. I swung my blade in a wide arc, cutting three pirates and driving all of them back a step. Behind me, Rupor and Harris engaged the pirates Martin and I had bypassed.

Confusion reigned among the pirates as a result of our surprise arrival in their midst. Martin and I took advantage of it and laid about us indiscriminately. I thrust my sword into the side of a pirate. He screamed as I ripped it free and slashed the man next to him. I blocked a swing from a third pirate and kicked him in the groin. Grabbing his collar as he doubled over in pain, I threw him into the back of a pirate battling with Rupor.

I looked for Quint and spotted him, Chapman, and his remaining guards heading for the airlock.

"Quint's getting away!" I hacked off a pirate's sword arm.

"Not if I can help it," Martin pulled his sword from the shoulder of another pirate.

One man stood between us and Quint's retreat.

I pointed my sword at him. "I want Quint, not you. Move."

The pirate's eyes widened in panic and indecision. Martin's sword flashed and the pirate crumpled to the deck.

"He took too long to make up his mind."

Clear of the pirates, Martin and I raced on as Quint and his men reached the airlock. The captain looked back at us and punched buttons on the airlock control with frantic haste. I had to reach him before he could disappear into the base.

Then a thunder clap drowned out all sounds of battle. Fighting paused as the docking bay reverberated with the sound of the explosions. Though I was looking in the wrong direction, the airlock door reflected the scene behind me.

Aashla's Hope floated free and was already moving ponderously toward the docking bay exit.

A BIG PITY PARTY

A cheer rose from the marines as our spaceship majestically glided out of the docking bay. Over the comm, I could hear the ship's crew preparing to pick up Callan, Megan, and the wounded marine. Around the docking bay, the fight went out of the pirates and they began dropping their swords to the floor in surrender.

"Cap'n David, sir," Heidi's voice held more life than I'd heard since her husband had dragged her off the *Aashla's Hope* many hours before. "A rescue team is assembling in the airlock. We'll have Her Highness and her companions back on the ship in two minutes."

Tightness I hadn't even realized was gripping my chest loosened. I released a long sigh and dropped Boost.

"It's over, Quint. My ship is free and your pirates are defeated. Do the smart thing and surrender."

Quint punched one more key on the airlock controls and the door hissed open. To my surprise, Quint didn't dash into the airlock. Instead, one of his men walked through the door.

"I don't think so, scout."

"You can't win, Quint. Do you remember the wormhole alarm a few hours ago? That was our messenger drone, launched just before entering your docking bay. The drone carries the location of this base, the approach path through the asteroids, and the identity of the senior captain. Honestly, I'm surprised a Federation Navy task force hasn't already popped out of that wormhole."

"I figgered out 'bout the drone when you done told us who you was, boy."

"If you knew we had alerted the navy, why did you bother fighting us? Why didn't you just let us go and get away while the getting was good?"

"Yer askin' me why, boy?" Rage filled Quint's eyes. "Take a gander 'round you. You think a place like this jest pops up all set and ready ta use? I remember when ol' Caudill and me stumbled 'cross this place. It was jest a big rock chock full o' caves. Me 'n Caudill got us some lads and worked our tails off ta build this place. My blood 'n sweat be in every nook and cranny o' this place. You think I's gonna let the man who be takin' it from me just fly away?"

The man in the airlock began handing something out to each of the pirates around Quint. I couldn't see what they were passing around, but all of my mental alarms began ringing.

"So this resistance of yours is just a big pity party because you're going to miss your old pirate base?" I sniffed and pretended to wipe away tears. "I feel your pain, Quint. Really, I do. I feel it so much, I wish all the victims of your decades of piracy could be here to shed a tear over your loss. But they can't because you or your men killed them. If losing this rock causes you pain, I say hurrah." I waved my sword toward Quint and his men. "Escape is impossible, so stop whatever it is you and your men think you're doing and surrender."

Quint's fingers danced across the keypad again.

"Yer right 'bout one thing, Rice. Escape be impossible fer most o' me men. But it ain't fer me and these lads with me."

"Martin, I'm tired of talking to this old man. Time to take him down."

We strode toward Quint. Quint's fingers touched two last keys then hovered over a button.

"Take another step, boy, and I'll drop the atmo shield and flush ya all out inta space."

We stopped. Four of us still wore vacuum harnesses, but none of the marines had them.

"You know you'll kill more than my men. You'll kill your men and yourself, too."

The pirate handing out stuff from the airlock came back wearing a vacuum harness. He carried another. As that pirate slipped the vacuum harness around Quint, the rest of Quint's guards donned harnesses, too.

Chapman looked wildly around him. "H-hey, where's my harness?"

Quint shook his head. "Now why would I be wantin' ta save you, Chapman?"

"But I've helped you! I told you who these men were. I've been *useful* to you."

"Yep, but there be plenty o' other useful idiots in the galaxy. I 'spect I's gonna find you right easy to replace."

Quint looked around the docking bay. "Sorry, lads. Wish I could save ya all, but that jest ain't in the cards today."

Quint looked me in the eyes. "An' now I got ta git busy makin' that impossible escape."

Then Quint's finger stabbed toward the button.

SPACE HIM

Time slowed to a crawl as I watched Quint's finger stab toward the button. Once pressed, the button would drop the atmosphere shield protecting the docking bay from the vacuum of space. The old pirate was too far away for me to reach him in the second he needed to press the button. Unbidden, my mind conjured the image of hundreds of men swept into the void, still living but beyond any power in the universe to save. And I would be swept into space with them, safe in my vacuum harness, mute witness to the last seconds of their lives.

"Nooooooooooooooo!"

Chapman barreled into the pirate captain. Quint's finger missed the button and the two tumbled to the ground.

There come times in every man's life when inaction is more dangerous than action. In that moment, even the coward can act decisively. Quint had pushed his useful idiot too far and Chapman had snapped.

Every man in the docking bay stood frozen, transfixed by the drama playing out beneath the keypad. The keypad with the still-active button that would drop the atmosphere shield.

"Now's your chance, lads. Get 'em!"

My cry still echoing around the docking bay, I charged to

Chapman's aid. With a roar, pirates and marines alike charged with me.

Quint's pirate guards saw the tidal wave of humanity sweeping their way. Abandoning their leader, they scrambled to escape into the airlock. A band of their fellow pirates piled in behind them. From the cries of rage and the screams of pain and fear, I was happy I couldn't see what happened inside that airlock.

Quint and Chapman flailed at each other, rolling around on the floor of the docking bay. Quint was a wily fighter and the stronger of the two men, but Chapman had gone berserk. The fight was too close to call.

"Martin, can you disable the button on that keypad?"

"Already on it, O Fearless Leader."

Pirates and marines joined me around the struggling pair, cutting them off from everything else. None of us interrupted the fight. None of us liked Chapman and we all agreed the man was nothing more than a useful idiot. But in this moment, he was *our* idiot. Even if he had acted in his own self-interest, Chapman's attack saved hundreds of lives. His actions hadn't earned him much, but they had earned him the chance to pound on Quint.

A moment later, it was over. Bloodied and battered, Chapman rose from the moaning pirate captain, Quint's vacuum harness gripped in one hand. With an animal roar of triumph, Chapman thrust the vacuum harness into the air. Hundreds of voices roared with him.

Chapman looked around him, his eyes bright with the fervor of battle.

"Let's give Quint a taste of his own medicine. Let's space him!"

I was elbowed aside as men pushed to reach Quint. A dozen hands hoisted the pirate captain over our heads. Marines and pirates alike passed Quint from hand to hand toward the entrance to the docking bay.

A chant broke out from the men. "Space him! Space him!"

The chant rose in volume and drowned out my calls to stop. Hemmed in by the crowd, I could do nothing but watch the mob

—for they were no longer pirates and marines—pass Quint, now struggling and flailing, toward his doom.

Martin's hand fell on my shoulder. "There's nothing you can do, David."

"I wanted Quint to face justice for all he's done, Martin."

"He *is* facing justice, lad. It's rough justice, I'll grant you, but so was beheading the pirate who tried to space Callan and Megan. Quint has earned this death a thousand times over."

Martin was right. It's not what I would have chosen, but I couldn't claim the earlier execution was right yet claim this was wrong.

I made myself watch as Quint, finally facing the terror he had inflicted on countless others in his long career, was heaved through the atmosphere barrier.

I made myself watch Quint's futile struggle for life as he drifted in the void.

I made myself watch Quint die.

HE'S AT PEACE

Quint's still and lifeless body tumbled away from the pirate base, shrinking until it was too small to see. I gave myself a mental shake and pulled my gaze away from the airless abyss beyond the atmosphere shield.

Chapman, a smug smile pasted on his face, stepped in front of me.

"Well, Rice, I guess you're pretty happy I was around to save everyone."

I punched him, flattening Chapman's nose.

"Ow! What the hell-?"

"Don't you *dare* proclaim yourself the hero."

"But I stopped Quint!" Chapman's voice rose with each word.

I punched him in the stomach and heard the breath whoosh out of him. Good. Maybe that would shut him up for a few minutes.

"This whole situation is *your* fault, Chapman."

I hit him with a left cross and he stumbled back a step.

"If you had simply kept your big mouth shut and stayed on our ship, *none* of this would have happened."

My right fist cracked into his eye and Chapman reeled back against the wall of the docking bay.

"If you had simply kept your big mouth shut, you wouldn't have been challenged to a duel."

I grabbed Chapman's shirt in both fists and pounded him against the wall.

"If you had simply kept your big mouth shut, I wouldn't have had to join the duel just to keep you quiet."

I smashed Chapman against the wall, again.

"If you had simply kept your big mouth shut, my wife and friends wouldn't have had to put themselves in danger just to keep our story intact. The story *you* were determined to reveal."

Chapman sagged as I thumped him into the wall a third time.

"If you had simply kept your big mouth shut, dozens, maybe hundreds, of men—marines and pirates, alike—would still be alive."

Thump.

"If you had simply kept your big mouth shut, *Milo* would still be alive."

Thump.

"He."

Thump.

"Was."

Thump.

"Only."

Thump.

"Sixteen!"

Thump.

I heard a voice from far away. "You're on a private channel, Your Highness."

"David? Talk to me."

I released Chapman and he slid down the wall to the floor.

"Callan? Are you safe?"

"Yes, darling, we're all on board the ship. We're all safe."

"Milo's not safe. He'll never be safe again."

"You're wrong, David. He'll never be in danger again. He's at peace."

"Do you truly believe that, Callan?"

"After all we've been through, how could I not?"

I paused to consider her words. Callan couldn't see it, but I nodded slowly and pushed my emotions down. Having mastered myself, I turned to survey the scene in the docking bay.

"All right, men, it's time to get back to work."

Rupor stepped forward and placed a hand on my shoulder. "We can handle this, David. When the fighting ends, a man must take the time to properly mourn the dead."

The marines did appear to have everything under control. Squads of marines herded the pirates into small, manageable groups and disarmed them. Others directed the collection of the dead and wounded from both sides. Medics moved among the wounded performing triage. And beyond the atmosphere shield, our ship's remaining pinnace detached and maneuvered into the docking bay. Tristan bounded out as soon as the hatch opened, rushing to tend the wounded.

And then Callan emerged and ran across the docking bay to me. She flew into my arms and kissed me. It was long and tender and I felt my emotions rising again. This time I did not try to hold them back and the tears flowed.

Tears of rage and relief.

Tears of loss and love.

Tears for Milo.

Tears for the marines.

Tears for Martin and Megan.

Tears for the woman who held me.

I sank to the deck and Callan held me while I cried.

Sometime later, I became aware a marine stood silently ten feet away. Callan and I rose from the deck and looked around the docking bay. The *Aashla's Hope* was inside again, floating on repulsers but tethered in position. Tristan still moved among the wounded, barking orders and tending patients. The pirates sat, hands upon heads, in small groups scattered around the bay.

"Yes, private? What can I do for you?" I said to the marine.

He snapped off a salute. "I'm sorry to interrupt, sir, but you're wanted aboard the ship."

"Do you have any idea why?"

"Yes, sir. They said to tell you the wormhole has opened."

WELL DONE, GENTLEMEN

"Your Highness?" a marine asked as we turned toward the ship. "Should we space Chapman, too?"

Callan glared at the man slumped against the wall. "No, corporal. I'm not kind enough to give him the easy way out."

Without another word, she led the way to the ship.

"Please excuse my ignorance, dear, but this must be some new definition of 'kind' I'm not familiar with."

"That's because you haven't spent enough time among the sycophants in court, David." With a smile Callan took my arm. "There are people for whom status is everything. They must belong to the 'right' groups and be seen with the 'right' people. Such people would rather die than lose status."

"You're saying Chapman is one of those people?"

"Absolutely. If we dig into his past, I'm sure we'll find a high status education and a high status job. All you have to do is look at Heidi to realize she's his high status wife."

"Okay, but that doesn't explain why he sucked up to the pirates like he did."

"Of course it does, darling. Different societies have different definitions of high status. Whatever gave Chapman his status before his capture did nothing for him in a society of pirates. He had to change who and what he was or face being a low status outsider. That's the one thing he couldn't accept."

That did explain a lot about Chapman's behavior. "And spacing him would spare him being dragged back into galactic society as a traitor against his fellow prisoners and a spy for the pirates. God above, even the other prisoners will despise him."

A grim smile played across Callan's lips as she nodded. "I have no sympathy for the wretched man. He brought it on himself."

We climbed the ramp into the *Aashla's Hope* and headed for the bridge. Crewmen hunched over each of the ship's sensor displays. Laura stood next to Heidi as the comm officer scanned subspace bands for any activity.

"Have you found anything, Heidi?" I asked.

She shook her head. "All of the bands are clear, David."

"Try broadcasting an SOS on all bands. And put the comm on speaker."

Heidi's fingers flew across the keyboard. The sound of the automated SOS signal filled the bridge. We received a reply within seconds.

"Unidentified ship, what is the nature of your emergency?"

The response was fast and professional. It had to be a naval ship.

"This is David Rice commanding the *Aashla's Hope*. We are currently moored in a pirate base docking bay~"

A new voice broke in. It held the no-nonsense, take-charge tone you find in experienced officers.

"How dire is your situation? We're on a hard burn toward the coordinates you provided in your drone. Can you hold out for another twenty minutes?"

"We don't need to hold out, sir. We've taken the base. The pirate captains are all dead and the surviving pirates are our prisoners."

There was a pause. "Well done, of course, but why did you broadcast an SOS?"

"We've taken the base, but have many wounded from both sides. We are woefully short of supplies and personnel to attend to them all."

"Understood. I have a fully equipped medical ship as part of my command. We will make all haste to the base."

"Thank you, sir. Rice out."

While waiting for naval aid to arrive, Callan and I went out to the makeshift hospital. My wife's eyes welled as she gazed upon the row of neatly laid out dead, each draped in the flag of his native country.

The marine commander approached and sketched a bow. "Your Highness? Perhaps you could say a few words? I believe it will mean a lot to the men."

"Of course, Commander." Callan touched her comm. "Heidi, please broadcast my comm throughout the docking bay."

"You're on, Princess Callan."

Callan walked in among the wounded, looking each in the eye and flashing her dazzling smile. She raised her head and her gaze took in the unwounded marines around the docking bay.

"My brave warriors, Tartegian and Mordanian alike, your world owes you a debt of thanks. You have fought well." She looked back to the rows of dead. "And too many of you have died well."

Callan turned back to the living. "Today, we have lost friends, brothers-in-arms. Back home, though they do not yet know it, families have lost fathers and sons and brothers. Yet these sacrifices will save lives untold. The lives of fathers and sons, of mothers and daughters, of brothers and sisters.

"We shall never know how many lives have been saved by your actions here today. More importantly, those you have saved will never know you saved them. They will sail peacefully through space and arrive safely at their destination, all because men of honor and courage dared to venture beyond the sky of their home world. Those saved will never know—but *I* know.

"And I swell with pride knowing our countries—our world—

produce men such as you. Well done, gentlemen. Well done, indeed."

The docking bay rocked with cheers as Callan knelt to speak with one of the wounded. She was still comforting the wounded when the navy arrived.

A ROYAL PROCLAMATION

The navy's medical ship came fully staffed and supplied. The ship's med team rushed to our wounded, injecting swarms of medical nanites into those with the worst wounds. Tristan could only watch in awe as wounds beyond his ability to heal closed as if by magic. Once those on the brink of death were safe, the doctor in charge of the medical team sought out our doctor.

"Sir, are you Doctor Agrilla?"

"I am, though after watching you at work, I'm not so sure I should call myself 'doctor' anymore." Tristan's gaze swept the organized chaos in his makeshift hospital. "From the bottom of my heart, thank you for saving those I am too unskilled to save."

"It's not our skill, sir, it's our technology. Without the nanites, my team would not have saved anywhere near as many men as they did."

Tristan's eyebrows rose. "Really?"

"It's God's own truth, sir." The doctor smiled at Tristan. "I sought you out because I want to ask you about some of the procedures you used."

Gesturing to some of the wounded men, Tristan and the naval

doctor fell into a technical discussion well beyond my capability to follow.

Once the initial rush to help the wounded and establish naval control of the docking bay was over, the navy reverted to its thorough, though tedious, routine. Armored marines swept the rest of the base section by section, rounding up the last of the pirates. The records of the pirate captains were secured and unsold plunder recovered. Naval repair crews even fixed the landing struts on the *Aashla's Hope*.

A long and busy thirty-five hours after they arrived, naval demolitions crews rigged the base with explosives and we finally set a course for the wormhole. All who were onboard our ship watched the vid display as the explosives detonated and blasted the pirate base into thousands of tiny asteroids.

The only thing worth noting during the trip to the navy base occurred shortly after we exited the wormhole. The trio of Rupor, Heidi, and Megan approached Callan in the recreation room.

"Your Highness?"

Something in Heidi's tone sent Callan right into princess mode. She stood straighter. Her shoulders drew back. Her gaze sharpened.

"Yes, Heidi?"

"I have a problem I hope you can solve, Princess Callan," Heidi continued with the formal tone. "In the Federation, divorces can be complicated, even if both parties agree to the divorce. I rather doubt Erwin will cooperate."

Heidi stopped and met Callan's eyes for a moment. Callan nodded for her to continue.

"Megan told me that you can issue a royal proclamation of divorce."

"I can, Heidi, but only for Mordanian citizens."

"Megan also told me you can grant Mordanian citizenship by royal proclamation."

"I can do that, also, but Rupor can do likewise for Tartegian citizens."

Rupor cleared his throat. "As I have a vested interest in this outcome, I feel it will be more seemly if the proclamations came from someone other than me." A bright smile crossed Rupor's face. "Besides, Callan, at one time my subjects expected me to marry a beautiful Mordanian citizen. I believe many of them are still rather partial to the idea."

Callan smiled in return. "Heidi, I don't have the oath of citizenship memorized, but I've accepted nontraditional oaths in the past. Do you swear to uphold the laws of Mordan, obey the monarch, and support Mordan in peace and in war?"

"I so swear."

"Then by the powers granted to me as a princess of the realm and heir to the throne, I accept your pledge and welcome you as a subject of the kingdom of Mordan."

Applause broke out around the bridge and Callan raised a hand to request quiet.

"Furthermore, it has come to my attention that you are unhappy in your marriage to one Erwin Chapman and wish to terminate the bond of matrimony between the two of you. Is that correct?"

"Damn right it is!" Heidi blushed when she realized what she had said. "I beg your pardon, Your Highness. Yes, that is correct."

"Again, by the powers granted to me as a princess of the realm and heir to the throne, I hereby grant your request for divorce and order your marriage to Erwin Chapman dissolved."

Applause broke out again, louder than before.

Callan looked at Rupor, who wore the widest grin I'd ever seen on his face. "For God's sake, Rupor, stop grinning like an idiot and kiss Heidi."

He did and we all cheered.

Thirty minutes later, we docked and emerged into a madhouse.

UNDER SIEGE

We docked at Velron Station, orbiting the border world of Darthan. Planets on the edge of Federation territory could rarely afford multiple space stations and Darthan was no exception. The single space station served both military and civilian ships and personnel. As seems to be typical in these situations, space for military ships was severely limited. Station control ordered the *Aashla's Hope* to dock in the civilian section.

The first hint of trouble came when some of our crew—all men and women formerly held by the pirates—ran out to help the station crew attach magnetic grapples and seal the airlocks. Thirty seconds later, they all ran back into the ship, sweat beaded on their faces and short of breath.

Martin and I exchanged glances before I spoke to one of the crew.

"Is there a problem, Natalie?"

Her wide eyes focused on me and her breathing slowed. "It's crazy out there, sir."

"What do you mean by crazy?"

"It's wall-to-wall newsies out there, sir. Half a dozen of them surrounded me when I tried to help the station crew, all of them pushing and shoving to get my attention, shouting questions the whole time. I- I'm not used to crowds like that after all the time I spent with the pirates and then you Aashlanders. I panicked." Natalie looked around at the others who went out with her. "We all did."

I patted her on the shoulder. "Why don't you and the others go to the med bay. Ask Tristan to give you something to calm you down."

Thumbing my comm unit, I said, "Heidi, please have the senior staff meet Martin and me in the Captain's office. Also, can you tap into the station's vid feeds and find a view of our docking bay?"

"I'm on it, David. Do you want me to scan the news channels, too?"

"Good idea. Be ready to route what you find to the screens in the office."

A moment later, we stared at the images Heidi sent to the office. Natalie hadn't exaggerated describing the docking bay. Hundreds of men and women pushed and shoved to get close to our ship's exits. Vid cameras swooped over the crowd, somehow managing to avoid colliding with each other. As bad as that was, the news vids were worse.

One newsie exclaimed, "Word on the station is those aboard this very ship stormed the base of the infamous pirate captains Caudill and Quint, slaughtering every last one of the pirates."

Another reported, "We have been told that these people from a long-lost human colony forgot all technological knowledge but may have gained powerful mental or mystic abilities. Frankly, viewers, it's the only logical explanation for how a band of barbarians could have defeated these pirates."

Callan, Rupor, and Tristan bristled at the speculation.

"Darling, did that man just call us barbarians?"

"Now, Callan-"

Laura pointed to a screen. "Look, it's David!"

An image of me in my cadet uniform filled one screen.

Martin burst out laughing. "Isn't he adorable?"

His laughter stilled when my image was replaced by one of Martin in *his* cadet uniform.

Megan wrapped an arm around Martin. "Don't worry, Martin, you look *much* cuter than David in that uniform."

Everyone had a laugh at our expense, but I'd seen all I wanted to see.

"Heidi, cut the broadcasts to the office and then get me the commander of the military base."

Several minutes passed before Heidi reported, "I've got an aide to the commander, David. It's the best I could do."

A harried face replaced Heidi's. "I have a task force docking as we speak and do not have time for civilian inquiries. You have thirty seconds."

"I am the reason the task force is docking, so you will *make* time for my inquiries."

"Look, I don't know who you are and I don't care. I-"

"I am David Rice, Scout First Class and captain of the *Aashla's Hope*, formerly the ship of the late pirate captain Caudill. I led the forces that took the base of the late pirate captain Quint. On board my ship are two future heads of state and diplomats representing a dozen other countries on the lost colony of Aashla. While you dither about your task force, my people are under siege by a mob of newsies."

I'd taken exactly the wrong approach with the aide.

"Then I suggest you stay on board your ship, Captain Rice. We'll contact you when we have time for you."

With a ridiculous flourish, the aide ended the call.

"I know too many men just like that twit," Rupor mused. "If we were back home, I could just order out some troops to clear away that rabble."

I grinned. "Then I say we pretend we're back home."

The diplomats and one hundred marines gathered in the cargo hold. The marines formed up around the civilians and diplomatic personnel and I ordered the cargo hold's airlock opened.

With the marine commander, I led the march through the airlock. Newsies surged forward when they caught sight of us.

"Commander, if you please?"

The commander's voice carried, even over the clamor of the newsies.

"Present. Arms!"

In unison, one hundred swords slid free of scabbards. The newsies ground to a halt.

"Marines. Give voice!"

A wordless roar rose from the marines behind us. The newsies closest to us began pushing backward. The commander motioned with his arm and the marines marched forward.

We stopped for no one and no one dared stand before the bared swords and roaring marines. Five minutes later, the base commander met us at the entrance to the military section. With no expression beyond a cocked eyebrow, she welcomed us into her domain.

MEDICAL WORKUP

Admiral McGillis, the base commander, turned our marine escort over to the base's marine commander with instructions to make them comfortable and debrief their commander concerning the fight for the pirate base. She led the diplomatic representatives, Martin, and me into a well-appointed reception room. The aide from my brief comm call waited within.

"I was in the middle of some rather important business when I received word of your approach." McGillis turned a steady gaze on me. "Scout Rice, you will never again bring an armed force onto my base without my express permission. Are we clear on that?"

I was prepared to acknowledge the statement and move on. Callan was not in as forgiving a mood.

"We most certainly are *not* clear on that, Admiral. Furthermore, David *did* contact your office, where this person," she waved at the aide, "made it quite clear our ship, our men, and our actions against the pirates were of no consequence when weighed against the arrival of your precious task force."

Callan folded her arms and gave Admiral McGillis her best princess glare. And it really was Callan's best. I only know of one person who could have stood against it unmoved, and Rob had been dead for nearly three years. I'll give McGillis credit, she figured out Callan was Someone Important long before her aide did.

"Admiral, I was-"

"I don't want to hear it, Smitts." The admiral's tone was so sharp the aide drew back as if he'd been cut. The admiral smiled at Callan. "With whom do I have the honor of speaking?"

Never let it be said I don't know my cue.

"Admiral McGillis, may I present Her Royal Highness, Princess Callan, heir to the throne of Mordan, and my wife." McGillis's left eyebrow rose and I turned to Rupor. "And this is His Royal Highness, Prince Rupor, heir to the throne of Tarteg."

Martin added, "Mordan and Tarteg are two of the most powerful and enlightened countries on the lost world of Aashla. Good relations with those two countries, as well as the countries represented by the rest of our diplomatic mission, will be vital if the Federation has any hope of bringing our world into the Federation."

McGillis got a faraway look for a second while she consulted her implant. "Scout Martin Bane, isn't it? I note that you refer to their world as your world."

"I've called Aashla home for eighteen years." He put an arm around Megan. "And, like David, I'll be marrying a local girl."

"My congratulations to both of you on your nuptials, past and pending. And please allow me to express the Federation's relief that both of you have returned safely after such an extended absence. No doubt you're both aware the Scout Corps wants to debrief you. Would you be averse to getting that out of the way as soon as possible?"

"Of course not, Admiral," I said

"Thank you, for your cooperation. Smitts will take you to the base scout commander now." McGillis nodded to Callan, Rupor, and the diplomatic personnel. "I'll personally see to their needs."

Smitts looked terribly uncomfortable playing escort to people he had snubbed earlier. Neither Martin nor I said anything to put

Smitts at his ease. Perhaps he would learn something from this, though I doubted it.

The Scout Corps office was a flurry of activity when we arrived. Smitts attempted introductions.

"Scout Commander Collins, may I present-"

Collins cut him off. "David Rice! It's good to see you hale and hearty. And Martin, the Bane of my existence, back from the dead! It is quite a grand day for the Scout Corps, indeed."

Oblivious to Smitts' discomfort, Collins said to him, "David was one of the best cadets I ever taught during my years at the academy. And Martin was one of the best troublemakers."

With a quick nod, Smitts excused himself and fled the office.

"Now that we're free of that idiot Smitts, let's get comfortable and start that debriefing, shall we?"

Martin raised a forestalling hand. "I would suggest a full medical workup, first, sir."

Collins gave Martin a quick up and down glance. "You do look as if you've had a rough time of it, recently, Martin."

"The navy took good care of me and I'm healing quite well, sir. It's David who should receive the medical attention."

"He looks remarkably fit to me, Martin."

"I'll admit David looks great on the outside. I'm worried about possible internal damage from over-Boosting."

Collins gaze sharpened. "Is this true, David? Have you been over-using Boost?"

"I Boosted only when necessary, sir. Unfortunately, there have been times when it was necessary to Boost rather more often than suggested."

"And longer than suggested, as well. I personally watched David Boost for thirteen straight minutes." Gasps sounded from the personnel in the office and the color drained from Collins' face. "We got his heart started again, but it was a close thing."

Fifteen minutes later, Collins had me inside the base hospital and about to go under anesthesia in preparation for a full scale invasion of my body by medical nanites. I refused to be put under until Callan arrived.

When she did, worry was etched across her face. "What's going on, David? Why are you in the hospital? Are you hurt?"

"This is all just a precaution, dear. Martin has gotten the scout commander worried about the effect Boosting has had on my body. They're going to send in an army of nanites to check me out."

"Martin's not the only one who's worried about you, darling." Callan kissed me lightly. "If you know what's good for you, you'll cooperate with the doctors."

She backed away so the doctors could get started. Her lovely face was the last thing I saw as I went under.

THE SPACEBABE

I hovered on the edge of consciousness, dreaming I was back home with my parents and sister. Mom was talking to a nurse about me. For a few seconds, I wondered why I was having such a boring dream. Then I came fully awake.

"According to your son's medical report, the nanites did a lot of internal reconstruction. Simple, though extensive, wear and tear from Boosting, it says. That kind of reconstruction puts a strain on the body, but it's nothing a little sleep won't fix," the nurse said.

"And you're sure he's just sleeping?" my mother asked.

"Well, I was, Mom," I said, my throat parched, "until you woke me up."

My mother, father, and sister all crowded around my bed, hugging and kissing me and generally making it hard for me to breathe.

"You should pour him some water, ma'am. He hasn't had a drink in two days," the nurse said, smiling. "And do let him come up for air every now and then."

"We've been so worried about you, David!" Tears rolled down Mom's cheeks. "You've been missing for nearly three years."

Dad clapped me once on the shoulder, a big smile on his face and tears welling in his eyes. Then my little sister pushed past him and promptly punched me on the arm.

"You had Mom and Dad worried sick, lunkhead. So don't go off and get lost again. Have you got that?"

Yes, she and Callan were going to get along famously. I sat up to pull her into a hug and then found myself simply staring at her.

"What are you staring at? Have I got something on my face?"

I shook my head. "No, Sandra, I'm just wondering when my awkward baby sister turned into such a beautiful young woman."

"Mom, something's really wrong with David. He's being nice to me."

A slight cough sounded near the door. Harris stood there, watching the scene with a broad smile. Seeing my eyes on him, he snapped to attention and addressed me in Mordanian.

"Her Highness only left your bedside to attend an appointment with a doctor." Alarm must have crossed my face as he added, "I'm told it is a routine matter. Perhaps it's associated with the implant she had installed yesterday. I've taken the liberty of informing her that you're awake."

"Thank you, Harris."

Harris nodded and withdrew.

"Who's that?" Sandra asked.

"Harris? He's a marine from the world I've been on for the last two and a half years."

"He's really cute. Does he have a girlfriend?"

"I have absolutely no idea, but I will be more than happy to introduce you." I looked past Sandra to my father. "Don't worry, Dad, Harris is as honorable a young man as I've met. We can trust him with the brat."

Sandra punched me on the arm again.

Rubbing my arm, I asked, "So, how did the three of you get here so quickly?"

"The Scout Corps brought us on one of their fastest ships," Dad replied. "We only docked at the station half an hour ago."

"Did anyone tell you anything about what had happened to me or where I've been?"

"No, son, the people we talked with didn't know anything except you'd crashed on some lost colony and had just resurfaced." Tears welled up in Mom's eyes again. "You can imagine how we felt when they brought us to a hospital."

"You always said you were going to find a lost colony someday," Dad smiled. "Looks like you're a man of your word, son."

Sandra flashed a wicked grin. "Yeah, yeah, so you found a lost world. Whoopee. I want to know if you found your spacebabe?"

A lilting voice spoke from the doorway. "What on Aashla is a spacebabe?"

Callan stood just inside the doorway, a fond smile lighting her face. Seeing Callan for the first time, Sandra's eyes went wide. "Wow, David. You really *did* meet her."

"I've got to say I'm impressed, son," Dad murmured. "That girl is beyond beautiful!"

I sat up straighter in bed. "Mom. Dad. Sandra. This is Her Royal Highness, Princess Callan, heir to the throne of Mordan and, more importantly~"

"Oh my God, are you serious? The spacebabe is a princess, too?" Sandra gave me a hard look. "You've *got* to be putting us on."

"Sandra, that was incredibly rude!" Mom blushed and attempted a curtsey to Callan. "Please forgive my daughter, Your Highness. She *has* been raised with better manners than that."

Callan laughed. "There are no apologies necessary. But the 'spacebabe' comment still intrigues me. What is that all about?"

Dad stepped in with an explanation. "When David was a boy, a retired scout lived across the street from us. He was a nice old man who filled David's head with stories of lost colonies, daring rescues, and a beautiful princess. Growing up, David swore he was going to become a scout, find a lost colony, have amazing adventures, and rescue a beautiful princess. Even if, to quote his seven year old self, it meant he had to kiss a girl."

"I see." Callan flashed her lovely smile again. "And am I supposed to be the beautiful princess?"

Sandra turned an incredulous look on me. "She's kidding, right? I mean, they *do* have mirrors on her planet, don't they?"

"Yes, we have mirrors, brat. But there's one more thing I need-"

Eyes dancing, Callan interrupted me. "And what about kissing a girl, David? Did that turn out to be as onerous as you feared?"

It was my turn to grin. "Well, I've found it rather tolerable when I'm kissing the *right* girl."

Sandra was much quicker on the uptake than my parents. "Oh my gosh! Do you mean you kissed the spacebabe?"

"Yes, brat, I kissed the spacebabe. Then I took it a step farther and I *married* the spacebabe."

Mom's hand flew to her mouth and she dropped onto the side of the bed. Dad gave me a big grin and a double thumbs up. Sandra even relented and gave me a big hug.

"I always said I wanted a sister. You done good, big brother."

Her eyes still dancing, Callan sat next to Mom and wrapped her in a big hug.

"David is far too modest to say it, but he did more than just kiss me and marry me. He has saved my life more times than I can count. His courage and conviction in the face of overwhelming odds gave me hope when there was little hope to be found. His love and compassion gave me the strength to carry on when all seemed lost. My people love him almost as much as I do." Callan kissed Mom on the cheek. "Thank you for raising such a son."

As Mom blushed, Callan took my hand in hers. "I only pray I can do half as well when our child is born."

I pulled back and looked into Callan's eyes. "*When?*"

"Yes, darling. I saw the doctor today to confirm it." Callan guided my hand to her stomach. "You're going to be a father."

I thought I could never be happier than I was on the day I married Callan. It turns out I could.

HOME AGAIN

Nothing that happened during the ensuing three weeks came close to matching the joy I felt seeing my family again and learning Callan and I were mere months from having a family of our own.

My wife, Rupor, and the other Aashlander political representatives benefited greatly from their new implants. They all received diplomatic implants—which provided language translations, cultural traditions, and the governing laws of the Federation, but *not* Boost—and made good use of their newfound knowledge. An agricultural assistance treaty was hammered out, along with an agreement to provide naval patrols on the Federation side of the wormhole.

Martin became a media darling, with the newsies playing up his "mischievous boy gone bad boy gone hero" story. Martin managed to pull me into the limelight, as well, and much was made of my adventures and my romance with Callan. I was never comfortable in front of the vid cameras and, after three dreadful interviews with me, the newsies decided to get all their stories from Martin.

Megan's music proved to be Aashla's first export. A musician touring military bases happened to hear Megan performing traditional and original songs for our marines. He whipped out a pocket recorder and captured the rest of her performance on video. The musician asked permission to upload the performance to the net. Megan agreed, but only after conferring with Martin and Callan. Two thousand years of isolation from the rest of humanity resulted in a musical evolution far from anything found in the Federation. With trillions of people looking for new and different entertainment, Megan's performance was an instant hit.

Callan's captivating beauty and animated interviews made her the face of Aashla. Newsies packed into her public appearances and vid cameras flitted all around her. Harris took it upon himself to organize an escort of armed marines for Callan, keeping the newsies at bay and clearing a path for her with bared teeth and, sometimes, bared blades.

Two days after my family arrived on the station, Harris requested a formal introduction to Sandra. My sister couldn't decide whether to be offended that Harris came to me rather than her or simply relieved that Harris finally picked up the signals she had been sending. Callan explained Mordanian dating customs to Sandra, explaining Harris simply followed the customs of his home world by approaching me. I had Martin advise Harris on Federation dating customs. Their first date went well right up until Harris got arrested for brawling.

According to Harris, a group of drunken young men voiced vulgar approval of certain parts of Sandra's anatomy. They refused Harris's demands to apologize to Sandra and then compounded their error by questioning Harris's parentage. Three of the men lay unconscious when station security took Harris into custody. According to Sandra, the offensive comment was nothing she hadn't heard before, but Harris's defense of her honor surprised Sandra and, according to Callan, pleased her no end.

We turned Chapman and the pirates over to Federation law enforcement and recorded hours of testimony for use against them in their trials. Chapman made matters worse for himself, challenging Heidi's Mordanian citizenship and the divorce granted by Callan. A judge ruled the matter lay outside of Federation jurisdiction and told Chapman he would have to argue his case in a Mordanian court. The day after the ruling, Chapman and the pirates were transferred to the planet below to await trial.

After three long weeks of preparations, the navy assembled the ships necessary to clear the Aashlan end of the wormhole. I'm told the clearing operation was quite a sight when witnessed from Aashla. It also served notice we were coming home.

A huge crowd gathered to watch the *Aashla's Hope*, escorted by half a dozen Federation Navy fighters, land outside Morda. Callan and I were the first to descend the ramp from the ship. Before us stood Callan's parents. Next to them stood Kim, smiling and craning her neck to see around us. The moment we both dreaded was at hand.

Kim focused on us as we approached. Our somber expressions told her we brought bad news. Tears ran down her cheeks even before we reached her. The queen put her arm around Kim as I told her of Milo's sacrifice and gave her a heartfelt hug. Leaving Callan comforting Kim, the marine commander and I undertook the daunting task of speaking with the families of each marine who gave his life on the mission. I will never forget the haunting look of the parents who lost their child, of the wives who lost husbands, and of the children who lost fathers.

At a reception that evening, Callan announced her pregnancy to the court. It lifted the mood around the palace, where Milo had been well-known and well-liked, and even drew a smile and congratulatory hug from Kim. Callan's parents rejoiced at the prospect of a grandchild and heir. The next day, the rest of the kingdom rejoiced with them when the news was proclaimed throughout the land.

In the following months, Federation delegations took up negotiations with many Aashlander countries and the first agricultural assistance missions arrived. Nist and Kim were married in a small, intimate ceremony. Martin and Megan were married in a huge, raucous ceremony. It made news across the Federation. Callan convinced her parents to fund a medical school in Morda and put

Tristan in charge of it. And, in the largest wedding Tarteg had ever seen, Rupor made good on his promise to Heidi. For the record, Heidi *does* look beautiful in Tartegian black and gold.

Nine months after we left on the *Aashla's Hope*, Callan went into labor. I sat by her side as Tristan guided her through the delivery and placed our newborn son in her arms.

"Welcome to the world, Robbill Milo Martin Edwar Rice Villas," she said to him.

"That's an awfully big name for such a little guy. Do you think he can live up to it?"

"Of course he can, David. After all, you're his father!"

Callan laid her head on my shoulder and our son caught my finger in his tiny fist. Then time went away and all was right in my world.

THE STORY CONTINUES...

David's and Callan's story continues in *Scout's Law*.
Available now!

If you enjoyed *Scout's Duty*, please post a brief review.
Reader recommendations are the best advertising.

ABOUT THE AUTHOR

Growing up, Henry worked at the usual range of menial jobs before ending up in software development. In between the menial jobs and the IT jobs, he achieved some small fame as the writer and co-creator of the small press comic book titles Southern Knights and X-Thieves. In 2006, Henry also took up the mantle of professional storyteller. He performs regularly throughout the state of North Carolina and has recently released his first book of children's stories.

Henry has been a fan of science fiction for as long as he can remember. He has loved space opera and planetary romance since the beginning, that is why his science fiction novels end up in those subgenres.

Henry currently lives in Raleigh, NC, with his wife, son, two cats, and lots of imaginary friends all clamoring to tell him of their adventures.

HenryVogelWrites.com

ALSO BY HENRY VOGEL

Scout series

Scout's Honor

Scout's Oath

Scout's Duty

Scout's Law

Scout's Training (coming soon)

Hart for Adventure (coming soon)

The Adventures of Matt & Michelle

The Fugitive Heir

The Fugitive Pair

The Fugitive Snare

Captain Nancy Martin

The Counterfeit Captain

The Undercover Captain

The Recognition series

The Recognition Run

The Recognition Rejection

The Recognition Revelation

Other Space Opera Novels

The Lost Planet

Illustrated Children's Book

I'm in Charge! and Other Stories

www.ingramcontent.com/pod-product-compliance
Lightning Source LLC
Chambersburg PA
CBHW050723180626
46814CB00002B/573